PRAISE FOR VIVIAN

"If you've never read a Vivian Arend book you are missing out on one of the best contemporary authors writing today."
~ *Book Reading Gals*

"The bitter cold of Alberta, Canada, is made toasty warm by the super-sexy Coleman brothers of Six Pack Ranch."
~ *Publishers Weekly*

"Brilliant, raw, imaginative, irresistible!!"
~ *Avon Romance*

"This story will keep you reading from the first page to the last one. There is never a dull moment..."
~ *Landy Jimenez*

"I definitely recommend to fans of contemporaries with hot cowboys and strong family ties.."
~ *SmexyBooks*

"This was my first Vivian Arend story, and I know I want more!"
~ *Red Hot Plus Blue Reads*

"Vivian Arend kicks off her new Heart Falls series with the emotional, heartwarming, and sensual story of a single dad hoping to make his daughter's lives better by hiring a nanny to help them as they grow and mature."
~ *Guilty Pleasures Book Reviews*

ALSO BY VIVIAN AREND

Six Pack Ranch
Rocky Mountain Heat
Rocky Mountain Haven
Rocky Mountain Desire
Rocky Mountain Rebel
Rocky Mountain Freedom
Rocky Mountain Romance
Rocky Mountain Retreat
Rocky Mountain Shelter
Rocky Mountain Devil
Rocky Mountain Home

Thompson & Sons
Ride Baby Ride
Rocky Ride
One Sexy Ride
Let It Ride
A Wild Ride

A full list of Vivian's print titles is available on her website
www.vivianarend.com

THE COWGIRL'S CHOSEN LOVE

THE COLEMANS OF HEART FALLS: BOOK 3

VIVIAN AREND

The Cowgirl's Chosen Love
Copyright © 2020 by Arend Publishing Inc.
ISBN: 9781999495763
Edited by Manuela Velasco
Cover Design © Damonza
Proofed by Angie Ramey & Linda Levy

---

*Z*ach Sorenson sat on the porch outside his best friend's home, pretending to enjoy a cold one while laughter echoed behind him.

The deeper rumble of Finn's chuckle meshed with his fiancée's lighter voice. Maybe Zach should switch to something stronger. Whiskey, or gin, or hell—maybe even tequila. Although that last one could be dangerous.

He leaned back on the porch swing, legs stretched in front of him as he crossed one boot-clad foot over the other and stared over the landscape toward the Rocky Mountains.

It wasn't that he begrudged anyone their good luck.

Begrudge? No. Be slightly jealous? Hell, he would admit to that one.

His name sounded. The door swung open beside him, and he twisted toward one of his new favourite people.

"Sorry it's taken so long," Karen Coleman offered. "Lisa and I will stop tormenting you. We're finally ready."

He rose to his feet as the rest of the party slipped out the door and headed to their waiting trucks. "Not a problem," Zach insisted. "Trust me. I know better than to tell a woman to hurry up."

He dodged to avoid being poked by Lisa. "You know it wasn't only us," she insisted. "Josiah takes *forever* to get ready."

Laughter rumbled again as the girls slipped into their seats.

Finn turned to Zach after settling Karen in place. "Glad you're coming to Rough Cut tonight. Sure you won't join us for the weekend?"

Oh, hell *no*. Best friends or not, the last thing Zach wanted was to spend the next forty-eight hours as a fifth wheel. "Thanks for the offer, but I've already made plans."

Finn's brow arched skyward. "Really?"

On his other side, Josiah stepped forward as well, curiosity written on the veterinarian's face. "First time I've heard this news. You keeping secrets?"

"Minding my own business," Zach drawled. He offered a wink to soften the words as he turned on his heel and headed toward the shed he'd commandeered to house Delilah, his 1955 powder-blue Corvette convertible "Catch you all at the pub."

He left the top up for the short drive from the still-in-development Red Boot ranch into the small town of Heart Falls. The trip was barely long enough for an attitude adjustment. He was pleased that his oldest best friend and his newest best friend had both found women who appreciated them and filled their lives with everything good.

The hint of green-eyed jealousy in Zach's gut got a quick, short blast of reality to knock its scaly claws out from under it. Someday he'd have that kind of relationship. Sure, life came with no guarantees, but he'd had enough good examples in his world to counterbalance the shitty situations.

When the time was right, *he'd* find someone. Someone who would be what he needed.

A soft snicker escaped. Thank God his friends couldn't

stroll through his brain right then, or he'd be teased mercilessly for the hearts-and-flowers turn his thoughts had taken.

Zach parked at the very edge of the lot and made his way into the pub, a blast of country music echoing over the wooden boardwalk as he pulled the heavy oak door open.

Inside, the strategically set lights were just bright enough to make everybody look good, and the rapid beat of boots against the dance floor set his fingers tapping.

And although they'd all arrived at the same time, his friends were thankfully focusing on enjoying themselves and not attempting to pull him into the mix. Lisa and Josiah hit the dance floor not even three seconds before Finn pulled Karen into his arms and twirled her against his body.

Zach lifted a finger at the bartender and ordered a beer.

The place was full of cheerful people, flirtatious glances, and a heck of a lot of sexual tension on the rise. He spotted a couple of the women he'd dated a few times over the past months, dipped his chin and offered a wink without any further promises.

Nice enough ladies, but there hadn't been the spark he was looking for. Which, again, probably made him a bit of a diva, as Finn had teased at one point.

He liked a good time as much as any guy. He'd enjoyed some wild one-night stands and a few longer relationships over the years that had been very physically satisfying, but now he wanted something different.

Hell if he knew how to define it, but at some point, he figured with his good luck, whatever he was looking for would jump up and smack him in the face hard enough he couldn't miss it.

He'd just drained his first beer when Finn danced Karen over to him.

Her expression was nothing but innocent as she held out a hand. "Dance with me?"

"Is the old man tired already? You should've picked me instead of him," Zach said as he put down his empty beer and accepted her offer. "I've got way more stamina."

Beside him, Finn thumped an elbow into Zach's ribs before responding, "Go on and tell yourself more lies if it makes you feel good."

Zach guided Karen to the dance floor, twirling her away from her man even as laughter drifted.

They moved together easily, a space between them as if they were brother and sister dancing—which was kind of how Zach considered both of these women in his life.

Amusement rose. As if he needed more sisters...

"What are you snickering about?" Karen asked.

He guided them past other dancers as he answered. "Figured you and Lisa would offer me sympathy dances. Just didn't think you would start this soon."

She hummed, following his lead as they moved past a tangle of less-coordinated two-steppers. "Heard some nonsense about you having big plans for this weekend. Considering Lisa and I were just talking about how you've been avoiding most of the local female population, you're either a lying liar, or you're a much better secret keeper than we imagined."

The woman was razor-sharp, which meant she was potentially dangerous to his plans. Avoiding a weekend's worth of watching his friends make goo-goo eyes at their ladies was high on his priority list.

But because she was so sharp, he felt safe offering a tidbit to tide her over *and* get her off his back. "Trust me. My plans for the weekend will make me happy."

Karen sighed dramatically even as he twirled her past where Finn was now chatting with Lisa and Josiah at a table in the corner. "Those were the magic words to get me to mind my own business." She gave him a stern stare, though. "As long as you're *happy*. That's all we want for you."

"I know," he said easily, slowing as the music segued into a new song.

He took a turn around the dance floor with Lisa next. Amusingly, almost the identical conversation escaped her lips the instant they started dancing.

"What's this nonsense about you having plans for this weekend? You should come with us. You don't need to stay here alone."

"Honestly, I have been taking care of myself for over thirty years," he assured her. "Go to the resort with Josiah. You all need a break before life gets busy again."

Lisa dipped her chin, but she still looked as if she wanted to interfere.

Luckily Zach had lots of experience dealing with interfering women—with five sisters, he'd learned at an early age how to handle feminine wiles. "I mean it. Go have a good time. I have plenty of things planned to keep me out of mischief."

She snickered. "Where's the fun in that?"

When the song finished, he guided her back to Josiah. A moment later, Zach slipped away to grab another beer and let them have time on their own. The bar was full enough it was easy to find other people to talk with, although he avoided making too much eye contact with any of his previous female companions.

Again, it wasn't them. It was all him.

He appreciated what his friends were trying to do. And by extension, their women. A kick of something warm struck his heart. It was good to know they cared.

Only—good *friends* weren't quite what he was wishing for at the moment.

Standing quietly to one side of the dance floor offered a great opportunity to observe. Zach sipped his drink and considered his options. Some companionship this weekend *would* be nice, but none of the ladies in the room—

Julia Blushing spun past on the arm of one of the local farmers, and all of Zach's mental ramblings stilled in an instant.

She wore faded jeans so white, he bet they were infinitely soft to the touch. She'd been dancing hard, and whatever jacket or overshirt she'd come in had been abandoned to leave her in a formfitting navy-blue tank top that caressed her curves in a dangerous way.

Her hair hung in waves, layers of red and gold shining under the lights as she twirled in the arms of a man Zach would give anything to change places with.

A green-eyed monster was back, but this one had a whole different set of teeth and claws that snagged his soul.

Here was the reason none of the other women in town had caught his attention in recent days. Zach had to admit the truth. He'd spent months trying to ignore the draw he felt toward Julia.

Talk about a complicated relationship, though. She was the recently discovered younger sister to Lisa and Karen. Definitely not someone to mess around with unless a guy wasn't fond of keeping his balls attached to his body.

Only...

He wasn't looking for someone to mess around with. Not anymore.

Zach wasn't quite sure when his change of heart had taken place. All he knew for sure was when he'd come to Heart Falls with Finn, it had been situation normal, everybody in for a good time.

Now he was ready for the next thing.

She's perfect.

His internal sidekick commented about the same moment Zach noticed Julia slide her dance partner's hand off her ass and back onto her hip.

I could break every bone in that man's hand without blinking.

Truth was truth, but the possessive streak wasn't something he was proud of.

She twirled her way off the floor at the end of the song, escaping from her handsy partner with a laugh. Zach memorized the man's face even as he forced his shoulders to remain against the wall, staying put instead of tracking the bastard down and offering a lesson in etiquette he'd not soon forget.

The beer in his hand wasn't enough. He'd wait until his friends left and he got home before starting a little more serious drinking, though.

The catchy music continued, and for the next few minutes, he entertained himself checking out the people in the pub. Making a few bets as to who would be going home with whom after last call.

It was only a few minutes later when the woman he'd been fantasizing about taking home himself reappeared. Not in some other guy's arms, thankfully.

Nope. Aimed at him and marching as if on a mission.

The tickle in his gut flared. That sixth sense he had set off alarms loud enough the place could've been on fire. It wasn't a warning to be careful, but a heads-up to stay alert and be ready to leap.

Was she in trouble? He scanned the room even as he braced for whatever it was she was about to lay on his doorstep.

He couldn't fucking wait.

Casual. Stay casual.

He worked to keep his smile low-key. "Hey, Jules."

"Hey." She was nearly his height, yet the breath she took was shaky enough to make him want to pick her up and protect her from whatever had hurt her.

He knew better than to offer that card right off the bat. Instead, he forced mild curiosity into his tone. "Problem?"

Even as she shook her head and offered a quick "nope," she messed with his mind by laying a hand on his arm and sliding in close enough that as she went up on her toes, their bodies made contact.

That rush in his belly lit up to DEFCON 1.

"Favour, stat. Kiss me." She whispered the words, but they rang in his head as loudly as if she'd shouted.

He caught hold of her hips to stop her from wiggling because his body had reacted far too quickly. Everything about having her in his arms was perfect...

And far too easy. He hesitated. "You playing a game again, Blushing?"

Her lips curled into what he recognized as a fake smile, her unnatural laughter scratching his nerves.

But her softness melted against him as she stroked her cheek past his until her lips met his earlobe.

Goose bumps rose on his skin.

"I swear I'll explain, but you've got to kiss me, now. Like a girlfriend. *Please.*"

Desperation rang in her tone, and the urge to protect roared to the surface. Whatever the hell was going on, he could fix this. The fact it was exactly what he'd been hoping for, wishing for—

Call it the luck of the Irish, but he knew a gift when he saw one.

Zach slid his hand around her nape, cradling the back of

her head. The other hand moved instinctively off her hip to her lower back, pressing her closer against him. Lifting slightly so they were lined up and body to body.

"No idea what you're up to, but I'm game."

A little gasp escaped her before their lips made contact. And yeah, maybe a gentle peck on the cheek or slow, soft kiss would've been a good place to start.

His instincts told him otherwise. He kissed her with everything in him, desire laid bare in his touch as he gave to her.

She needed his help—she had it.

She also had all of him, because his gut said *she* was who he'd been waiting for all this time.

He jumped with both feet.

THERE WAS a fine line between being out of control and scared to death, and out of control and thrilled. Being kissed senseless by Zach Sorenson fell into the second category.

Thrilling wasn't always a good thing.

Still, Julia buried her hands in his hair and felt the bubbling rush of heat in her veins for just another moment. Because, damn, the man could kiss. His lips against hers were firm and demanding. His taste rushed through her. Her cheek tingled from where his five o'clock shadow had scuffed.

By the time he let her up for air, her face wasn't the only part tingling.

Still, she reined in her libido best she could even as she savoured the hard muscles under her.

Their gazes met. His pupils were wide, his breathing slightly out of kilter, although nowhere near as erratic as her own gasping inhalations. People were watching—murmured words swirled as people swung lips close to ears to share secrets. A slow examination of the way their bodies aligned.

His hand at her back slid downwards. It stopped before it went into dangerous territory, but now it rested on the swell of her ass.

A shiver rippled over her.

A soft chuckle danced against her skin as he twisted her head just enough to hide her face against his chest while he spoke in her ear.

"Come on."

An instant later, cool air filled the space between them. With strong fingers tangled around hers, he guided her toward the side of the hall and the emergency exit door.

She hesitated before he could tug her from the pub. It took a sharp squeeze on his fingers to get his attention.

He curled himself around her so he could hear her words.

"People need to see us," she insisted.

"*Some* people need to not see us until I know what the hell is going on," Zach insisted. "Talk first."

She let him lead her, glancing over her shoulder to try to see if any of the key gossips of the community had spotted them.

Her gaze fell on her sister's fiancée. Finn Marlette's alert gaze followed her and Zach, and a rush of *oh shit* arrived.

She had damn good reasons for what she'd started, but she hadn't thought this through before acting.

At this point the only choice was to go forward. She ducked her chin and slipped out the door at Zach's side.

The ice-cold wind stole her breath and sent goose bumps rising over her heated skin. A second later a warm, soft jacket settled around her shoulders, right before Zach grabbed the lapels of the coat—his coat that she now wore like a shawl—and tugged her to face him.

"Why?"

A man of few words. She could work with that. Only when laughter rang from the front entrance barely fifteen feet to their right, Julia paused before diving into her explanation.

A group of three women were staring at them, gazes darting up and down. Were they the ones Julia had overheard? She supposed it didn't matter, except for the fact she had to sell this bit of bullshit with everything in her.

She turned her focus on Zach, draping her arms over his shoulders and pressing their torsos together again. "I swear I will explain, but right now you need to lose that frown."

"It's hard to look like everything's peachy keen when I don't know what's going on," Zach said, but his lips curled upward, and his hands wound around her waist again.

Big hands, strong and controlling—

A shiver that had nothing to do with the cold evening air shook her from top to bottom. Julia fought the fear inside her and nodded briskly even as she let her fingers drift up to play with the curl of brown hair that had fallen over his forehead.

"Someone was gossiping. Really mean shit. Maybe even those women, and I guarantee you will agree to help when you hear the whole story. But for now, trust me?"

He didn't answer. Then she couldn't ask again, because his lips were on hers once more, the kiss making teeny electric zaps fly up and down her spine.

Her body *liked* this man. Which was a weird thing for her to acknowledge, all things considered.

At her back, footsteps echoed on the boardwalk. Feminine giggles rang as the group of ladies passed by.

Zach teased his tongue against hers, and a moan escaped. Honestly escaped, because the last thing she wanted him to know was how much being pressed against him affected her. Although—*hello*—the thick length of a healthy erection pressed against her belly.

So. She wasn't the only one reacting to their little *tête-à-tête*.

Julia broke the connection between them this time, pressing a hand to his chest to open up enough room so she could gasp for air.

Under her fingers, his heart pounded.

His bare biceps flexed as he caught hold of her elbows. "Enough. We need to talk."

"My place?" Having him come under her roof had the added benefit of adding fuel to the rumour mill if anyone saw them. Which, considering where she lived, chances were high.

He didn't argue. Just wrapped that big hand around hers again and guided her down the boardwalk to the corner where they turned to the west.

They moved quickly. Zach remained quiet and didn't ask any more questions, which was good, because although she intended to make everything clear...

Her brain whirled. How had this evening gone from amazing to hell and then to being kissed senseless by Zach Sorenson in such a short period of time?

He stopped at the front door of her apartment building before swearing softly. He turned on her almost accusingly. "Why is there no security?"

Her snort wasn't very ladylike. "Gee. Not sure. Maybe because this is the cheapest place in town, and things like a doorman or a security system are low on their priority list?"

Zach's blue eyes flashed for a moment, but he opened the exterior door and gestured her past him.

Across the street on the bench outside Connie's Café, a couple of young guys whistled and shouted rude suggestions. Julia ignored them like usual.

She took the stairs to the second floor, automatically stepping around the worst of the stains on the carpet. It was impossible to tell which were old and which were new, and after one misstep into a fresh pile of vomit, she'd learned avoidance was simpler.

Key already in hand, she had her door open in seconds, this time waiting for Zach to enter first.

He put a hand on her back and guided her ahead of him, his silence growing louder. Which was fine, because all the voices in her head were shouting at the same time. What she really wanted was to make a cup of tea and sit in the dark for a while to let her world settle down.

What she wanted would have to wait.

She twisted toward him instead. "Explanation. Okay."

He folded his arms over his chest, biceps bulging in that position. He examined her from top to bottom then shook his head. "Dammit, Jules, you look like shit. What the hell?"

There was no anger in his tone, just very controlled annoyance, but on top of everything else, it was the last straw.

Tears arrived as a sob burst from her lips.

2

*G*reat move, asshole.

Zach stepped forward and wrapped his arms around Julia. He cradled her carefully, so he wasn't smothering her but at the same time offering as much support as possible.

Tears poured out of her as if he'd somehow turned on a tap with his words, and, dammit, he wished like hell he could take them back.

And yet he was floored to see her react like this considering what he'd learned about her over the past months. He'd expected a snarky comment or, worst-case scenario, for her to kick him out of her place for being an ass.

Her shoulders shook as she buried her face harder against his chest, arms squeezing tight around his torso.

Zach stroked the top of her head for a moment before realizing if she did snap out of it, petting her like a puppy was probably not a wise move. Instead, he rubbed her back and took horrified stock of her apartment.

It was clean. Empty to the point of a monk's cell sparseness, the few personal touches were limited to some bright throw cushions and a couple of pictures on the wall.

The place was also extremely small. Four walls and one other opening that led to a tiny bathroom. A couch sat across from an old travel case. The kitchen ran the length of one wall. That was it. No bookcases, no frilly curtains or plants. Austere to the extreme.

It didn't make him think of Julia at all.

Behind him, the doorknob rattled before the hinges creaked and a man stepped into view. The stranger wore a dirty T-shirt half tucked into his pants, half stretching over the round of his beer belly. He drew back with a curse upon spotting Zach, hands rising as he retreated to the landing. His sprint down the stairs was impressive considering his loose paunch.

When the door opened, Julia had jerked to attention. She stepped in front of Zach to shout at the vanishing intruder. "I told you to never do that again."

Fire flared inside, and the only things that stopped Zach from running after the man were Julia's fingers now tangled in his T-shirt.

"What the hell is going on?" he demanded again.

She pressed her free hand to her head as if trying to keep her brains from spilling out. "One thing at a time. Just...sit down and I *swear* I'll explain."

It took everything in him to ease away. Two steps brought him to the small dining table, and he settled into the wooden chair on one side.

He fought down a growl as she took the second chair and jammed it under the front doorknob.

Unbelievable fury roiled in Zach's gut.

Somehow, he kept his cool as she turned to face him. Tear lines streaked her cheeks, but she straightened her spine. "I was in the bathroom at Rough Cut and overheard some women gossiping. There's a rumour going around Heart Falls that I'm having an affair with Brad Ford."

Even as pissed off and in hyperprotective mode from everything that had happened over the last few minutes, her words floored Zach. "Someone thinks you're having an affair with your *boss*? The guy who just got married a month ago and who is obviously and stupidly in love with Hanna?"

His disbelief must've rang clear because Julia nodded. "Isn't it absurd? But you know what small town rumours are like. Somebody's going to find something to prove it—the fact I came to Heart Falls to mentor under him because we met each other a couple years ago at the EMT training center could be enough to get some people to believe."

Okay, Zach hadn't known that part. It added a layer of concern to the situation. Not that he thought she and Brad were doing anything wrong, but it would give the mean-spirited gossips something to chew on. "So you kissed me...?"

A little bit of her bravado faded. "I kind of panicked. I heard them talking, and the only thing in my brain was to make sure the rumours don't continue. And maybe if I had a boyfriend already, that would stop the stupidity in its tracks."

He wasn't sure if the fact she picked him for this honour was a good thing or an insult.

Being a glass half-full kinda guy, he went with it being a good thing. "You're saying I'm a convenient boyfriend?"

She hurried to explain, stepping forward to finish even as she wiped her eyes and tried to pull herself together. "*Temporary* boyfriend. It's just for a short time. My trainee position is done at the end of October, and then I'll be gone. But yeah, if people think *we're* together, they won't think I'm fooling around on the side with Brad."

This was getting messy. "Yeah, I can see how all that works. Great. Fine." He met her gaze straight on. "What about your sisters? And my friends? What are we going to tell them?"

She opened and closed her mouth a couple of times, and in spite of the tension in the room, he had to admit to being slightly charmed. She was damn cute.

The impulsive thing had caught him off guard, but her heart was in the right place and considering *his* long-term goals, being offered guaranteed time with the woman had to be counted as a win.

Julia's nose twitched. "Umm. I haven't thought about that. Like I said, I didn't really think any of it through. I just reacted. I was doing triage before the situation bled out."

"Yeah, I can see that. But we have to come up with a different spin to the story. Because as much as my friends love me, if they think I screwed around then dumped you, I'm the one who'll be bleeding."

She looked confused. "You won't be dumping me. And I won't be dumping you. It's just a little... I don't know, a short-term thing."

"Short-term?" He eyed her, making sure he didn't let his gaze linger too long where it shouldn't. "Yeah. You mean like a one-night stand? Because I can see your sisters hanging me by my nuts if I had the crassness to try."

Her cheeks flushed. "We're not having a one-night stand. The whole point of this is to make it look as if we're involved enough that Brad is clearly out of the question."

"Great. We'll fool around from now until the end of October when you leave. Then your sisters, who will still be here, will kick my butt every time they see me. Which, considering one of them is deep in cahoots with my best friend, means every damn day."

Julia shook her head, the crease between her brows forcing him to fight to keep from smiling. "They won't be mad at you.

We'll explain. Just to them, and Finn and Josiah, of course."
She paused. "And maybe Tamara as well."

That last part wasn't said with as much confidence.

"So what you're asking me to do is either lie to my friends
or lie to *some* of my friends."

She looked a little more uncomfortable but stuck to her
guns. "*Please.* We have to find a way to make this work because
Brad is a good friend and I can't let him be hurt. Not him or
Hanna. I owe him too much."

Another layer of mystery added to the situation. What had
happened at that training school to connect the two of them so
tightly?

She headed to the counter and plugged in the kettle,
glancing over her shoulder. "I need a cup of tea. Want one?"

It wasn't the whiskey he was looking forward to, but it
would have to do. "Sure."

He waited and let her fuss at the counter for a few minutes.
Meanwhile, his gaze kept returning to the chair blocking her
doorway. This entire mess would take some time to untangle,
but the one thing he knew for certain?

She was not staying one more night in this damn
apartment. It clearly had major security issues. Zach kicked his
own ass for not finding this out sooner because the thought of
her being in the apartment alone while someone marched in
on her—

He took a deep breath and concentrated on pulling his
temper back to normal levels.

A couple minutes later, she placed two cups on the table
along with cream and sugar before settling across from him.

The three-legged stool under her was shorter than the
chair he sat in. It put her chin about four inches above the
surface of the table, and she looked like a little kid having a tea
party.

Anger returned. "You want to discuss why you've got a chair in front of your door?"

A soft sigh escaped. Julia lifted her gaze but didn't meet his eyes. "The locks don't work very well. I drag the trunk in front of the door before I sleep."

That comment only strengthened his resolve. "I see."

He drank the tea without tasting a thing. He returned the cup to the table surface then placed both palms on either side of it. "We have some problem-solving to do. Pack a bag. You're coming home with me."

Her eyes widened. "I can't do that."

"My place or one of your sisters," he offered. "But considering we need to talk about the dating thing..." Zach kept as still as possible, but his usual easygoing nonchalance had vanished sometime in the last minute. "I swear nothing will happen that you don't want, but I need to get you somewhere safe before another person comes through the door and I hurt them."

He said it calmly. Peacefully, even, but Julia's eyes widened.

He had to assume that it'd been a hell of an evening. Julia was a caring, kind woman, and even though she was tough enough to be a damn good EMT, everything that happened tonight was breaking down the barriers.

And as good as his control was these days? He wasn't kidding about the need to protect.

Julia took a final swallow of her tea before placing her cup beside his. She rose to her feet, pressed a hand on top of his briefly, then moved to pack as ordered.

THERE WASN'T a whole lot of talking going on. Zach had

grabbed the duffel bag she'd filled, thrown it over his shoulder, and then firmly taken her hand in his as he guided her back toward the parking lot outside Rough Cut.

His strong fingers wrapped around hers were comforting after the chaos of the evening.

The start of the trip between town and the dude ranch Zach and Finn were setting up passed in silence. Julia barely registered she was getting a ride in Zach's famous convertible, her brain scrambling to find a solution for what came next.

Impulsively tossing Zach into the mix had been brilliant and yet totally wrong. Annoyance crawled up her spine. Trying to do the right thing and still having things backfire was exasperating.

The cold stone in the pit of her stomach that she hated with everything in her grew heavier again. Fear didn't always make sense. What triggered it, what caused the memories to return.

This wasn't going to be the same, she told herself. She knew better what to watch for, and she had a whole lot of support in the form of her newfound sisters.

Sisters who would wonder what the heck was going on when they heard through the *grapevine* that she was seeing Zach.

Shoot. She rested her head in her hands and listened to the tires bump against the uneven highway asphalt.

"Stop tormenting yourself." Zach's deep rumbling voice slipped over her like a warm blanket. "We'll figure this out. I mean that."

His strong features were clearly visible in the light from the dashboard. His expression was a lot harder than usual. As if all the easygoing fun that she'd seen in him over the past months was boxed up and contained.

"I'm sorry." She said it sincerely, even as she knew the apology wouldn't change anything.

The honest truth—if she had to temporarily screw up her life and somebody else's to save Brad Ford a world of hurt?

She'd do it in an instant.

That wasn't something that she could up and say, though, without complicating the situation even more than it already was. But considering she owed Brad her life, a little emotional upheaval, even within her newfound family—

Just the thought of that truth made her pause. She had family again.

Lots and *lots* of family, and while on one level she was thrilled, there was another part of her that remained in denial.

Zach once again caught her fingers in his, squeezing them tight. Which was nice and reassuring, but when he didn't let go and let their linked hands rest on the seat between them, Julia's pulse kicked up a notch.

She liked the man.

When she'd come out of that bathroom, struggling to come up with a solution, seeing him had felt as if she'd rounded a corner into an ocean inlet and left behind the rough waves. Calmness had wrapped around her and let her take a full breath.

Holding hands seemed far too natural considering how unnatural it was. Up until now they had always been a part of a group. Activities with her sisters, dancing at the pub, that kind of thing.

Still, she had stitched him up about a month ago when he'd accidentally been shot. The feel of his firm muscles under her fingers—

It was a little creepy how often that scene replayed itself in her head. Considering her issue with stalkers, the last thing she wanted was to be one herself.

Zach slowed as they entered the gate to the Red Boot

ranch. Julia peered out the window at the outbuildings around them.

The guys had been working on the place since the spring, rapidly at first but with a slowdown recently. Although it was getting closer to winter, so she figured that made sense. They just didn't seem to have the same urgency to get the place up and running that she'd noticed in the beginning.

The buildings and grounds had changed since the last time she'd been there, though, and Julia was fascinated. "Where are you staying these days?" she asked.

He pointed to the far end of the row of small cabins facing the Rocky Mountains. "I've got the biggest one. Two bedrooms —you'll have space to yourself."

His words came out a little more clipped than usual, his body tight as he parked his classic car in an old wooden shed on the far side of the cabin. His truck sat outside the makeshift garage.

They both got out and met at the trunk.

Zach took a deep breath before turning to face her. "I'll let you in and you can get settled. I promised Finn I'd take care of a few chores tonight. I'll be back in about an hour."

She glanced at the small cottage beside them, a cozy glow shining out the window. The temptation to run away for at least a short time was strong, but something told her it wasn't the right move. With where her head was at, she'd do nothing but fidget and worry the entire time he was gone.

Julia shook her head. "I'll drop my things, but let me come and help you."

He hesitated. "This whole situation we need to talk through—I don't think that should be done while we're wandering around the barns."

"I agree. But honestly, I wouldn't mind a bit of labour while I'm thinking. It's how I figure stuff out."

His big shoulders lifted in a lazy shrug. "Okay. I'll get your help mucking out a few stalls." He took her bag again. "As long as you remember which end of the shovel is the working bit."

The soft snicker that escaped her felt good. "Trust me. I've got that part down pat."

They crossed to the cabin. She slipped into his bathroom to change out of her good jeans. It was too short a pit stop to do much more than admire the concrete vanity and the pinewood trim on the mirror and cabinetry. She caught a brief glimpse of blue and brown tiles, but the rest she'd take a closer look at when they returned.

She tucked her bag beside the corduroy-covered couch in the living room and met Zach at the door.

He had also changed into work clothes. He examined her before giving a brief nod. "You'll be happy to know we have rubber boots you can borrow."

"Any good dude ranch has extra rubber boots," she said cheerfully.

He strode toward the main barn. "Not sure this is a good dude ranch quite yet," he admitted. "We'll get there, but right now it's a bit of a reach."

Zach got her situated with footwear and a shovel, pointed to the three stalls he wanted her to take care of, then left her alone.

He stepped farther into the barn and got to work, so she followed his example and got down to it.

The physical labour of lifting pellets into the wheelbarrow calmed her racing thoughts.

It had always been like that. The repetitive motion helped her step away from her brain fluttering on repeat. By the time she went through the final motions, her leg and back muscles ached in different places than from the earlier dancing.

Plus, she'd figured out some possible bartering chips to toss toward the upcoming conversation.

Zach paced past, nodding his approval. "Good job. And thanks—you saved me a bunch of time."

Julia shrugged. "Caused a bunch of trouble already, so it's the least I could do."

He tilted his chin toward his cabin. "Grab a shower. I'll finish up and join you in about half an hour."

This time as she let herself into his place, Julia allowed herself the luxury of taking a long, slow look around.

For some reason, Zachary had moved into what would eventually be a family bungalow. It wasn't decked out yet like it would be down the road. She knew that from talking to Karen about the level of clientele they hoped to attract to Red Boot ranch.

This looked more bachelor chic. A comfortable couch sat opposite a sturdy coffee table, the surface well-scuffed from where countless feet had rested. A couple of scorch marks marred the wooden surface, one large enough to proclaim a pizza pan had gone straight from the oven to the tabletop.

She hurried into the bathroom, this time able to appreciate the high-quality tile around her. The rain shower fixture overhead delivered a heck of a lot more water pressure than she'd had in her admittedly disgusting apartment.

Between the chores, the shower, and the bit of time to breathe, Julia had come up with a plan.

It would still be awkward, but she felt a whole lot more in control as she met Zach in his living room, settling in the easy chair to the side of the couch.

Settling might've been the wrong word—she perched at the front, hands folded in her lap to keep from fidgeting.

Zach had returned to being the poster child for relaxation.

He leaned back on the couch and propped his woolen-sock-covered feet up on the coffee table.

His gaze drifted over her, examining her before nodding decisively. "Okay. It's problem-solving time. You need a temporary boyfriend to stop some nasty rumours. I get that, and I can agree, because wiggling lips don't stop once things get rolling." He lifted his chin and looked her straight in the eye. "But first you need to come clean. Why the hell *did* you come here? To Heart Falls, and to this job? Because it sounds as if there was something between you and Brad in the past. While I don't believe for one second that you're fooling around with him now, I don't want to get blindsided in the future."

Thank goodness she was dealing with an intelligent man. "We didn't have that kind of a relationship."

"Great. What kind of a relationship did you have?"

So much for keeping the truth a secret. "He rescued me."

Zach's casual relaxation vanished. He rocked forward on the couch, blinking hard. "Excuse me?"

It was Julia's turn to raise a brow and relax a little. "He saved my life. If I feel anything for Brad, it's a bit of hero worship, because without him, I'd be dead."

3

*J*ulia's unexpected confession simultaneously relieved a few fears while driving Zach's protective instincts back into high gear.

"You're going to need to explain that a little more." Zach sat upright, giving her his full attention. He made sure he kept his voice gentle, though, because the last thing she needed while talking about bullshit would be for him to go ape shit on her.

Julia took a moment as if getting her thoughts together before meeting his gaze full on. "The short story is while I was at the training center for EMTs, one of my classmates mistook me being friendly as encouragement far beyond what it really was. I don't want to go into the details, but he kidnapped me. He was very gentle about it. I thought he was just kidding around until I was tied up and trapped with no way to escape."

The curse that slipped from Zach's lips made her lips twitch.

"Yeah. Pretty much what went through my head when I realized Dwayne hadn't been kidding about the *keeping* part of *keeping me safe*. Brad was one of the trainers at the school, and we'd developed a good relationship—very much a big brother thing as he mentored me through my first semesters of extended schooling. Brad noticed right away when I went missing."

Zach was going to buy the man a bottle of anything he wanted. "How long were you missing?"

"Five days. It would've been longer, or forever, if Brad hadn't figured it out. But it comes down to this. Brad nearly lost his job for doing what he needed to find me, mostly on a hunch. There's no way I could repay that by allowing him and Hanna to be hurt."

Zach rested his elbows on his knees even as he nodded. "I'm fully on board. We'll make sure everybody knows you're taken. It shouldn't take long to knock the knees out from under this rumour."

She deflated slightly, the worry in her eyes slipping to relief. "Thank you."

His own concern rose. Talk about complications.

He wanted to be with this woman and give dating a try. What he'd wanted to say was he'd take care of her going forward, but a take-over, take-charge approach was out of the question. No way did he want to cause the slightest hint of a reminder of her past trauma.

Yet his gut rarely steered him wrong, and his first impulse was to tell her a partial truth.

To hell with it. He leaned back again, getting comfortable. "Couple more things to talk about."

Julia nodded. "I'll tell my sisters, and Finn and Josiah, but I think that's as far as we can share that us dating is not real. I mean, I trust Tamara as well, but as soon as I tell her, Caleb will know. He's got so much close family underfoot—it's kind of hard to know where the story will stop."

"What if we don't tell anyone it's not real?"

She snapped upright at his comment. "You said your friends would be upset. And that my sisters would break out the ball busters."

"That's if we were just fooling around." He let his gaze drift over her, appreciating the firm muscles and soft curves. "I have zero problem actually going out with you."

The little frown between her brows was back. "Stop kidding around."

"Oh, honey, this isn't my kidding around face." He offered a wink. "You're a beautiful woman with a great sense of humour and a very giving heart. You intrigue me."

She looked as if she was struggling for words. Then she shook her head. "Remember the bit where I'm leaving at the end of October?"

"You said your internship was done at the end of October. Doesn't mean that you'll be leaving. Lots more jobs available in the Heart Falls area. But that's not something to worry about at the moment." He checked her over again, gaze lingering on her cheeks that had flushed red at his bold appraisal. "Julia Blushing, would you go out with me? Breakfast tomorrow morning?"

Her head shook from side to side.

"Is that a no, you'd prefer lunch or dinner? You know, we both like to dance. I'd love to take you back to Rough Cut."

"Will you be serious?" Julia had her hands in her lap, tangling her fingers together over and over.

Zach took a step back, figuratively. He lowered his tone and spoke softer. "I'm not trying to trap you into anything, but I'm telling you the honest to God truth. I like you. I would very much like to get to know you better. If you don't think I'm a terrible bet, this would solve things on all sorts of levels. My friends won't think anything of us dating, and your sisters won't freak out as long as we're upfront and honest from the beginning."

"Finn saw us," she confessed. "When we were getting ready to leave the pub. I think he saw us kiss, and he definitely saw us slip out the door."

Which was something that could play in his favour. Still, Zach took the cautious route. "And if you absolutely want this to be nothing but pretend, then we will deal with the four of them. But I'd be honoured if you'd consider dating me for real."

Her expression grew bemused. "I don't think I'd be a very good girlfriend," she cautioned.

"Maybe you need some practice," he offered dryly. "We'll grade on a curve."

Her gaze snapped to his, a whole lot of what-the-hell attitude back in that moment, and something inside him clicked.

This was the real Julia. *This* was the intriguing woman he'd seen glimpses of off and on. He wanted to get to know her better, wanted to spend time with her.

And while it sounded as if she had some pretty major events in her background, he was a patient man. He'd be able to help if she needed him to. Otherwise, having a good time together would not be a hardship.

Julia rubbed her eyes as a huge yawn escaped. "I'm sorry. I can't think about this anymore tonight."

"Sleep on it. We'll talk more in the morning when I take you to breakfast."

Her glare could've cut diamonds. He winked in approval.

They stood at the same time.

He gestured toward the back of the cottage. "You take the bed. I've got an air mattress somewhere I'll toss in the second room."

"I don't mind sleeping on the floor."

He turned her by the shoulders and pushed her toward his room. "You're too tired to argue with me. Save it. We can have a really good, knock-down verbal spat about who sleeps where. Tomorrow."

She held on to the door for a moment, staring back with eyes that were exhausted and slightly haunted, but a smile twisted her lips. A real smile instead of the awkward fake one that had shown up before. "Zach?"

"Yeah?" He deliberately walked past her, heading into the chaos of the room he'd used to toss his shit.

"Good night." A gentle whisper that slipped over his skin like a caress.

He found a spot to place the air mattress, stretching out in the middle of a mishmash of boxes and other possessions. Her voice continued to drift through his ears as he fell asleep.

He was awakened by strange sounds coming from his bedroom. Zach rose, caution tossed aside as he cracked open the bedroom door.

In the middle of his king-size bed, Julia's head flipped back and forth on the pillow, the sheets tangled around her.

A moan of fear slipped from her lips, and her hands scrambled at the covers. That's when he noticed that the quilt was pinned under her body, trapping her in place.

Poor girl. "Julia. Wake up, sweetheart. You're having a bad dream."

She continued to move frantically. He spoke again, sliding closer to the bed. Her eyes were squeezed shut as her fingers plucked at the material pinning her in place.

Hell if he wanted to scare her more, but the sounds escaping her lips were breaking his heart.

Zach spoke louder. "Julia. Wake up. Everything's going to be okay."

When she kept rocking in place, Zach took a chance. He laid a hand on her shoulder then quickly removed it. "Julia."

The third time he made contact, her eyes popped open, gaze snapping to meet his. The fear on her face was stark, and something went brittle inside him.

She opened her mouth. He expected to be screamed at, but what escaped was his name.

"Zach?" A hushed whisper. Barely there and very much a plea.

"You're all tangled up. Okay if I give you a hand?"

Her chin quivered as she nodded. He rearranged the blankets until she had full range of motion once again. "There you go. That should be better."

Before he could pull back from the bed, her fingers wrapped around his wrist. Her big eyes locked on him, and she looked uncommonly like a deer caught in bright headlights. "Thank you."

He cautiously settled a hip on the edge of the bed, smoothing the sheet over the quilt. She settled back, and he stroked her hair from her face.

The entire time, she watched him.

She didn't say anything. Just stared with that pleading expression. As if she wanted something but couldn't say the words.

No way in hell would he make too broad an assumption right now. Not after what she'd shared earlier.

So he sat where he was, gently stroking his fingers through her hair.

Her eyes closed to half-mast before popping open, as if desperately fighting sleep.

He couldn't help it. She was so timid at that moment, like one of his little sister's rabbits. Really wanting to believe it was safe, yet uncertain of moving closer.

31

Zach made a judgment call and went with it. If he was wrong, they could get their heads straightened out later. "Go to sleep," he told her. "I'll stay and keep you safe."

For second a flash of fearlessness crossed her expression. "I can take care of myself," she insisted.

He kept his smile in place. "Of course you can. But tonight, I'll help."

FROM THE DRYNESS of her mouth and the ache at the back of her skull, Julia knew she'd had a nightmare.

The fact she wasn't curled up in a ball on the floor or stuck in a corner of the room freezing to death with her arms tangled around her thighs made her less certain, though.

Part of the night came back to her. The bit that involved a pair of blue eyes, steady and kind, watching as sleep returned. Zach's voice as a thread of calm that had slipped into her ears and tangled around her nervous system, soothing away her tension from the inside.

She sat up and glanced around, almost certain she would find him stretched out beside her on the king-size bed. When she discovered she was alone, it was with equal parts of sadness and contentment.

She didn't need the complication of a real boyfriend. She *definitely* had appreciated his warm presence by her side last night.

Knowing it was impossible to balance the two parts of that equation, or decide which was more important, Julia threw back the blankets and got out of bed.

A quick glance at her watch said it was well past eight. She was used to working all sorts of shifts, and throwing herself out of a solid sleep into work mode was already second nature. But working in emergency services meant she also knew how to thoroughly enjoy her sleep when she could, such as going without a morning alarm and waking once her body was rested.

She walked into the kitchen, the scent of coffee pulling her to the side counter even as she had to ruefully admit she was a very good sleeper *most* of the time.

Damn nightmares.

She squared her shoulders and poured herself a cup, sniffing the liquid before taking a sip.

It wasn't *fresh* fresh, but it also wasn't tar. After working at the fire hall around people who didn't know two things about what a good brew was supposed to taste like, Julia was very happy to discover Zach's coffee was drinkable.

There was no sign of him. At least not until she opened the fridge to discover a note taped to the side of the milk carton.

If you're starving, help yourself. But if you can wait, I've got that breakfast date to take you on. Give me a call or come find me in the barn.
—Zach, your boyfriend

That final word sent a shiver over her skin, but this time she didn't think it was concern so much as simple shock.

She stood in front of the picture window and stared at the mountains as she drank her coffee. She systematically went through every step of what had happened the previous day, analyzing where she could've done something different.

But by the time she reached the bottom of her cup, the only thing she'd change was to not have a nightmare, and it wasn't as if she had any control over that. Talking about her kidnapping usually triggered a bad night or two.

For the rest of it, she would give Zach all the points in the world for being a gentleman *and* extremely understanding.

She still wasn't going to date him for real.

Oh, she was tempted. During that first kiss at Rough Cut, there'd been a very real physical draw, albeit unexpected.

Yet all the reasons she had for keeping to herself were still valid. Top it off with the fact he was her sister's fiancé's best friend. Coming back and seeing him every time she visited? It would be much simpler to pretend. In six weeks she'd be gone, and this whole mess could be put behind her.

With that decided, she pulled on her boots and made her way to the barn. A man stood in the distance currying a horse, his broad shoulders moving easily as he worked the brush over the horse's withers.

Only when Julia stepped close enough to realize it was Finn and not Zach, it was too late to change direction.

Finn stopped what he was doing, a slow smile barely disturbing his lips. "Julia."

She hadn't spent that much time around the man, and to be honest, she found him a little too solemn. Every time she'd been with Karen and Finn, Zach had been along as well, and it had been his lighthearted humour she'd been drawn to.

Still, she knew Finn was rock-solid when it came to taking care of her sister Karen. Plus, he and Zach had been friends forever. There had to be something to him that made everyone trust him that hard.

Julia tangled her hands behind her back and waited, figuring he'd say something about spotting them the day before. Then something out of place struck her, and the question blurted free. "What's wrong?"

He raised a brow.

"You guys were supposed to be gone this weekend. Karen and Lisa told me at Rough Cut that they'd see me on Monday morning, but you're still here."

"Small change of plans." Shockingly, his always modest

smile broadened until it was a full-out grin. "Karen and I are getting married."

She knew that. Maybe the man was drunk and not quite in his right mind. "*Right*. You're engaged."

His soft snort echoed in the small space, and one of the horse's ears flicked in surprise. Finn soothed the animal before turning toward Julia again. "Last night we got to talking and realized neither of us wants any kind of big shindig. Then Josiah got some tickets to a show in Vegas from his brother for Sunday night. One thing led to another, and we've decided we're heading out this afternoon."

Holy cow. "You're getting married in *Vegas?*"

He dipped his chin.

All of the tension that had been weighing her down vanished in an instant. As distractions went, this was tip-top. She clapped her hands in excitement. "That is very cool. Congrats."

"I'm glad you think so. You can save the well-wishes until we make it official. Go pack a bag, because you're coming with us."

Oh my God. "Really? I mean, why would I come?"

That brow of his shot up again.

"*Julia*." This time his tone was full of disappointment, as if scolding her for doubting her place in the family.

Okay, she was a sister to Karen, but it still seemed kind of sudden. Wasn't going to hurt to roll with the situation, though.

She offered her own grin. "I'm happy to come and support you. Thanks for the invite."

"Karen said you had the weekend off already. If you can get an extra day, we'll all fly back on Monday. If you can't, we'll put you on a plane Sunday afternoon so you can make your Monday shift."

Julia nodded. "I'll give Brad a shout. One of the guys owes

me a favour, so I bet I can flip my first shift to later in the week. I'll let you know as soon as I can."

"Sounds good." He paused, suddenly very serious. "So. You and Zach?"

Oops. "I kind of hoped you'd already talked to Zach."

"Haven't seen him yet. Left a message so he knows when we leave."

Right. Because Zach would be at the wedding as well. A teeny knot of concern slipped in before she shoved it aside.

The man had been a knight in shining armor last night. They were going to make this thing work between them. Besides, the last thing she wanted was to get Finn all riled up and concerned before heading to his own wedding.

She faced the music. "Zach and I are just good friends. Last night we had a situation to deal with. Gossips were saying some nasty things, so he and I decided to pretend date for a bit. That's all."

Finn's lips didn't budge, but the lines at the corners of his eyes tightened. "He's a good man, Julia. The best. Whatever you've got going on is your business, but you need to know you can trust him. He'd never do anything to hurt you."

"I know that," she assured him. "It's part of what makes him so perfect for this. I'll let Karen know, and Lisa, but other than that, we're keeping this quiet, okay?"

He dipped his chin. "Secrets have a way of eventually getting out," he warned.

"It's only until I leave at the end of October."

A slow frown spread on his face. Finn took a deep breath. Seemed to consider speaking, paused, then shook his head. "Don't hurt him."

She blinked. "Of course not."

Finn examined her face steadily before turning back to the

horse to finish his job. "He's got a heart of gold. I imagine he'd do anything for you. Don't take advantage of that."

The twist in the conversation was beyond her, so Julia stepped away in search of Zach.

She found her sisters first.

She'd looked all over the barns and arenas before heading toward the ranch house Finn and Karen were renovating for their personal use. When she spotted the women on the back deck, she slowed her pace. That gave her time to examine Karen and Lisa—two of the three unexpected additions in her life.

What was she saying? *Three* additions? Try three sisters, one father, and a whole mess of cousins she hadn't a hope of untangling without a roadmap and a *who's who* of the Coleman clan.

After spending her life as a single child with just her mom, then losing her mom a couple years earlier, being thrust into the noisy, curious mob was invigorating and terrifying.

The thin thread of anger that rose up and tangled around the thought of her mother was ignored for now, because staring at two people who wore her face was enough to focus on here and now.

Lisa was only a couple of years older. She'd recently cut her hair to shoulder length, and blond highlights shimmered in the loose strands. She was a live wire, constantly coming up with some kind of mischief, and Julia was drawn to her in a way that felt all sorts of uncomfortable.

She wasn't used to having confidants. Her few friends over the years had proven to be more fair-weather opportunists than real soulmates.

Lisa's completely out-there and honest personality was a little daunting at times, but Julia was smart enough to know it was the change in circumstance that made the interaction feel wrong, not her sister's open and honest caring.

At seven years older, Karen was less bubbly and enthusiastic, but her eyes were kind, and she definitely had that big-sister vibe going on.

All three of them did, as Julia included Tamara Stone in the mental gathering. The other three women also seemed to have a tangible connection. Roots that were so deeply meshed together, Julia both craved being a part of it and worried how she could keep following her own goals without being overwhelmed.

Yeah. Being grafted into the juggernaut called *family* would take some work.

Julia was about to announce her presence when Lisa spotted her. The true delight on her sister's face helped ease more of the tension about having forced herself in where she wasn't wanted.

Lisa opened her arms as Julia hit the top of the stairs. "Glad you're here. Have we got a surprise for you."

The hug Julia got felt good, and so did the flash of inspiration. "I bet you want to tell me we're going to Vegas."

A snicker slipped from Karen as Lisa rolled her eyes then offered a glare. "Someone told you."

"The imminent groom-to-be," Julia admitted before turning to Karen. "I'm really excited for you. Is there anything I can do to help?"

Her sister pulled her hair back into a ponytail, tightening the scrunchie to hold it in place. "Not much we need to do. Josiah's brother has taken care of most of the details for us—he's already in Vegas. We've got accommodations, the wedding chapel, and reservations for dinner at the Paris."

"And there's the show on Sunday night, if you can stick

around." Mischief rose in Lisa's eyes. "Of course, if you want to go dancing, we can work that into the schedule."

"I need to make a couple of phone calls," Julia assured her, ignoring the dig about dancing. Had Karen also seen her with Zach? "I'll let you know as soon as I can if I have to come back early."

"Hey, ladies, flight is confirmed. Two o'clock, so we need to leave by noon at the latest." Josiah marched onto the deck, a small, tan-coloured terrier at his heels. They both strode to Lisa's side where Josiah picked her up and spun her in a circle, Ollie barking enthusiastically the entire time.

"Put me down," Lisa said with a laugh.

"I'm hoping if I spin you hard enough, you might agree to a spontaneous wedding as well."

Julia blinked at his comment, but Lisa only laughed as she tapped her fingers against his shoulders. She shook her head.

"Stop that. I already said no. This is Karen and Finn's party. We'll just have to continue shacking up."

He shrugged. "Can't blame a guy for trying." His gaze shifted to take in Julia. "And you. Ready for a little time in sin city?"

"I've never been. I'm pretty excited," she admitted.

Strong hands caressed over her shoulder, fingers squeezing briefly. Zach slid into position beside her. Close enough the heat of his body meshed with hers.

Staying there was tempting—far too tempting—but for her own peace of mind, Julia took a half step away.

Karen was too distracted by Finn's arrival, and Josiah only had eyes for Lisa. But Lisa?

She didn't miss a thing. Her smile kicked up a notch as she examined Zach and Julia. "I think it's going to be a very interesting trip."

4

*Z*ach was doing his damnedest to try and give Julia some room, but it was the hardest thing ever.

It seemed every time he turned around, she was right there, chatting with her sisters with boundless enthusiasm. She projected so much life and energy, he was constantly drawn to her side.

It took far too much effort to stop reaching for her hand every chance he got.

Piling into the extreme back seat of the Coleman minivan put him right next to her, though. An accident of fate he was happy to enjoy as the Coleman girls continued to chatter.

Behind the wheel, Tamara glanced in the rearview mirror, her laughing eyes taking in the six of them. "You guys are all a load of trouble, but I hope you have a wonderful time. You deserve it. I mean that, sis."

The last said directly to Karen, who was seated beside her in the front passenger seat.

Karen twisted so she could see everyone in the back better.

"We'll make sure we get a video of the wedding for you and anyone else in the family who wants a copy."

Tamara waved a hand. "We'll be there in spirit. I agree with the concept of keeping it small and fun, considering I never invited any of you to my wedding."

A snicker escaped Lisa. "You set a bad example."

"I set the *best* example," she corrected, gaze once again fixed on the highway. "I proved the most important thing you need for a good marriage is the right partner."

"Amen to that." Finn leaned forward from where he was seated behind Karen to lay a hand on her shoulder.

She pivoted and offered Finn such a blinding *I'm in love with you* smile, it damn near filled the van with sparkling unicorns and rainbow dust.

Which was exactly what Zach hoped to see. His friend deserved every bit of happiness headed his way.

Beside him, Julia listened intently, but her expression wavered between excitement and concern. "Are you sure we'll make it to the airport on time? If our flight's at two o'clock, don't we have all sorts of security we have to get through first? How far is the airport from us now?"

To hell with it. Zach pressed his fingers over hers where her hand lay on the seat between them, squeezing gently. "The plane won't leave without us," he assured her.

In front of them, Josiah twisted. His quick glance took in both Julia's face and their linked fingers, but he blinked back his surprise and addressed her. "Have you flown before?"

"Once. Well, I suppose twice. Vancouver to LA and back when I was about twelve."

"Disneyland trip?" Lisa asked.

"Just the beach and some winter sunshine," Julia told her. "That's all we could afford, but I loved it. The flight was pretty much all the Disney rides wrapped up into one. Someday I'll go officially."

She glanced at Zach, that crease back between her brows. Her gaze shifted to their hands.

Dammit. He had unconsciously began rubbing his thumb over the back of her knuckles. When she didn't pull away, though, he decided to keep her anchored. He knew the bomb Josiah was about to drop.

"We're not flying commercial," Josiah said casually. "Finn and Zach have access to a private plane, so you're in for a special treat."

Julia stiffened. "A private plane?"

"It belongs to the corporation." Zach squeezed her hand. "Remember you met Alan Cwedwick, our lawyer, that one time."

The time she'd had to stitch him up after he'd been sort of shot—which wasn't something he wanted to spend a lot of time talking about. Although it had to be said. Having a woman who could deal with a little blood without panicking was a good thing.

Not that he planned to get shot again anytime soon.

In front of them, Lisa pivoted until she could lay her arms over the backrest and speak to Julia. "The fact they have their own plane is out of this world. I can't tangle my brain around it either. But I will say, after Josiah and I flew first class to London a month ago, I'm very willing to be spoiled."

"Spoiling is good," Julia said, smile fixed in place.

But she tugged her fingers free a moment later, staring out the window as the conversation continued around them.

Screw this. Zach slid his arm along the back of the passenger seat then angled to whisper in her ear. "You okay?"

She glanced toward the front of the van before meeting his gaze. "It's a little overwhelming."

"The fact our corporation owns a plane? Or that we can use it to make two people who are very important to us extremely happy by letting them get married on their own terms?"

"When you put it that way..." That cute little nose wrinkle was back. "It's still overwhelming. How many other people do you know who own a private plane?"

"Julia, let it go."

She offered him a heated glare but changed the topic. "I didn't have a chance to tell anyone about our fake dating. Except Finn. I caught him in the barn before I met up with you. But my sisters don't know, and neither does Josiah."

"Is that really something to worry about right now?" Zach asked. "This is a fun, celebratory getaway. Nobody in Vegas knows us, so it's not as if we have to put on an act."

"Right. So there's no reason for you to hold my hand."

There was every reason he needed to hold her hand. Also on the necessary list: he needed to stroke her skin and lean in close while he breathed deep enough to send her scent ricocheting through his system.

Give her some damn space.

Easier said than done. He pulled back far enough to offer her a wink. "I like showing my affection. Everyone knows this. Hugs, holding hands..."

"Then you go right ahead and hold Finn's hand all you want," she said with a smirk for a second before her jaw dropped. She leaned past him, gaping out the side window. "Holy *crap*. Is that our plane?"

Tamara had turned down the drive at the small airstrip where the company plane was stored.

"We'll definitely be taking off on time," he assured Julia.

She stared in fascination, unaware her entire body was pressed up against his side. She might have been trying to put more physical distance between them when she was alert, but it

43

was clear she was just as comfortable around him as he was around her.

Still, he didn't want her to realize where she was and panic. He eased back to give her a better view, describing what he knew of the plane and what would happen over the next few minutes so she wouldn't be taken by surprise.

Julia nodded as he spoke, offering him a real smile as the car came to a stop. "That sounds a lot simpler than the security I remember going through before."

"Stick by me. If you have any questions, I'll help."

Only the instant they poured out of the car, it was clear he had no chance of being the one by her side as they headed onto the plane.

Tamara gave everyone final hugs and kisses, including Julia, who was looking a little wide-eyed.

At least until Tamara stuck a finger in her face. "These two are terrible at taking pictures," she said, gesturing toward their sisters. "It's your job to do better. And don't forget, we want lots of selfies so you're in the shot as well."

Brilliant. The tension in Julia's body vanished as she accepted her walking orders. "I can do that."

Then she was off, Lisa and Karen sweeping her with them toward the freestanding stairs.

Finn met Zach at the back of the van, passing bags to the crew coming forward to handle them.

His best friend eyed him for a moment.

Josiah stood waiting to one side, arms folded over his chest. The veterinarian had only been a part of their group for the past six months or so, but it was clear he knew how to read a situation.

His lips twisted into a smile as he met Zach's gaze. "So. What happens in Vegas, stays in Vegas?"

"I doubt that's what Karen had in mind, considering she plans to marry this jackass," Zach drawled.

His best friend walked past him, shoulder-checking him and *accidentally* shoving him off balance.

Zach laughed as he scrambled to keep his feet.

Josiah placed a finger against his lips. "I will swear I see nothing until somebody tells me that I'm allowed to see something."

He winked then marched after the women, leaving Zach and Finn alone.

Finn paused in the middle of the tarmac, a far enough distance between them and the rest of their party that they couldn't be overheard.

"Had the strangest conversation with Julia this morning," Finn said.

"Really?"

"Yeah. Something about you two being in a fake relationship." He hesitated. "Doesn't sound like something you'd be keen on. Especially considering..."

Zach waited in silence.

He wasn't going to make it easy on Finn. They'd been best friends for enough years and gone through hell together. They'd also gone through some of the best times of their lives, and he considered it a privilege to be invited to witness this momentous next step in Finn's life.

Still wasn't going to spill the beans unless Finn outright called him on it.

"Considering I know you think marriage is a pretty important relationship." Finn raised a brow. "Adding in how you already feel about the woman, this fake thing sounds like a bad idea."

Damn the man for being able to read him too well. "Are we going to write poetry and braid each other's hair now?"

Finn's solemn expression flared into a wide smile. "Julia's a good woman."

"Damn right she is." Zach lowered his voice. "Still to be seen if she's the good woman who wants to be with me. Don't worry about us—this trip is about you and Karen. No matter what, we're going to have a hell of a good time."

Finn pounded him on the back then headed to the plane. "Sounds like a plan to me. To Vegas, and to forever."

His best friend's plans for forever were slightly ahead of Zach's, but he agreed with the sentiment. They marched forward, ready to chill and enjoy the weekend.

When they got back to Heart Falls, there would be time enough to have a good, long talk with Julia about their future and how to make both their dreams come true.

Julia wasn't sure where to look, and she most definitely didn't know where to put her hands.

The looking part—that was because she was enthralled. The private plane wasn't some gigantic boat with luxurious overstuffed leather couches like she'd seen in movies.

It was a smaller, seemingly more practical plane. Although the fact that Zach and Finn owned the damn thing still knocked it off the practical shelf and onto the *oh my God* list.

Who owned a plane?

Well, obviously they did, but no matter how many times she tried to wrap her brain around it, the details refused to compute.

The chairs were cushy, and there was a lot of legroom. The plane was set up with seats that faced each other, front and back. After they'd gone through the necessary security, the guys settled on one side and Karen and Lisa pulled her into their conversation.

Takeoff was fascinating. Julia stared out the window the entire time, shocked to discover she'd grabbed hold of Lisa's fingers at some point.

She thought back over the past months and the time she'd spent with her sisters. It had been good to slowly get to know them, and her father, although George Coleman was usually only around for short periods on the weekends.

That worked out fine as well because she wasn't really looking to have a dad figure jump in too fast.

But they'd done so much normal stuff. There'd been a lot of hamburgers and homemade meals. Comfortable evenings around the fire.

There'd been no sign during the wiener roasts in Lisa's backyard that any of them were casually jetting off on a regular basis to wherever people with private planes went.

A soft giggle broke through her mental ramblings. Julia glanced to the side to find Lisa shaking her head.

"You need to take a deep breath. Then, either pretend you're in the middle of a make-believe story or find some way to balance your brain." Lisa tilted her head. "You kind of look like Ollie when she's desperately trying to decide whether she should spend the day under my feet or follow Josiah."

"Great. I remind you of your dog," Julia drawled.

Karen laughed. "Considering Lisa loves that dog like a human, it's not a bad thing."

"Where is Ollie for the weekend?" Julia asked before including Karen in the question. "And *your* fur baby. Unless you brought Dandelion Fluff with you."

"We did discuss the possibility," Lisa admitted. "But this is an adults-only trip. We didn't want to have to worry about puppy potty breaks or the rest of it."

"Tansy and Rose are taking care of our pets," Karen said. "They're having some work done at their place, so they'll stay at the ranch for a few days."

For a moment, Julia's thoughts went sideways in a different direction. The Fields sisters had become good friends over the short period of time Julia had been in town. Partly because they had a monthly girls' night out event with a number of women, including Julia's mob of sisters.

Rose Fields was a beautiful Black woman with long dark hair that always seemed to fall to perfectly frame her face. Her effortless beauty made Julia feel ruffled.

Julia glanced across to where the guys were chatting together, elbows resting on knees, happy contentment pouring out.

"Do you think—?" *Oops.* She slammed her lips shut before the question could reveal the direction of her thoughts.

Dammit. Not fast enough. Two pairs of eyes stared at her intently.

Karen lifted a brow. "Sister rule number twenty-seven. Start any kind of sentence with *do you think* then stall out, and I can guarantee we will poke until we figure out what you were about to ask."

Lisa nodded briskly. "Uh-huh. You may as well spill right now and save yourself some time."

Damn her mouth for getting away from her. "Zach took Rose dancing. That's all."

Her sisters exchanged a glance before Karen took charge. "Considering that sentence didn't start with *do you think*, now is when we start guessing."

"Do you think...Rose would mind if I took Zach dancing?" Lisa asked sweetly, before qualifying. "The *I* in that statement being Julia, of course."

Karen responded instantly. "Rose wouldn't mind at all. She insisted she was done with him."

Lisa snorted. "That just sounds so wrong. But you're right, she did say that."

As embarrassed as Julia was at the twist in the conversation, the teasing from her sisters was gentle-hearted. Julia's cheeks heated, though. "That's not what I was going to ask."

Lisa ignored her, speaking to Karen. "Do you think...Zach wants to take Julia dancing?"

"Is *that* what they're calling it these days?" Karen quipped.

A snort escaped Julia, and her sisters turned happy faces toward her, leaning in to speak in conspiratorial tones.

"You like him, don't you?" Lisa asked.

"Of course I like him." Julia was shocked at the question. "He's Finn's best friend, which means he has to be awesome or else that wouldn't have happened. Plus, he's really nice to Karen."

"*Pshaw.*" Karen waved a hand. "He's nice to everybody. He's just plain nice."

A mischievous smile slid over Lisa's face. "You know, the nice ones are usually the dirtiest in the bedroom."

"*Lisa.*" Both Julia and Karen spoke in a scandalized tone at the same moment, and suddenly the guys glanced over as if very interested in their conversation.

Karen stuck out her tongue at Finn. "Never mind. Nothing interesting happening over here."

Julia met Zach's gaze and wondered what she'd gotten herself into. Between the pretend boyfriend business that could wait until after this weekend, and the way he'd taken charge and refused to let her stay in the apartment—

All things she would deal with come Monday.

Now she needed to focus on not getting distracted by a man with sparkling blue eyes. A man whose gaze seemed intent on stroking her skin and making bits of her tingle that hadn't for a long time.

Would she like to do a little...dancing with the man? *Dancing* never seemed to turn out the way she wanted it to. Sadly, she was enough of an optimist that she still hoped at some point to be able to experience more than what she'd had in past relationships.

Cold drifted over her skin. A memory she hated, that refused to leave her be. Tied up and alone, not sure what was going to happen the next time her kidnapper returned.

A shiver escaped, rocking her briefly.

The next thing she knew, Zach was out of his seat and kneeling beside her. "You okay?"

He said it quietly, but he settled his hand on her knee, the warmth of his palm stealing over her skin. Her sisters had barely registered something had gone wrong, but he'd already known.

Equal parts wonderful and creepy, if she were honest.

She ignored the questioning gazes from Karen and Lisa and focused on Zach.

"It's fine." She leaned closer to whisper in his ear. "You're complicating matters."

His slow, lazy chuckle drifted over her. Then he squeezed her knee and stood, his smile back to a just-friends level of intimacy. "Julia says she wants a drink. I think that's a great idea."

Whether or not they believed him, they all accepted his excuse.

Finn got to his feet as well. "While I plan to be sober when we exchange our vows, I do have a few bottles of champagne with us. No reason why we can't open one now."

What followed was a great reshuffling, because of course

Karen had to sit next to Finn, which meant Lisa had to sit next to Josiah.

Which left Zach and Julia snuggled up beside each other.

The comfortable seats had no armrest between them, which placed her thigh against his. Hip to hip, their elbows bumped briefly as she accepted a glass from Josiah, who had claimed maître d' status.

Zach tapped a finger against the crystal, the clear sound ringing through the plane cabin. "Within my responsibilities as best man *and* the closest thing to a male relative of the bride—"

"Since when?" Karen demanded.

"Don't interrupt the man when he's pontificating," Lisa whispered. "That's when they give away all their secrets."

Julia hadn't even had a sip of her champagne, and she already felt slightly drunk. "Is that how it works? Now I know exactly how to execute my evil master plan."

Beside her Zach winked before raising his glass a little higher. "As I was saying, the real best man toast will come once you've done the deed—"

"You might want to rephrase that one as well," Josiah drawled.

A chorus of snickers rose from the entire group.

Zach waited even as his grin grew wider. "To two of my favourite people. We watched you fall, and fall hard, and now we look forward to celebrating the next chapter in your life."

"Awwww, that was totally sweet," Karen said.

"Nobody diabetic should hang around the man for long," Finn muttered, but even he cracked a smile. "To good friends and a memorable weekend."

Crystal clinked. Shining eyes reflected all around before Julia lifted the glass to her lips. The champagne slipped down her throat, bubbles rising to hit her nose. She sneezed. Zach held out a tissue, taking her glass from her even as conversation rose again and laughter surrounded them.

It was not at all what she had expected at this stage of her life. Being surrounded with people—family, dear God, some of them were *family*—had never been a part of her dream.

She stared over at Zach and considered the upheaval of the past couple of days. He was a good man, sweet and yet strong enough to be protective, and she did another round of debating whether it was worthwhile to take a chance.

Not at falling in love—she didn't have nearly enough imagination to think about that impossibility.

But a short-term real boyfriend? The way Zach had suggested?

You'll just disappoint him.

The thought dashed into the moment of happiness, and she grabbed it with both hands and flung it away like a disc. It might be true, but it didn't have to come into this place and time.

The man was positivity and happiness. If she was smart, she'd simply enjoy having some of that in her world for a weekend. She didn't need to think about the long-term.

It took a split second to make a decision. Pretty much the way it had in the bar the night she'd gone looking for a way to save Brad's reputation.

No long internal debate, no weighing the positive and negative. There was just taking one little thing that felt good and letting it ride.

Julia eased against Zach's side so she could enjoy the heat of his body as she nestled into him.

Nobody noticed.

Nobody, that is, except Zach.

He cautiously slid a hand around her back and let the

strength of his arm cradle her. Gentle, but most definitely surrounding her and letting her know he was there.

To hell with it. They were headed to Vegas. What could possibly go wrong if she let down her guard just a little?

A hell of a lot.

Once again, she pushed away the negative thought. She would have to be completely unlucky for this to turn out badly. And really, at this point in her life, she deserved for something to be unexpectedly wonderful instead of an unmitigated disaster.

It was time to take a brief, but hopefully memorable, break from reality.

5

A freight train was running beside his bed. It was so damn loud, and so damn close, the entire bed vibrated, but still, Zach's eyelids remained glued shut.

He really hoped nothing fell out of the train cars, because at that moment, he couldn't have rolled over to save his life.

There also seemed to be a furry sock in his mouth.

Something warm and soft moved against his side, and if he had any muscles left in his body, the surprise would've made him flinch. As it was, he lay still enough that whatever was nuzzling against him began tickling his ribs.

A loud and very enthusiastic yawn broke the silence, which struck Zach as one of the funniest things he'd ever heard.

"Damn wild freight train," he muttered.

"Where?"

Something other than insensibility slipped in. That had been a female voice. Zach peeled one eye open far enough to glance down.

Long red-highlighted hair lay tousled over his naked chest...

And that's when he realized there was a whole lot of naked going on.

He stilled, because he didn't want to freak anybody out. Easing up on one elbow, he blinked against the bright light stealing in through the narrow slit in the curtains. That was enough to offer a vision that set his heart pounding along with his head.

He lay on a massive king-size bed. The quilt was who knows where, leaving nothing but a sinfully soft sheet draped over his and Julia's bodies.

Naked bodies—had he already thought that? The naked part.

He kept staring, but it didn't matter how often his gaze drifted over her, he couldn't put together the bits and pieces that had led to this moment. Which—

Christ on a cracker, not good.

She moaned as she rolled, making full body contact with his entire torso. "Where's the train?"

The fact that she still sounded three sheets to the wind wasn't a good thing. Damn it all to hell.

Zach lay back, careful not to disturb her, because the last thing he needed at that moment was both of them in panic mode.

Thinking. Thinking.

They were in Vegas. That much he remembered. He ignored the warm skin pressed against his side and frantically attempted to replay the last twelve hours.

He made it as far as remembering the post-wedding dinner at the Paris Hotel. Memories were just sneaking to the next point, which involved waving off Karen and Finn, who, rightly enough, had other things planned for the rest of the evening.

Then the four of them, Josiah and Lisa, he and Julia, had slipped out...

Somewhere?

To do something?

"Oh, for fuck's sake." Julia said.

It took about twelve syllables to get the words out. Her intonation was classic pissed-off, hungover, regret-filled partier. Fifty percent *what the hell have I done?* and fifty percent *I'm going to kill whoever did this to me.*

Amusement began in his gut then rumbled its way up until his chest shook. The sound made his own head ache, but it was impossible to stop. The fact that he might end up in her crosshairs in the next thirty seconds didn't do anything to reduce the amusement factor.

When she snickered as well, that was it.

Laughter filled the room, surrounding them and tickling hard until he gasped for air. He clutched his stomach as he rolled away.

Even with a headache from hell, he laughed.

When he caught himself under control enough to be able to glance across the bed at her, Julia snorted.

That was it. They were both gone for another five minutes.

They ended up flat on their backs on the king-size bed. Julia had wrapped herself up toga-like in the bedsheet. Somehow in the midst of their giggle-fest, Zach had found a pair of sweatpants, so at least his junk wasn't hanging out in all its glory.

They glanced at each other another few times before it seemed safe enough to speak. "I'm so sorry." Zach said it as sincerely as possible.

"For what?" Julia asked.

He hesitated then decided *what the hell.* "I have no idea. I was hoping you would tell me."

She shook her head then instantly squeezed her eyes shut

and slammed a hand up to her forehead. "Ouch. Okay, note to Julia. Do not make any sudden moves."

He snickered.

Her face contorted. "Dear God, please let's not start that again."

"Agreed." He cautiously curled upright, waiting on the edge of the bed until the room stopped spinning. "Drinking was obviously involved."

Behind him, she moved slowly, the mattress adjusting as she sat up. "I have no clothes on."

She stated the fact as if it were a weather report.

"I noticed." Dammit, there still had to be alcohol in his system. "I mean, I noticed because I also had no clothes on, not because I currently have the ability to do anything whatsoever regarding said nakedness."

The bed creaked just the slightest bit. Zach twisted to watch Julia pace toward the window.

It was a nice enough hotel room. Spacious, luxurious. All the things he'd really like when he actually got a chance to take Julia somewhere. The hangover pounding at his temples? Not so much.

She had her nose pressed against the window, the sheet draped around her dipping low in the back. The long line of skin becoming visible tempted him to follow after her and check out exactly how soft it was.

Which meant at least some of the alcohol had evaporated out of his system.

"It's pretty." She turned toward him, her eyes squeezed shut. "It's very bright. You know what time it is?"

Zach checked his watch. "Ten a.m."

She lifted a hand in the air and swung it as if cheering. "Yay. I slept in."

Their eyes met, and he stared into her face as the reality of what might have happened struck. "I really do have no idea what happened. But I'm sorry. I promise to take care of you, no matter what."

Because while he very much wanted to be involved with Julia, being naked with not much memory of what had happened the previous evening was not a good way to begin.

Add in the fact that a quick glance around the room showed two closed suitcases still stacked against the wall, which meant if they had done something that they didn't remember, *dear God he hoped not*, they would've done it without protection.

Julia blinked a few more times, gaze fixed on his. Her nose wrinkled as she considered his words.

Her lips curled into a perfect circle as understanding fluttered in. "Oh. *Oh.*"

She glanced to the side for a moment, her body tightening from top to bottom. Unexpectedly, she relaxed, releasing a breath hard enough it made her long hair wave.

A very decisive headshake followed. "It's okay. Whatever we did get up to last night, we didn't have sex."

Oh, really? "And you know this how?"

Her lips twitched. "Wait. I suppose we *might've* had sex, but it's very unlikely. Tell me, Zach. How big is your penis?"

The unexpected question floored him. "*Uh...*"

Her smile widened. "And on that note, I'm taking a shower. And finding some clothes. Then I want bacon. Lots and lots and *lots* of bacon."

He was still reeling from the penis question.

Room service was a thing he could handle even while discombobulated. "The shower's yours. Want me to bring your bag into the bathroom or put it on the bed?"

She considered for a second. One arm shot out to grab the wall for balance as she involuntarily swayed.

When she refocused on him, an endearing hiccup escaped her lips. "Excuse me. The bed would be fine. You can have the shower when I'm done."

"Okay."

Julia bent to scoop up the mass of material gathered at her feet, the swath of fabric barely draped over her body as she regally marched past him into the bathroom.

The lock clicked shut.

Zach was left standing with a rising semi, a full-on violent hangover, and a wicked level of respect for the woman who teased and tempted him to his core.

AFTER A SCORCHING hot shower that left the mirrors so steamy, teeny rivulets streaked down the surface, Julia was only a half step toward feeling better.

She had zero idea how long she'd spent soaking herself, alternating between hot enough to turn her skin lobster red and ice-cold in the hopes the combination would drive the remaining alcohol out of her body.

It hadn't worked.

Or, it hadn't worked completely. She was now sober enough to be able to look around the massive bathroom and appreciate the layout and conveniences. The shampoo smelled heavenly, the soap as well, and when she cracked open the body lotion, that's when she knew for certain they were staying somewhere very expensive.

Even the body lotion smelled good.

With the fluffiest towel she'd ever used in her life wrapped around her body, and another twisted around her hair, Julia sat on the padded bench in front of the vanity and stared at the steamy surface in front of her.

Way to go, Blushing. One night in Vegas, and you've already gotten naked in bed with the man.

She squeezed her internal muscles again, ninety-nine point nine percent positive she was right. They hadn't had sex. If they had, she would've felt it. Her muscles, unused for a long time, would have been sore.

Sex had been off the table for Julia for a while. Vaginal intercourse, to be precise, because she knew sex was so much more than just penis in vagina action.

Actually... Any kind of sex other than masturbation had been missing for a long stretch of time. Solo fun times? She was a champion.

She leaned forward and smeared a hand across the fog, wiping a section of the mirror clean. Her haunted eyes were visible for only a second. Being able to reassure Zach was a good thing, but as her brain started to clear, the other realization slid in.

He wouldn't let her declare her truth without more explanation. He would be the type to dig for more.

She liked that about him, except now when it would lead to a very blunt and embarrassing conversation.

The fan was doing its best to clear the steam from the air, and her face came into sharper focus. Her eyes seemed far too wide and innocent considering the way she'd boldly pretended waking up naked with him hadn't thrown her for a loop.

The bits and pieces she did remember needed to be seamed together with his.

Before she left the bathroom, she gave herself a stern warning, finger pointed at the mirror. "He's a friend first. We shouldn't try anything more, especially considering our luck doesn't seem to be very strong at the moment. It's too bad, but the fates have spoken. Zach will be a fantastic friend."

She dipped her chin decisively, wincing at the move. "*Owww.*"

Her time in the bathroom had been long enough for Zach to work magic. Her suitcase rested on the bed, but more importantly, the entire room was filled with the scent of bacon.

"You are a god among men," she told him as she made her way to the table in front of the window.

Zach pretended to tip his imaginary hat then pulled out a chair for her in front of the feast. "It was a bit of a rush order, but there's plenty of protein and fat. And orange juice," he added. "Help yourself. I need the shower."

Julia barely noticed him leave, the crisp bacon breaking off in her mouth and sending a mini food orgasm through her system. At the last second, she remembered her manners and called after him. "Thank you."

He lifted a hand, strolling through the bathroom door, his amazing butt vanishing from sight.

She glared at the piece of bacon in front of her and told herself sternly, "Noticing his butt is not a thing that *friends* do."

A quick snap of her teeth, and the bacon shattered into deliciousness on her tongue.

Zach wasn't gone for long, but by the time the bathroom door opened, Julia had enough food and juice and coffee into her system that the room was no longer spinning.

She'd also taken breaks from her feast to dig into her suitcase and pull on underwear and clothing. Nothing fancy, but tidy enough they could leave the room without looking as if they'd spent the night in drunken debauchery.

Her phone was absolutely dead. She plugged it into the wall and went back to the bacon as quickly as possible.

"Just a second. Forgot my stuff." Zach strolled across the room to his suitcase. The towel wrapped around his waist hung precariously low. The ends were tucked in to hold it in position as he used both hands to pull things out of his suitcase.

He stood close enough his iliac crest was visible, the long lines leading down to his groin standing out in firm relief. Abdominal muscles flexed as he picked up a T-shirt and jeans, pivoting to head back into the bathroom.

Dear God.

Julia wiped at her lips, not certain if it was bacon grease or drool at the sides of her mouth. She filled her cup of coffee again and tried not to think about it too hard.

A moment later Zach marched out and joined her at the table. His hands moved decisively, piling bacon, a fried egg, and at least three slices of ham onto a piece of toast. He slathered the entire thing with ketchup and lifted it to his mouth and took a giant bite.

"I'm really glad I'm not nauseous," Julia said.

"It's always like this after I drink," Zach informed her. "I'm starving."

She gestured magnanimously to her leftovers. "Have at 'er."

He was too busy eating to answer, but his eyes flashed with amusement.

She sipped her coffee and waited until he finished his ravening beast imitation.

The pause gave her time to look around the room. The view from the window had been spectacular. They were directly across from the fountain she'd seen so many times on television and in movies. Inside the room, it was decadent and relaxing, and obviously not a standard double room.

From the king-size bed to the sitting area, this was nowhere she would've expected in her wildest dreams.

"We're not in Kansas anymore, Toto," she whispered.

Zach gave a snort of amusement. "In other news, now that

my head seems to have decided to remain attached to my shoulders, maybe we should talk."

"Talking would be good. I remember Karen's wedding."

"Dinner at the Paris. I had a massive steak." Zach frowned. "You had pasta, Karen and Lisa had some kind of seafood, and Finn had ribs."

"Josiah had the vegetarian lasagna."

Zach grinned. "Lisa told him he was committing veggie-cide, eating all of those poor earthborn creatures."

So they both remembered dinner. They remembered going out dancing afterward with Josiah and Lisa. Only when her sister and her beau had started making goo-goo eyes at each other far too often...

"We went drinking," she told Zach. "Josiah and Lisa wanted to go off on their own, but they also didn't want to leave us alone, so you and I said we wanted to explore."

He nodded, waving a hand excitedly. "That's right. We found that private club on the twenty-seventh floor."

"Really? You can't remember what we did, but you can remember what floor it was on?"

Zach looked shocked. "Of course I remember what floor it was on. How else am I going to go back if I don't know where it is?"

A snicker escaped, and she curled her arms around her stomach. "Don't make me laugh. My stomach hurts."

Zach's lips twisted in a wry smile. "We did tequila shooters, didn't we?"

A second later, the memory was back. "You said they were your favourites."

He cursed. "When I'm already drunk, they're my favourites. You know that song 'Tequila Makes Her Clothes Fall Off'?"

Julia was finding this far too entertaining considering she was still partly hungover herself. "That's you?"

"Obviously."

"Way to warn me, baby."

He offered her a mock glare. "I don't know where you found that high horse to ride in on."

"Guilty as charged," she said, raising a hand in the air. "Tequila and I get along *real* good."

Zach frowned. "Where's my phone? I bet we probably have pictures of our drunken revelry."

"Mine was dead. I put it over there to charge." Julia glanced around. "I haven't seen yours."

What followed was a very time-consuming game of hide-and-go-seek, which involved picking things up and putting them back down.

In a fancy hotel room like this, there were an awful lot of things to pick up and examine, from magazines on the long rosewood bureau to a fancy box filled with tea on the side counter. Julia moved cautiously to not reawaken the hangover that threatened to leap back at any moment.

"Found it," Zach announced from his position half buried under the bed.

Watching him wiggle out meant she was once again staring at his Very Fine Ass.

In self-defense, she turned back to the desk and spotted a bottle of champagne with the silver ribbon around its neck. Seriously, this was one fancy-schmancy room. A closer glance and she noticed it said *Wedding Congratulations* on a tag hanging from the ribbon.

"Hey, Zach. We must've bought a present for Karen and Finn." She picked up the bottle and twisted toward the table, pausing when the writing on the folder on the desk under the bottle finally sank in.

Your Wedding.

That part wasn't the bit that got her heart pounding and her stomach churning far too hard considering her current delicate post-hangover condition.

It was the large words at the top of the folder that were the troublesome bit. The uber-fancy, written in silver with glittering sparkles, two-inch-high letters that read:

Jules & Zach 4ever

_____

6

"*D*amn, my battery is dead as well." Zach got to his feet and headed to his suitcase for a charging cable. He glanced at Julia. "You have enough juice to be able to text Lisa?"

Julia didn't move. She just kept staring at the bottle of champagne as if it were a snake about to strike.

"Sorry. You said something about a wedding gift?" He moved toward her at about half his regular speed. He was no longer about to fall over but far from recovered.

"Oh, shit. Shit, shit, *shit*." Julia picked a shiny black file folder off the desk, flipping it open.

Curious what could produce that kind of a reaction after she'd faced the rest of their weird morning so calmly, he slid in behind her, reading over her shoulder.

Congratulations as you begin the rest of your life together. Here at Mile-High Memories, we believe that moment that you said "I do" is one to be treasured forever. With that in mind, remember you can access your entire ceremony online by using the case-sensitive code YeHaWeDIDit!!! *on our website.*

"How come we brought home Karen and Finn's wedding mementos?" Zach asked in confusion. The name of the wedding chapel seemed wrong, but at that moment, who knew?

Julia let out a stuttering breath. She firmly closed the brochure and turned to face him. "Because it's not Karen and Finn's. Not according to this."

She violently shook the file from side to side.

He still had to be intoxicated because two and two were currently adding up to something way different than four. "How come that's got *our* names on it?"

She pressed the file against his chest, shoving past him and heading to her phone. He twisted and followed hard on her heels, glancing into the file folder again for further clues.

Behind the page with the access code was a picture.

"Oh, shit," he echoed her sentiment.

It wasn't a bad picture as far as that went. Actually, it was kind of cute, but it didn't look as if they were hanging out at a high-class bar doing shooters. He had his arm around her, huge smiles on their faces. Julia wore a sparkly tiara with a massive wad of white fluffy stuff sticking out the back. He supposed that was the equivalent of a wedding veil.

For his concession to formalwear, a lopsided bowtie had been placed around his neck. It looked extra ridiculous considering he wore a plain black T-shirt with the word GROOM across the chest.

It matched her white one that said RIDE.

RIDE? The hell?

"What's that access code again?" Julia demanded before cursing softly. "My phone is charging at the speed of a drunken gnat."

He passed her the piece of paper without taking his eyes off the picture. "It seems we had a hell of a good time."

"I'm still hoping this is some sort of elaborate hoax Lisa concocted," Julia confessed. "Here. I got it lined up."

They huddled together on the bed in order to keep the charging cable plugged in. Julia held out the phone, and Zach placed his hand under hers to tilt the screen so he could see the images beginning to roll.

A bright-red loveseat held centre stage, small end tables on either side filled with massive bouquets of white roses.

"This way, mademoiselle, monsieur." The man's far too cheesy and very fake French accent sounded against the delicate background of piano music.

The next moment, it was them, Julia and Zach, sliding into view.

Video Zach sat, and the couch made a distinctly rude noise.

Julia snickered, seating herself beside him and crossing her ankles demurely. "Excuse you."

He scooped her up—him, Zach on the screen—ignoring Julia's giggles as he settled her in his lap. "Be nice," he warned.

"I'm always nice." The sexual innuendo in the words was strong, especially when combined with the sultry glance she tossed him.

Beside him on the mattress, real-time Julia shuddered. "Dear God, I do not do sex kitten very well."

Zach wasn't about to argue because he liked his anatomy where it was currently located. She didn't need to know how instantly he'd just reacted to her tone. "I hope this isn't a sex tape."

Julia stabbed at the phone screen, hitting the pause button. She twisted toward him, one fist landing on her hip as her jaw dropped. "You did not just say that."

Holy hell, the places his mind leapt to. "Why? Because you hope it is?"

"Of course not!" She pinched the bridge of her nose. "Be quiet."

A snicker escaped before he could control himself. "Yes, ma'am."

Ignoring him, she put the phone back into position and hit play.

That voice echoing in the background began again. "Before we get to the official ceremony, we like to start with something we call the True Love Test. I'm going to ask you questions, and you get a chance to show how much you truly know about your dear soon-to-be-wedded partner."

"This part should be good," Zach muttered.

On the screen, Julia laid her head against Zach's shoulder, one hand patting him on the chest. "Smoochy Bear and I are ready."

The groan from here-and-now Julia was loud and sincere.

"What is Zach's favourite food?"

Julia answered instantly. "Ice cream!"

"And Julia's?"

"Meatballs and sausage." Online Zach said it with a straight face, staring at the camera as if his life depended on it.

Beside him on the bed, Julia snickered harder than the drunk version of her did. But then again, only one of them was alert enough to have caught the joke.

"And what is your partner's favourite thing to drink?"

The unanimous response came back with such perfect synchronization they might've practiced for a month. "*Tequila!*"

"There's our confirmation of how we got into this mess," Zach said.

Another half dozen questions and answers followed,

interrupted when last-night Julia got an attack of hiccups. Online Zach tried to help by patting her violently on the back. Fortunately, that ended only a few seconds later when he slid off the couch.

Both of them vanished onto the floor and out of sight.

The video cut off briefly, returning to a new location. The Mile-High Wedding chapel had a distinctively western theme. The man standing at the front with Zach at his side wore a ten-gallon hat in a less than pristine white tone.

A few folding chairs were arranged on either side of the room to make a path to the altar. There were actual people waiting to watch the ceremony. All turned toward the camera, waiting for Julia to arrive.

Zach tilted the phone toward himself a little more because what he was seeing couldn't really be real. "How did you convince Dolly Parton to come to our wedding?"

"I'm very proud she's there. Dolly is awesomeness to the extreme." Julia lowered her voice. "I'd like to confess that I would also kill to have a set of tatas like hers."

A sharp burst of laughter escaped him. "Your tatas are just fine. It looks as if we also got Roy Rogers, but I don't know who the rest of them are."

"I'm bitterly disappointed in you, Zach Sorenson."

She said it with such an absolute conviction he hit the pause button, stopping the wedding march that had just begun to play. "What?"

Julia folded her arms over her chest and blinked hard, annoyance dripping from her expression. "You did not ask a single Elvis impersonator to attend our wedding."

Dear God, he was going to die. His grin was so wide his face hurt, but the back of his head ached, and his brain swirled with unanswered questions. "What the hell did we do, Julia?"

She let out a big sigh, the phone resting in her lap. "We got drunk. That much is obvious."

"I guess the good part is, my mentor always said if you're going to do a thing, do it to the best of your abilities."

"Well, then. In our Wild Adventures for Beginners class, we just scored a hundred percent." Julia held a hand in the air, and he gave her a high five.

They both groaned as the shock of impact vibrated through them. "No quick moves," Julia reminded him as she pressed a hand to her forehead.

"Got it." He pointed to the phone. "You want to watch the rest of it?"

This time when she hit play, they managed to sit quietly and let the travesty unfold before their eyes.

Part of it was Zach didn't feel like making any smart comments anymore, because there was something about watching Julia walk toward him and take his hand, and the expression on his face that seemed too real to tease about.

The vows were short and to the point, but the instant the *I do's* were exchanged and the faux French speaking administrator asked about rings, the solemnity of the occasion fell apart.

"Dammit—no rings." Last-night Zach glanced around the room. "One second."

He stepped to the wall and grabbed down a decoration. One of the lariats that had been draped on a hook.

Online Julia squealed, ducking behind Dolly Parton as Zach twirled the lasso. Chaos ensued. Chairs tipped, the witnesses scattered...

When Julia made a break for it, headed back down the aisle toward the camera, Zach neatly roped her, pulling the loop tight around her arms and bringing her laughing self back against him.

The instant he released her, she lifted her hands to his face, leaning in.

There on the bed, Zach's heart pounded. Dammit, he was turned on and waiting with breathless anticipation for online Julia to kiss him.

At the last second, she twisted his head and pressed her lips against his cheek, blowing a solid raspberry that echoed over the recording equipment.

The half dozen witnesses returned to the screen, cheering loudly. Rose petals flew in the air, then Julia and Zach were being marched down the aisle toward the camera. Huge grins in place.

Julia jerked to a stop. She glanced down at her shirt and caught hold of the B in BRIDE. One solid tug ripped the cheaply fastened letter from her chest. She twisted and handed it daintily to Dolly before coming back and grabbing Zach by the hand again.

His head tilted to one side. "RIDE?"

Her cheeky grin flashed. "Hello, cowboy. You're the one who lassoed me."

Fortunately, the video ended at that moment, except for continued music and credits.

Julia let it keep playing, but she placed her phone on the end table beside the bed and shot to her feet. "Well. That was exciting."

Yeah. That was one word for it. "Still don't think we had sex?"

Strangely, that was the trigger that made her cheeks bloom with colour. "Yes. I mean no, we did not have sex. More to the point, what do we do now?"

It was the wrong answer. Zach knew it before he said it, but he could no more hold back than stop the seasons returning. "I suppose we should go on a honeymoon."

JULIA NEARLY PULLED a muscle rolling her eyes as she headed back to the table. "There's got to be some bacon left."

There was no correct follow-up to that video they'd just witnessed. Married? The whole idea was complete bullshit, and they both knew it.

But his teasing suggestion of a honeymoon hit her interest buttons way harder than she'd have ever imagined possible.

Stick to facts. Stick to friends.

"We'll figure out something," Zach said in a far more serious tone of voice. "Sorry, but this has just been one ridiculous thing after another. We should find out if there's actually a wedding chapel called Mile-High Memories."

That was somewhat reassuring. "What time are we supposed to get together with the others?"

Zach frowned as if thinking was still hard. "Lunch."

She nibbled on the lone piece of bacon she'd discovered hidden under a lettuce leaf. "Okay. We have time to do some research and formulate a plan before we get together with anyone."

He joined her at the table and poured a new cup of coffee. He lifted the carafe in a silent ask.

More caffeine? Desperation shoved her mug forward. "Okay, since our phones need a few more minutes to recharge, let's make a list."

Her purse was within reach—thank goodness she hadn't lost that along with her mind last night. It only took a second to pull out her journal and open it to a fresh page.

Zach's lazy smirk was back. "That's awesome."

"What?" Julia demanded.

He wiggled a finger at the open journal. "Boy scouts got nothing on you."

An enormous sigh escaped before she could stop it. She put down her pen and folded her arms over her chest. "Okay, get out all the teasing at once so we can be done with it."

Shock slipped into his expression. "*Umm—*"

"Carrying your spare brain, Julia? What's on the agenda today, Julia? Want some gold stars for your notebook, Julia?"

Zach held up a hand. "Whoa. I hit a sore spot. Didn't mean to. I mean, I'm impressed. And thankful."

She paused, the anger inside wavering with uncertainty. "Thankful?"

"We need ideas. The way my brain feels at the moment, we could come up with the solution to world peace, and I'd forget it three seconds later. I'm glad you're taking notes."

It was her turn for sheepish discomfort to sweep in. "Sorry I overreacted. Journaling helps me focus, and I've done it for as long as I can remember. But people can be shits."

He laid his hand on her arm and squeezed. "Nothing but respect here. Honestly."

She picked up her pen and wrote a simple *To-Do* at the top of the page. Even with his reassurance he didn't think her journaling was silly, she didn't bother to try and make things fancy. "Check for the wedding chapel—although I'm pretty certain it exists. Having an online portal is a bit far for an elaborate hoax."

"You're right. I was being hopeful." Zach reached for the file and reopened it, digging a little deeper and pulling out pictures and papers. "...and it looks as if we have an official marriage certificate. Drat."

He placed it on the table between them.

"*Gah.* Okay, so if it's not filled out correctly, are we off the hook?" She leaned in, suddenly hopeful. "The cover of the file has my name as Jules, and I'm definitely Julia."

He groaned, running a finger under the spot with their

names. "Julia Gigi Blushing." A blink of surprise then amusement arrived as his gaze lifted to hers. "Gigi?"

"No idea why Mom inflicted me with that, other than to cause me unending torment during junior high."

"I hear you on that." He pointed to the next line.

She snickered as she read his full name. "Zachary Beauregard Damien Sorenson? Seriously?"

"I know. The whole thing is so pretentious.

"Beauregard is different, but Damien as well?"

He sighed mightily. "I was named for my father and both grandfathers."

"That's...a mouthful." Julia grabbed a glass of water, suddenly needing something to do with her hands. She knew so little about Zach, really, that this moment of cracking the door seemed important.

Seemed intimate.

He leaned back and nodded. "After having four girls, I think my parents wanted to make sure they used all the masculine familial names possible while they had a chance."

"Four girls..." She gaped. "You have *four* sisters?"

"Five. My little sister turns thirty this year."

Recalibrating. The urge to up and apologize struck all over again, and Julia went for it. "I am so sorry for mixing you up in my nonsense."

"What are you talking about? This isn't your fault." Zach shrugged. "Well, it's both our faults for drinking too much, if we're honest, but otherwise, don't go blaming yourself for the midnight-marriage thing."

"I meant for hooking you into the whole fake-girlfriend thing in the first place." It wasn't easy to continue, but she had to. "I didn't think very hard, and now I realize I don't know you very well. It was wrong to tangle you in something without being aware of what dragging you into my mess could mean."

His body was still relaxed, but that lazy expression slipped into something more solemn and forthright. "It's okay, Julia. I mean it. I'm glad I can help you deal with the rumours, and we're going to deal with this as well. Trust me."

The problem was—she did. Far too much, all things considered.

Still, she met his gaze head on. "Thank you."

His chin dipped decisively. "Okay, problem-solving time."

"How old are you?"

Another question that slipped out, but Zach took it in stride, pointing to the paperwork before them. "Thirty-three. Thirty-four on December twenty-seventh. And this says you're...*damn*. You're just a baby."

That earned him another eye roll. "Stop that. I'm twenty-five."

"A perfectly good age for a bottle of scotch."

"Don't be annoying, Beauregard." His lips twitched at her comment. "No? You like *Beau* better, baby?"

"I like *baby*, better," he confessed. "Okay, to-do list. As far as I can tell from looking at this certificate, it could be totally legit or bonfire kindling. I think we need to contact a real lawyer."

She wrote down *lawyer*. "You have someone on speed dial, if I remember correctly."

"Yeah." Zach shook his head. "Alan's going to be far too entertained by this."

"If it's real, will he be able to help us cancel it? Or annul it, or whatever it is you do to bogus marriages. I mean it's not as if we need a divorce."

He stretched again, drinking his coffee thoughtfully. "That's one part we can relax about. Alan will know what to do. You want me to call him now?"

A quick glance at the clock on the wall and Julia said, "Before noon on Sunday? That's just mean."

Zach waved off her protest. "He gets paid to deal with the nonsense we fall into, but I'll send him a message instead. That way he can respond when he wants. We probably can't do anything about this until we get home anyway."

Which meant they had to tell her sisters. "My sisters are going to laugh themselves silly when they hear what we did."

Zach made a face. "We could skip sharing the 'imagine our shock when we woke up naked' part of the experience."

That was an easy answer. "Agreed." Julia nodded vigorously before remembering that wasn't a smart move. "*Owwww.*"

He hummed in sympathy. "We're both a little delicate right now. For the to-do list—want me to find us a spa to help work out some of the kinks?"

"If we're supposed to meet the others at noon, it would have to be after." She tapped her pen on the notebook. "Problem-solving, first. All we have is *contact lawyer.*"

"Which is pretty much all we need." Zach stroked his fingers against his shadowed jaw. His gaze fixed on her, growing more intent. "Except I need to be utterly serious here and embarrass the hell out of both of us. Regarding that waking-up-naked business."

Julia braced. "You're really going to ask this again?"

"The problem is, I'm not one hundred percent certain we didn't have sex. And while there is nothing wrong with us having sex at some point, the fact I can't remember is terrifying me. I'm not the kind of guy who sleeps with a woman after she's been drinking, Julia. The fact you were three sheets to the wind should have meant sex was off the agenda."

He really was one of the good ones. Which made it easier

to pony up the details that would reassure him even as she hated having to share something so personal.

She lay down her pen and leaned forward. "We were *both* drunk. But I believe you, absolutely, that you wouldn't have taken advantage. The way I was acting all handsy in that wedding video, it's possible you had to call *me* off. Not probable, but possible." This was kind of like tearing off a bandage—easier if she just spat it out. "I haven't had sex in a couple of years. If we'd had sex last night, I'm pretty sure I would feel it today."

"Oh." Zach lifted a hand as if he was going to say something else, but he closed his mouth and his brow furrowed. He nodded slowly, eyeing her with curiosity. "That's a long dry spell."

"Self-inflicted. Don't worry, I'm not about to combust or anything."

She could tell he was itching to ask more but wasn't sure where the line between them stood and how far politeness would extend. And while there was more she could share, it wasn't necessary.

Instead, Julia went back to her notebook and wrote down *physical.* "Well, if anything sexual did happen, I'm due for one of my regular checkups sometime this coming month. Which means I'll be tested for everything anyway, what with my position as an EMT. Any possible social diseases I need to be aware of?"

His lips twitched again. "This is like having a conversation with my RN mother. Far too blunt, and yet I know better than to try to avoid the interrogation. No, I'm not carrying any communicable diseases."

"Your mom's a nurse?"

"Retired now, but yeah." His grin widened. "I begged my dad to give me the birds-and-the-bees talk, but no. By the time he got around to it, my mother and older sisters had already traumatized me."

She could imagine. "My mom—"

The memory stalled before she could even share it. Her mom had shared about the mechanics of sex at the appropriate time. Looking back, the very dry and clinical descriptions hadn't been the best introduction.

Realizing that sent another sharp jab through already painful memories.

Then damn if Zach wasn't there again. Kneeling beside her and looking up with concern written all over him. "You okay?"

She forced a smile. "I guess I've developed a little baggage when it comes to my mom. Sorry. Didn't mean to go off on a tangent."

He winked. "No problem. I'll grab my phone and send off that message to Alan. You want to touch base with Lisa? Maybe set up a meeting spot. We can share the dreadful details in person. Together."

"That sounds fine."

He squeezed her knee then headed to where his phone was charging.

Julia watched him for a moment before purposely rising and opening her own device. This was all just a momentary glitch. After they'd dealt with the teasing, it would be easily solved.

Yet this royal screwup made it much easier for her to reaffirm her conviction that it would be best to strictly play pretend once they went back to Heart Falls.

Zach was a good man, and he didn't need to get tangled up more than she'd already got him. She would keep them on the friend side of the page. Honestly, that would be special all on its own.

She opened her messages and clicked through to her sister.

7

*Z*ach found them a corner booth in the restaurant where the six of them met. Private enough that his and Julia's bomb could be presented without too many others overhearing. Public enough that he knew he wasn't about to be skewered by anyone—especially by the most dangerous members of any family: sisters.

As they settled, he examined his friends, looking for clues as to how they might react. Josiah wore the same gloating expression as Finn. Karen and Lisa looked relaxed yet deliciously content.

For a moment Zach fought his first instinct, which was to grab Julia by the hand and haul her back to his suite to put that same expression on *her* face.

The idea was tempting, but it wasn't his right, dammit.

With the two other couples seated on the inside of the circular bench, he and Julia sat on the outside edges opposite each other.

He was just about to bring up the funny thing that happened the previous night when Julia beat him to the punch.

"Hey, Lisa. Bet you twenty bucks I've done something in Vegas that you haven't."

Which was the perfect way to get all their attention. Lisa and her bets were notorious.

Lisa lifted a brow. "*Really?* What did you get up to after Josiah and I left you on the dance floor?"

"So many cool things. Like, Zach found us a private club on the twenty-seventh floor and somehow got us access."

Josiah looked impressed, dipping his chin at Zach. "Room with a view? *Nice.* You must've really sweet-talked somebody to get access without an invitation."

Considering Zach didn't remember what strings he'd pulled, he simply grinned as if he was a magician. "When you've got it, you've got it."

"That was only part of our adventure," Julia said. "I also met a Dolly Parton impersonator, tried some really good tequila, Zach and I got married, and I discovered that room service bacon is—"

"Hold your horses." Karen shot up a hand, fingers spread wide. "Did you say you *got married?*"

Julia nodded then winced. "Excuse me. Slight headache. Yeah, it was kind of one of those *one thing led to another* deals, ending in an *oops*. It's okay, though. Zach's already contacted his lawyer dude, so we'll get it fixed up in no time."

The entire time she shared, her tone remained light. She was so obviously amused it was impossible for anyone at the table to get upset.

Only Finn was examining him with that impenetrable gaze that said *he* knew exactly how fucked up this was.

Thankfully, his best friend didn't speak. On the practical side, Finn wouldn't have been able to get a word in edgewise because Lisa, Karen, and Josiah all spoke at once.

"Are you kidding?" Josiah said with a laugh.

"I can't believe you did that."

"Was there an Elvis impersonator as well?" That last one from Lisa, which made Julia snort.

"No. I'm so disappointed." She turned her attention across the table to Zach. "See? If we were going to have an impromptu marriage in Vegas, Elvis was *supposed* to be involved."

"I'll remember that for next time," Zach drawled. "You may as well show them the video."

"There's *video*?" Lisa reached for the phone Julia had all queued up, and a moment later the four of them had all leaned into watch the travesty.

Zach met Julia's gaze across the table. She smiled and offered a wink. Everything about her said she was relaxed and happy...

Except it was a complete lie.

A repeat of the moment when it seemed she had been about to share her amusing birds-and-bees story. A veil had fallen, bringing in something heavy and sad.

Now? She was putting on a great show to make light of the situation for their friends and family, but inside, she was hurting bad.

The insight struck him on so many levels. First and foremost because he wanted to fix her pain. She didn't deserve to be sad, and this hurt seemed to go beyond the mixed-up mess of here and now.

Second truth that hit him—

He could read her like a book.

Julia Blushing was a very good liar, but he was even better at spotting her tells. And while laughter swelled at the table as the video continued, Zach struggled to keep his new awareness from showing on his face.

What a tangled web.

He'd always been lucky. His gut instinct had always told him when it was time to take a chance. When the time was right.

Everything in him said Julia was hiding something deep, maybe even keeping truths from herself. But more than that, his gut told him that they belonged together. Sham marriage, fake boyfriend, none of that mattered.

He and Julia were meant to be.

Hell of a thing to discover, though, considering everyone at the table was now highly entertained at the idea of them as a couple.

His phone buzzed with an incoming message, and he pulled it out to discover a response from Alan to his *what do we do next?* query.

Alan: *well, I can honestly say you boys keep me entertained. Plus, you keep me in business. I'll do more research, but at first glance this isn't going to have a cut-and-dried solution. Just a heads-up. This might end up more complicated than you hope.*

Zach put his head down and typed under the edge of the table where nobody could see him: *aren't you a ray of fucking sunshine?*

Alan: *you don't pay me to blow smoke up your skirt.*

Zach: *thank goodness. A kilt in Alberta would get mighty chilly at times.*

Alan: *ha ha. You want me to rush down to Vegas or wait until you're back at the ranch on Monday?*

Zach: *the ranch. This is supposed to be Karen and Finn's gig. Julia and I will meet you at the house Monday evening and we'll get the mess straightened out.*

Alan: *pass on my congratulations to the newlyweds. I mean, the couple who* intended *to get married this weekend.*

Zach: *will do*

Now he understood why Finn always teased that Zach's jokes weren't that funny. Alan had the same issue.

Zach tucked his phone away before the rest of them noticed, which was good. He didn't want to share the whole *it's going to be more complicated than you hoped* revelation. Monday would be soon enough to start fixing their mistake.

A cheer rang out and then wild applause as the video came to an end.

Lisa met his eyes. "I've got to give up my *Most Mischievous Whiskeyteer* badge after that bit of shenanigans. Well done, Julia and Zach."

Zach laid a hand over his chest. "Don't disappoint me. Tell me you actually have a badge to give Julia."

"Oh, no, Lisa doesn't need any encouragement to produce strange membership paraphernalia," Karen said. "One year she tried to make a set of ears for us all à la Mickey Mouse."

"They were really good ears," Lisa insisted.

Karen raised a brow. "You stuck a set on Tamara's head before the glue was dry. I had to cut the damn thing out of her hair."

Lisa's nose wrinkled in a move that was strangely reminiscent of Julia's favourite expression. "Oh. You're right. I forgot about that part."

"I'm pretty sure Tamara hasn't. In fact, she already told me about that event, so I think it was very memorable," Julia shared.

"*Memorable* is one way of saying *traumatic.*" Karen gestured toward where the waitstaff was bringing their lunch. "Clear the runway. Food's about to arrive."

And that was it. Zach had to admit that while he had a way with people, Julia took it to the next level. No one other than Finn seemed to have any concerns whatsoever about the current situation.

Well, no one other than Finn and himself, of course. Because the layers of questions were getting deeper instead of falling away. Still, Zach focused on enjoying the meal and the company of friends instead of worrying about the situation.

It wasn't until they hustled the women off to enjoy a luxury spa package for the afternoon and it was down to just the three of them that things got complicated again.

Zach settled with a contented sigh into the high-back leather chair in the whiskey bar, the scent of cigar smoke drifting on the air just enough to be pleasant. The waitress brought glasses of heavenly scented amber liquid then vanished as if she'd never been there.

To his left, Finn raised his glass and peered into the whiskey. "One hell of an *oops*, my friend."

Josiah didn't even pretend to be casual. He leaned forward on his elbows, drink ignored. "Top it off with the gossip I just got from my receptionist back home, can I ask what the hell you're doing?"

Drat. "What's the gossip?"

"Word is you and Julia are a hot item." Josiah's usual easygoing expression had gone blank.

So. The small-town rumour mill had done its job. Man, they would have a field day when the updated news hit.

"You're my best friend," Finn began. Paused. His gaze

lasered in. "What's the plan? Is this a mistake to be solved or an opportunity to take hold of?"

Josiah blinked. "Whoa. Did not see that one coming."

Zach could appreciate their newer friend's confusion. "Our mentor, Bruce. It was one of his sayings. One of the lessons he taught us—too many times people see what they think is a disaster headed their way and do everything they can to avoid it or get out of the path."

"When what they should be doing is figuring out how to harness the energy and aim the river in the direction they need it to go," Finn finished.

Josiah hesitated. "Accidentally getting married might be a good thing?"

Finn shrugged. "Nothing to panic over, that's for sure." He met Zach's gaze again. "You know you've got my support. The whole situation is a little twisted because Julia is Karen's sister, but since I don't think you would want anything that's not in Julia's best interest, I see no potential conflict."

He held out his hand, and Zach took it gratefully. "You're the best."

The three of them all sat back a lot more comfortably now that Finn had stated where he stood, which put Zach in a better position.

Taking advantage of the moment's pause while they all sipped their drinks let Zach run through what he wanted to say. Both of the men beside him were trustworthy. As partners to Karen and Lisa, both of them had high-stakes interest in how his and Julia's relationship turned out.

It wasn't reasoning that made him speak. His gut made him do it.

"I want this," he admitted. "Not sure why or how to get to the point where this is more than a messed-up-yet-good idea between two people, but no matter how we got here, me and Julia being hitched is not a mistake."

The corners of Finn's lips twitched upward. He made eye contact with Josiah. "Looks as if we're backup for what might be the strangest reverse-courtship ever. Marry first, fall in love later."

Josiah lifted his glass in the air in a toast. "To brothers-in-arms and the brave women who love us. When the dust settles, may Julia be counted among that number."

A shiver slid up Zach's back. He raised his glass in silent agreement.

He'd always loved a challenge. Finding a way to forever with Julia would be worth every bit of the struggle.

He just hoped she'd agree sooner rather than later.

PUSHING ASIDE the unreal situation with her and Zach, Julia was discovering a whole lot of things to appreciate about Vegas.

Like now. She rested her head on the soft towel rolled up at the edge of the pool and let the warm bubbles of the spa bath break around her like hundreds of heated kisses against her skin. "This is heavenly."

"I could use one of these in my backyard," Karen said. "Just think. After you finish chores or a long hard ride, you could soak in one of these until you're good as new."

"Speaking of long hard rides..." Lisa let her sentence trail off, but the innuendo was there all the same.

Julia wasn't touching that one unless she had to. Redirecting... "How was the wedding night, Karen?"

"You tell us," Lisa said with a snicker.

"You're terrible," Karen scolded before speaking in a softer tone. "Okay, I avoided the topic for an entire hour, but I'm at the limit of my patience. Julia, what gives?"

Julia went for the best wide-eyed doe look she could manage. "Isn't it just the wildest thing? Accidentally getting married. Blows my mind, but it'll be okay—"

It was obvious the two people staring back at her were not buying her innocent act.

She shrugged and went with honest. "Okay. This time with a little less enthusiasm. It's not a big deal. Zach is a great guy, and the whole thing was just an evening fueled by too much liquor." She hurried to explain because both their expressions had changed enough to cause concern. "Nothing happened between us other than the sham wedding. Nothing's *going* to happen other than being friends. His lawyer will help take care of the mistake. Other than that—" *Oops.* Good time to get the fake boyfriend thing into the open. "Well, there is this *one* other thing."

"The part about how you and him were burning up the sheets back in Heart Falls?"

Unexpectedly, the comment came from Karen, not Lisa.

Lisa gaped. "They are?" She somehow looked horrified and offended at the same time. "You *are?* I can't believe you didn't tell me!"

"Because there's nothing to tell," Julia insisted. "We just... it's complicated."

"It's also the rumour de jour back home. Tamara texted me this morning that she heard it from at least five different people in the span of an hour." Karen poked her toes out of the water and examined her polish critically. "So...what gives? Sisters share secrets."

The words triggered an awkward sensation, but Julia was trying to embrace the changes in her life. Add in the two women with her now were some of the best she'd ever met, blood-related or not.

Julia gathered her courage, sitting a little straighter. "Okay, here's the scoop."

By the time she'd explained the situation with the gossip, somehow the events of the entire evening had flown from her lips. The only thing she didn't explain fully was the situation with her stalker-slash-kidnapper. The less time spent on that topic, the better.

Her sisters listened without comment but with great concentration.

When she finished, Karen nodded. "One of the first things Finn shared when we were getting involved again was how much he trusted Zach. He considers the man a brother—and I sort of do as well. Already."

The slight hesitation from Lisa was only noticeable because of how she usually leapt before looking. Concern lingered in her eyes. "I have no way to say this without being blunt. You've been in our lives for nearly six months. In all that time you've never talked about past boyfriends or girlfriends. Tell me to butt out if you want, but even pretending to be with Zach will require some physical contact. Will that be a problem?"

Julia wasn't about to lay out all her issues, but this much she should share. "I'm not looking for a long-term relationship. If I was, it would be with a guy, I guess. Then again, my turn to be blunt, I don't miss penis time."

A soft cough sounded.

The three of them glanced up to discover a young man with flushed red cheeks standing at the edge of the hot tub, a tray of snacks in his hand. "I'll just put this here."

He vanished before Julia could sink under the water to hide her embarrassment. Of course, both Karen and Lisa were smirking and not even trying to hide it.

"Thanks for the warning," Julia muttered.

"Poor guy." Lisa ducked away from Karen's swing. "Hey."

"Poor guy? Poor Julia," Karen corrected. She smiled softer now. "Teasing aside, we've got your back. I can see why you want to make things better for Brad. The rumours you and Zach are together should help, but beyond that, you're not required to do anything that makes you uncomfortable. You can do what you need to with Zach just as a friend. Okay?"

"I know that. And..." Maybe it was stupid, but she believed the best of Zach, confirmed by how horrified he was at the possibility he might have taken advantage of her. "I don't think Zach is the type to push. He'll tease, but he's not an Alphahole wannabe."

"Agreed." Lisa wrinkled her nose, her eyes flashing with mischief. "Although, if we're talking about sex appeal factor, for all that he's not a 'my way or the highway' kind of guy, Josiah is very demanding in the bedroom. Truth. Sexy sex appeal isn't only granted to the guys who growl *mine, mine, mine*."

"I do like it when Finn growls, though," Karen admitted before shaking a finger at Julia. "You tell us if you need us. Call —day or night. You're our sister, but you're also our friend. We're here for you. If all you want to be with Zach is friends, then that's it."

Her throat was tight. "Thanks."

Lisa stood to offer a hug but slipped, vanishing from sight for a second. When she popped up, dripping wet and laughing, the seriousness melted away into a warm fuzzy feeling that lasted the rest of the evening.

The guys grabbed them from the spa, and while Julia ended up sitting next to Zach during dinner and the show, his company was comfortable and easy.

He leaned close a few times during the performance,

whispering comments. She did the same, and with the sweet thought of *friend* wrapped around them, their connection was natural and fell into the *just right* category.

"Thank goodness my headache is gone," she murmured in his ear after a particularly boisterous stage number.

"I hear you." His smile flashed. "No more tequila for us?"

"No more tequila." She held out her pinkie.

His snort was loud enough to draw attention from her sisters. Lisa shushed him with a wink.

Zach pressed a finger to his lips, but as soon as Lisa looked away, he leaned in again, his lips brushing Julia's ear. "Wait until you meet my sister, Petra. She pinkie swears all the time."

That's a meeting that will never take place.

The thought sent Julia's mind wandering for the rest of the show.

The pack of them finished the night with one final drink in Karen and Finn's suite before Lisa and Josiah walked them down the hall to where Julia's private room was, a few doors away from Zach's.

"Sleep in if you want," Josiah reminded her. "Our flight home isn't until the afternoon, so I booked brunch for eleven-thirty, after checkout."

"Sounds good. Night, all." Julia offered a quick wave before slipping into the cool darkness. Their voices sounded in the hallway for a couple more minutes before fading away.

She wandered across to the window, staring out at the sparkling lights. It had turned out to be a fantastic day, and now she was ending it with a king-size bed all to herself and no alarm to wake her in the morning. What a treat.

The nightmare seemed to arrive only seconds after she'd turned out the lights and pulled the covers to her chin.

Waves rocked her, knocking her feet out from under her

every time she attempted to escape. When her back hit the sand, the water rose rapidly and covered her head as the current swept her away from shore. Long strands of seaweed tangled around her body, dragging her relentlessly to the bottom of the ocean.

Julia woke, cutting off a cry of fear in mid-shout.

Heart pounding, she swallowed hard and tried to tell if her throat was dry or rough. How long had she been screaming? Or could she at least hope she'd been whimpering this time?

The sheets were tangled around her, the pillows shoved to the floor. A glance at the bedside clock said only two hours had passed since she'd entered the room.

She eyed the mattress and wondered if she risked trying to get more sleep.

Call us if you need us. Day or night.

Karen's offer from earlier that day whispered through her head. It had been honestly given, and Julia was tempted to reach out. Except...

No way was she interrupting either of her sisters' getaway nights with their guys. Which meant she had two options. No, three.

Suck it up and try to sleep again.

Give up and stay awake. She'd be exhausted tomorrow, but at least she didn't have to work.

Or...

Julia pulled out her phone. Put it down. Picked it up. Put it down.

Dammit. Decide already.

She let fate decide and sent Zach a text. If he'd shut off his phone for the night, so be it.

Julia: *if you're up...can I come sleep on your couch? I had a nightmare.*

She stared at the phone for a minute, not sure if she wanted an answer or hoped she'd have to wave it off as a lark in the morning.

A soft knock on her door sent a rush of adrenaline through her. Julia leapt up and peeked through the spyhole.

Zach.

She let him in right away. "I'm so sorry—"

"Don't apologize." He slipped past her into the room, his words whisper-soft as if they weren't alone. "Get back in bed and go to sleep. I'll use your couch."

The idea was all kinds of wrong. "That's ridiculous. I'll take the couch. I insist."

"Julia Gigi Blushing, get your ass into bed this minute." He caught her by the shoulders and gave her a gentle shove toward the bed. "Come on. Compromise. I'll sleep on top of the covers, then."

Her body still quivered from the nightmare, and she was exhausted after the previous night and all the activities of the day. Crawling under the covers felt good, and the way the mattress tilted slightly as Zach lay down beside her was like the slow, comforting sway of a porch swing.

She curled on her side like usual and ended up staring straight at his face. He'd closed his eyes, long lashes resting on his cheeks. His chest rose and fell in an even rhythm that mesmerized and calmed her.

His breath washed over her, sweet and reassuring, and just having him there warmed her.

Relaxation slowly slipped in. Julia caught herself reaching out to brush back the lock of hair that had fallen over his forehead.

His lips curled, and he caught her fingers in his, guiding them to the bed between them. Cupping her hand loosely, he whispered again, "Sleep."

She did. A solid, comfortable rest that lasted until the sun streaking across the bed woke her.

Zach was gone, and his side of the mattress was cool to the touch.

8

$\mathcal{T}$he trip home Monday morning had been a blast. Julia had to admit that was mostly because Zach and Josiah kept up a running commentary worthy of any comedy routine.

Between the comfortable accommodations in the plane and their pickup at the airport in Alberta being Red Boot ranch's foreman, Cody, they were back outside Karen and Finn's future home without spending more time and energy discussing her and Zach's accidental wedding.

Julia was thankful Tamara hadn't been their pickup ride, though. One less person to explain things to would make moving on from here that much easier.

They sat in what would eventually be a grand living room with tall floor-to-ceiling windows facing the Rocky Mountains. Now it was still filled with construction materials and a set of folding lawn chairs.

Zach's lawyer sat across from her, his expression unreadable. He kept picking up his pen and flipping it over, point down, clicker down, point down—

The entire time staring at her face as if waiting for her to confess to some dire crime.

"Are you charging by the hour for this trip, Alan?" Zach drawled.

Alan Cwedwick didn't even blink. "Just figuring out the best way to proceed."

"Don't give me that. You've already got a checklist and a timeline, and you just need to explain what you need from us." Zach propped one foot up on his knee, tapping his fingers on his thigh. "Unless you're saying you don't know what to do this time, which would disappoint me."

"Oh, I know exactly what is on the books in this kind of circumstance. Just don't think you'll like it much." Alan's focus sharpened, and his gaze snapped to Julia. "Have you been married before?"

Julia blinked. Instinctively, one hand rose to point at her chest. "Who, me?"

"Engaged to be married?"

What the heck was going on? "I don't see how that relates to Zach and I getting this mistake annulled."

The clipboard in Alan's hands dipped, his pen moved rapidly over the papers. "Would you say you've had a difficult time maintaining long-term relationships, Miss Blushing?"

Zach was no longer relaxed or lighthearted. He leaned forward and glared hard at his lawyer. "I don't know where you think you're going with this, but watch yourself, Alan."

"I'm doing my job." The man tossed the clipboard on the table and folded his arms across his chest. "Julia, if I gave you a lump sum of money, would you agree to leave Heart Falls immediately and never come back?"

Julia had thought waking up naked in bed with Zach had been mind-bogglingly unreal, but this conversation topped even the bizarre video of their wedding. "Excuse me? I have a job. I'm not leaving Heart Falls until after my internship is done, and even then, I have family here. Of course, I'm going to come back. Why are you asking such ridiculous questions? Zach and I just want this wedding thing to go away. It was an accident, okay? And both of us were involved in making that mistake, so I don't appreciate the implication I did something immoral."

"Were you aware that your sister Karen received a large sum of money once she became involved with Finn Marlette?"

Zach was on his feet. "Enough, Alan. Get to the point. Also, you talk to me and leave Julia out of this since you seem to have lost all trace of professionalism."

Being ignored felt as unreal as having Alan's intense attention.

But the lawyer turned his gaze on Zach as requested, pointing him back to his chair. "Unfortunately, you will remember that Bruce liked to consider possible situations that might arise. One of those involved you and Finn eventually finding relationship partners. Certain criteria were flagged as potentially dangerous, not just to yourselves, but to the inheritance he passed down to you."

"You think Julia and I drunkenly getting married is dangerous?"

Alan sighed, some of his rigid tension slipping away. "Zach, it doesn't matter what I think. What matters is what's required by the contract both you and Finn signed when you took over Bruce's holdings. You got married without a prenup, and also without any kind of previous interaction between your new partner and myself as the representation of Burly, Evans, and Ives. Those two items have now triggered certain consequences."

"We've had a previous interaction," Julia reminded him. "I met you the night I stitched up Zach and another of your clients after they got shot." Julia offered her best *so there* glare.

"While that was a charming interaction, and I can speak highly of your caregiving skills, I was thinking more of social interaction than emergency medical procedures." Alan tipped his head in her direction. "I will acknowledge you seem to have the ability to keep your mouth shut when required. That doesn't change what happens next."

Zach perched at the front edge of his lawn chair. "Still think it's absolutely ridiculous, but fine. Tell us the damn consequences."

"If you'd like, we can discuss this privately," Alan began.

Zach waved the suggestion off. "Julia's involved, accidentally, but still. She deserves to be here while you get to the damn point."

For an instant Alan looked borderline apologetic as he glanced her way, then he went all businesslike and pulled the clipboard toward himself. "Very well. The policy in question states that if either partner participates in an activity that could cause potential financial detriment to the—"

"In English," Zach commanded. "And for God sake, the Coles Notes version."

"You have to stay married for one year." Alan slammed his lips together.

Her reaction was utterly wrong considering how serious the man looked, but Julia couldn't help it. She snickered.

Both heads swiveled toward her. Alan was shocked, Zach looked puzzled.

"I'm sorry, but you just said we have to stay married for one year. There is no way that could possibly be the legal advice you want to give. Especially considering you asked me a bunch of questions that implied I'm some kind of moneygrubbing gold

98

digger looking for a sugar daddy."

"I'm glad you find this amusing," Mr. Cwedwick said dryly. "But rest assured, as convoluted as Bruce's thinking was, this is what's on the books. You are to remain married for one year. At that point if you'd like to have the marriage dissolved, I will be happy to put the papers through ASAP."

"And if we do what I think is more prudent and go to another lawyer to deal with this?" Julia asked.

The man glanced at Zach. "I wouldn't suggest that idea. Your finances are tied up with your partner's, and under these circumstances, your choice also affects him. I believe Bruce thought that limitation would be a good way to stop your friendship from causing you to make an unwise move, followed by Finn simply bailing you out."

Zach's confusion hadn't faded one bit. He looked as tangled as her brain felt. "So, we have to stay married?"

"Yes."

Zach shook his head, his gaze meeting Julia's. "I agree with you. This is pure bullshit. This can't possibly be true."

Finally, someone else in the room who wasn't talking nonsense. "*Thank* you."

"That said, I have never known Alan to bullshit before in his life." Zach made a face. "Mind if I talk to him for a minute by myself? He can throw legal jargon at me, and I can swear in his face easier if you're not in the room."

Shoving to her feet felt good as restless energy returned with a vengeance. "Fine. I'll be outside, communing with nature and discussing with any birds that happen to land within listening distance about how criminally stupid the legal system appears to be."

Outside, the cool fall air wrapped around her, bringing a certain calm to her fevered thoughts. She wandered to the nearest arena and leaned her elbows on the wooden railing, her gaze drifting over the horses herded together at the far end.

Stay married for a year? Laughable that she'd even heard that come out of the lawyer's mouth. Zach would figure something out.

She didn't even know what she was going to do past a month from now. And while she planned to come back to Heart Falls for visits, it was beyond time to accept a position for the coming winter. There'd been one in High River she could take. The town wasn't that far away, so she could continue to spend time with her sisters.

A soft nudge against her fingers brought her attention back to the arena. The little colt Karen had rescued stood on the other side of the railing, his nostrils flaring as he sniffed Julia's hands.

"Hey, little guy." She reached through the fence and caressed the white spot on his brow. Scratching lightly, she eyed him thoughtfully. "You're looking better than the last time I saw you. Putting on a little weight. Good for you."

Moonbeam dipped his head then pranced back, almost like a puppy, dancing his front hooves on the ground then spinning away before returning.

Another amazing moment to add to all the others she'd had while in Heart Falls. She would miss it when she was gone.

Julia glanced back at the house where Zach and Alan Cwedwick were visible through the window. Zach must've just dragged a hand through his hair because the ends stood tousled in every direction.

This ridiculous situation would be solved, and then she'd be able to move on to her next thing.

Although the teasing thought remained—*life's never that simple.*

THE INSTANT JULIA left the room, Zach thrust out a hand toward Alan. "Okay. Give me the letter."

Alan shook his head. "I don't know what you're talking about."

The urge to snap his fingers was strong. "Bruce *always* did this. He would come up with these farfetched situations, and then he would write us a damn letter explaining what he was trying to accomplish. It's exactly what happened with the whole challenge to get the dude ranch running. Hell, he wrote a letter to *Karen* before he even knew she existed. You can't tell me there's no letter from Bruce this time."

"Oh, there was a letter from Bruce," Alan agreed.

"*Ha.*"

"But not for you."

Zach paused, his hand still hovering in the air. He jerked it back. "For Finn?"

"For me." Alan shoved his hands in his pockets and shook his head. "Look. I don't like this either. I apologize for sounding like a shit back there with those questions for Julia. But I have to do my job."

"Which right now would be figuring out how to get Julia and I a quick and dirty divorce." Even as he said it, Zach hated the words.

"I *can't.* And you can't. This is serious, Zach. If you go ahead and make that decision, it will trigger a dissolution of your entire holdings. Yours and Finn's."

Ridiculous had just gone into impossible territory. "You're telling me that Bruce Travers, himself a divorced man, had such a negative reaction to myself or Finn needing to call off our potential future marriages that the entire corporation is on the line?"

"Oh, Finn can get a divorce if he wants. You can't. Not for one year."

And impossible went into fairytale land. "Now that's just silly."

"Agreed. Yet it's one hundred percent legal—I double-checked all the loopholes myself." Alan made a face. "And I'm a damn good loophole closer. Sorry about that."

The urge to go get a bottle of tequila made zero sense, but it was there. Zach pinched the bridge of his nose. "Alan, we've enjoyed a long relationship, so I hope you take this the right way. Right now, I hate your fucking guts."

"I'm sorry," Alan repeated. "Hate me all you want, just don't go getting a divorce from someone else."

Zach met his gaze. "The kicker is, I wasn't planning on it," he confessed. "But this whole bullshit situation is going to make it a lot harder to convince Julia that my interest isn't just financially motivated."

The first entertaining part of the last hour arrived. He'd managed to shock his lawyer. Alan stood there, his mouth opening and closing a few times before blinking back to alertness. "You—*want* to stay married?"

"You are not to repeat that, especially not to Julia. Not at this point. But yes, getting married was an accident, but it wasn't a mistake." Zach dragged a hand through his hair. "Okay. Somehow I have to figure out a way to make this work."

Alan had lost a lot of his attitude in the last five seconds. "Well, then. That's interesting."

It was too much to hope for. "Does that mean you're changing your legal stance?"

"Oh, hell no. Just...interesting." Alan grinned. Then he reached into his pocket and pulled out an envelope. "Not the letter you were hoping for, but the ground rules regarding your marriage. Again, if you want to complain, take it up with Bruce."

Zach snatched the envelope from him. "Have a good trip home. I suggest you leave before Julia decides to practice her autopsy skills or something."

"Let me know if you need me for anything. As always, it's been a pleasure working with you," Alan said with zero hesitation.

"Everybody's a comedian," Zach grumbled, following Alan out the door.

He waited until the other man left the yard before joining Julia beside the horse arena. This wasn't going to be easy. A juggling act between convincing Julia to do what was right because it was necessary and because it was what he wanted—

It wasn't often that he tossed curses his mentor's way, but this time? Bruce Travers had fucked up royally.

Julia folded her arms over her chest. "The fact that Alan left without paperwork for us to sign does not seem like a positive thing."

Zach shook his head. "I'm sorry. I don't even know how to explain how they managed it, but it's a completely legal convoluted mess. Us getting a divorce means both Finn and I lose financial control of our corporate holdings. Like, they're gone. That's it."

"A corporation that's big enough to own a private plane." She seemed rightly dumbfounded. "It was one drunken night. We can't stay married after getting hitched while under the influence."

"Not staying married could cost a lot of people everything. Me. Finn, which would also mean changing Karen's life radically."

Her face twisted. "I'm supposed to complete my trainee status in October. Then I'm gone from Heart Falls."

"You can find a new job."

"That easy? Plus, I only have a place to stay until the end of the month."

Zach wasn't about to let that one go. "You're not staying at that deathtrap any longer, remember? Also, look around you. Dude ranch. Multiple buildings with your name on them. Although I feel as if there might be a line in here that says we have to share. To make the marriage legit. Alan said these are the rules."

He pulled out the envelope and shook it in the air.

She reached for it. "Mister Cwedwick has been oh-so-helpful. I'm definitely putting him on my Christmas card list."

"Can we send him a letter bomb?"

She paused before sliding the envelope open. "I need to be sitting down before we open this."

"Your idea is much smarter than mine. I was going to suggest tequila, but all things considered, that might not be wise. Don't worry. We'll figure this out."

Julia marched ahead of him, headed to the cabin he'd claimed for his own.

"Everything is simple, isn't it?" She glared so hard he could have sworn his hair sizzled. "I could tell you I was betrothed to a vampire, and you'd wave it off and offer to be our third."

A snort escaped. "Sorry, no. The fooling around with a guy thing doesn't cut it for me. Unless your vampirical arranged marriage is with a lady. Then we can talk."

Her glare broke from annoyance to amusement as she paused on his front porch. "It's the grouping of the sexes in the ménage that makes you hesitate, not the actual threesome?"

"My biggest complaint is the whole sucking-blood thing, but yeah...whatever. When it comes to sex, I have zero beef with whatever turns a person's crank. *My* engine is attuned to ladies, though, like sexy emergency rescue chicks with feisty attitudes."

He opened the door, but she detoured instead to the hardback chairs he'd placed to one side of the porch—the ones with a great view over the panoramic scenery.

She stilled even as she took a seat. Her gaze met his, and she seemed to calm herself before ignoring his last comment and speaking with complete seriousness. "I get that this is important. I'm not about to run away or do something to hurt my new sisters. Or Finn."

Zach ignored her complete failure to mention not hurting *him*.

Julia stared over the landscape. "This is uncomfortable for many reasons, so let's say we agree to do this thing."

"Stay married?"

"Stay *pretend* married," she clarified. "If we're going to be roomies, we need ground rules."

Made perfect sense. Also, his gut told him to stop worrying about the wild situation and roll with it. Enjoy it, even. "What kind of ground rules?

She shook the envelope in the air. "We check what your meany-pants lawyer tossed at us and find out how close we have to live. Sharing a house, I can work with. Sharing a bed is out."

Zach pulled himself upright even as he laughed at her assessment of Alan. "I am perfectly capable of sharing a bed without anything happening you don't want to happen."

"I like my space," Julia drawled. "Sharing a bed is on the *no* list."

"Fine, but may I point out that we've already sort of shared a bed a couple of times and nothing terrible happened."

Her jaw swung open. "*We. Got. Married.*"

Oh. Right. The jury was still out on whether that was the most brilliant mistake he'd ever made or the worst.

"Fine. No shared beds." He hid his sigh—she was far too fine to be living celibate for a year...

Wait.

He stiffened. "I have an item for this list."

9
_____

*J*ulia tugged the stool beside her closer to use as a table as she pulled her ever-present notebook from her purse. "Go ahead. I'll make notes. We can run them by Alan later to make sure they're kosher."

Brilliant idea as well, but he was too focused on the rule he wanted to emphasize to tell her that. "This year, if you want to fool around with anyone, it will be with me."

Her expressions were priceless. This time it was a raised brow and an *are you kidding me?* look.

"Trust me, I am not interested in finding *anyone* to fool around with, and that includes you." She jabbed a finger at his chest. "You will not cheat on me during the year, though. Because if you're off fooling around with someone else, people will think I might be cheating, and considering this entire mess started from trying to stop rumours involving my sex life —nope."

Considering the only person he wanted to fool around with was sitting two feet away from him? "Agreed. Which brings me back to my point—you want to have some fun, let me know."

"Thanks, but I've got it covered," she said dryly as she wrote RULES at the top of the page. "Number one. No cheating. Number two on the list, so it's clear. No sex."

He hesitated. "For a year?"

That brow went back up. "Balls really don't explode or turn blue, you know. Also, there's this fantastic thing called masturbation. It feels good and only requires you, yourself, and... Well, the saying is me, myself and I, so I'm not sure what the last part is when I change it to third person."

"*Third* person? That's the trouble. You've got way less than three in this picture." She rolled her eyes big enough he laughed. "Look at us talking about masturbation like it's a thing I'd be willing to do for an entire year."

"You don't like it, you don't have to do it," she pointed out. "*I* don't want to be married to you for a year, but I will suck it up and make the best of it."

Not remotely the same thing in his books, especially considering he liked her. Wanted her.

Wanted more than this sham relationship they'd begun.

Still, seemed the best thing to agree for now and deal with changing her mind over the months to come—

Dear God, a year of no sex?

Screw that. He wasn't some hound dog who couldn't keep it in his pants, but he liked sex, and he liked Julia, and he wanted...

Right. At the moment what he wanted and what he was negotiating for were two different things.

"If we're spending a year together, I want this to be something we enjoy." He tapped the *No Sex* line in her book. "I hear you on that rule, but seriously, you've had some shitty boyfriends if the only thing you're negotiating on is sex. We have a lot of time to get through while we make this look real enough people don't figure it out. We should write down things we *want* to spend time doing together."

Other than sex, dammit.

Julia nodded then on the opposite side of the page added a new heading. *Activities to Do Together.* "That's a good idea. How about you think of three things you want, and I'll think of three. We can start there."

Finally a place he could lay a few ground rules in his favour. He considered before nodding. "Got my three."

She dragged the pen against the surface of her notebook, doodles of flowers appearing on the page. "Hang on. Give me a minute."

Zach sat back. With her frowning at her notes in the most adorable way, it was too easy to slip into admiration mode.

The twist of her lips right before she bit down on the bottom one...

Fuck it. Zach twisted in his chair and prayed that she didn't glance his way until his erection no longer threatened to burst from his jeans.

Her eyes lit up, and she wrote something down only to scratch it out a second later, her frown growing deeper.

"Having troubles?" Zach asked.

Julia nodded then shrugged. "You start. I bet that'll give me some ideas."

Okay by him. "First. We go dancing once a week."

She blinked. "Really?"

He nodded vigorously. "I like dancing. It's great exercise, I love the music, and it's a good way to make sure people see us together."

It would also put her in his arms on a regular basis.

"I guess."

"Don't try to tell me you don't like dancing, either. Rose and Tansy and Karen and...damn, all of your girl posse pulled me aside at some time over the past four months to tell me how much you like it and wished you could go more often." He held up his hands in a modest shrug. "And I am a fantastic partner."

Her nose wrinkled up in the most adorable way before she wrote down a number one followed by *Go Dancing*. "Okay... but we dance. We don't need to make out in the corners of the dancehall or anything to have people think this is real." An evil smile crossed her lips. "I know."

This time she wrote decisively in her book on the rules side of the page.

Zach slipped over to read over her shoulder. "No public displays of affection." *Screw that.* "I agree."

Shock flashed. "Really?" she repeated.

Hell no. "With one addendum."

He stole her pen and inserted the key word in his favour.

Julia sighed. "No *unnecessary* public displays of affection?"

"You said it before. People need to believe we're a couple. If we never hold hands or anything, people will wonder what the hell is wrong." He gave her his best puppy dog grin. "The local women I dated have kind of gotten used to me being...affectionate."

"You mean handsy," she drawled.

He didn't want to grin, but it was impossible to stop.

"None of their business what we're..." she trailed off. "Fine. My thing I want us to do is ride. Since, as you said, dude ranch and all. Is that possible?"

"Definitely." And an activity he'd enjoy as well. "My second—I need you to come with me when I do research for my brewpub."

Suspicious Julia was back. "Research?" Her head tilted, and she eyed him as if he were bug on a pin. "You're going to make me drink beer?"

"You don't like beer?"

Her head wavered. "I like *some* beers, but I've been warned by Karen what your experiments involve."

"Trust me. I'll only give you the good ones to try." The research would require her to travel with him to as-yet-undisclosed locations, but he'd work up to that. Getting the opportunity to spoil her a little would go a long way to finessing them into the relationship he wanted.

Julia's lips twisted into the barest hint of smirk, but she wrote it down before adding another of her own. "My second... I want us to do yoga."

"Wow, really? That was going to be my third thing," he said as seriously as possible.

She glared. "You're not funny."

"I'm hilarious. Okay, we do the pretzel business on a regular basis. You are totally in charge of that, by the way. I know nothing more than it's fun to watch."

The sound that escaped her was mostly a laugh, but she choked it down fast. "That's terrible."

"I'm a guy. For my final request, once a week we have supper together. Homemade, home-cooked, clean up together, no TV."

That request made her stop harder than his other two. When she lifted her gaze, her expression was a mixture of confusion and suspicion. "That's very domestic."

"My parents do it. Family night. It's..."

He paused, not wanting to freak her out. He skipped his first choice of words which were something about important family traditions because he figured that would make her run for the hills.

Zach went for the safe route. "It's cheaper than taking you out once a week, but it's the kind of thing everyone will eat up. Make this seem more real."

She sighed again, but it was obviously for dramatic effect.

A moment later, a yawn escaped her. "Sorry. I'm still beat from our night turning our world upside down." She glanced around the yard before turning back. "I start work tomorrow at noon. You mentioned me not staying in my apartment anymore. I'm not willing to argue because I know the truth—staying there was a crisis waiting to happen."

"We'll set you up here. We need to go through Alan's rules then grab your stuff, including your car."

Julia nodded, but something was still on her mind. It took about three attempts for her to start, but when she got rolling, it came out decisively. "I don't want Karen to know the details. The part about if we don't follow through on this, she and Finn lose their stuff."

He hesitated. "Okay?"

She met his gaze square on. "My sisters had a lot thrown at them when I appeared. For me to suddenly have that much control over them would be horrifying. I mean, I sort of do, but I don't want her to know. Please, I expect you need to tell Finn something, but that specific part needs to stay secret. I mean, can we just tell them that there's some complication and because we don't have a prenup, we have to stay married so *you* don't lose out? I don't want to involve Karen. I don't want our growing relationship burdened by something that's not her responsibility."

The fact she'd thought of it before he had was humbling. But then again, he wasn't looking for ways this might fail.

He hadn't kept a secret from Finn since...

Well, frankly, *ever*.

Still, he saw the wisdom in it and slowly nodded his approval. "I'll get in touch with Alan as soon as I can to make sure he knows to keep the details quiet."

Julia examined him before offering a faint smile. "Thank you. Really. Thanks for understanding."

"Hey, these are unknown waters for me. The whole year-long relationship business. I figure we're going to have to keep the lines of communication open so we don't end up killing each other over senseless shit, and what you just brought up is far from senseless."

"Yeah." She tapped her notebook, changing the topic. "I don't have a third thing right now."

"Don't worry about it. You figure out something later, and we'll add it." They still had to read the damn envelope, but he figured it was time for action instead of letting her brood over what couldn't be changed. "Tell you what. I'm sure you want to update your sisters about what's going on, and we need to grab your stuff from your apartment. Why don't you give them a shout and ask them to meet you there? I'll drive you over, and between our three trucks, we can get you settled out here at the ranch pretty quick."

Julia made another face, this one a little uncomfortable. "I don't think it's going to take three trucks."

"It'll take whatever it takes." He pushed the envelope back at her. "Give them a call, then you can read this to me on the drive to your apartment."

It was the calm before the storm. Julia glanced around her silent apartment and wondered when she'd lost control of her own life.

Zach had escorted her upstairs and waited until she'd barricaded herself in before leaving to find extra packing boxes.

Her sisters were both on their way, the promise of a full explanation once they got there probably even now sending them over double-quick.

Julia shoved a hand in her pocket, and paper crinkled. The

damn note from the lawyer with more inexplicable demands. Thankfully the list had been short, but the three requirements had been more than enough to make it clear there was no wiggle room to simply live separate lives.

You shall reside under one roof.

You will not be apart for more than two days/nights during any month, barring medical emergencies.

Once a month you will write and exchange a letter listing any concerns you are currently facing. While there is no specific word count required, anything less than one page will be deemed unacceptable. [Contents of these letters will not be read by anyone else, but you need to inform me that you have complied.]

Zach had growled at that last one and made a comment about *bloody homework.*

Her lips twitched into a smile before she could stop it. At least the man was keeping his sense of humour.

At least the man *had* a sense of humour—God, she couldn't imagine being trapped in this situation with some stick-in-the-mud who didn't know how to laugh.

And the ability to laugh was going to come in handy, considering starting any minute now she was going to have to bullshit her way through the biggest lie of her life.

The door banged against the trunk blocking the path, and she shook herself alert. "Coming."

"Dammit, Julia." Karen stood on the other side, peering in through the slight crack she'd managed to open. Julia dragged the trunk aside and found herself caught up in an ironclad hug a moment later. "Hey, kiddo. You're having one hell of a weekend."

The concern in her sister's voice just about did Julia in. "Oh, it's been exciting, all right."

"Coming through. Box delivery." Lisa arrived, a stack of cardboard in her arms as she pushed into the bachelor suite. Her nose wrinkled. "Okay, I can finally admit how much I hate this place. Let's get you packed."

"Only if you can pack and talk at the same time," Karen said, letting Julia go with a final squeeze.

"I'll do the kitchen. Karen will do the living room. Julia, start with your clothes. And yes, talk while you pack." Lisa handed out boxes along with the orders.

"She likes to run everybody's life," Julia said dryly.

"I still hope to break her of that habit," Karen offered. "Of course, now that she's got Josiah to boss around, we should get less of it."

Lisa stuck out her tongue before turning to the tiny kitchen and opening the cupboard doors. "What's the news, Julia?"

Maybe with a little more practice it wouldn't feel so weird to say. "Zach and I are married."

"We heard that part already," Karen scolded.

"We're married and staying that way for one year. There're complications with the estate-slash-inheritance Zach was given. Us getting married without a prenup messes him up financially. So, I don't know exactly how everything's going to work, but I agreed I would stick around for the year."

She'd been placing clothing out of her chest of drawers into a box, straightening the edges of each article carefully as she spoke.

The room went quiet.

She glanced up to discover both her sisters blinking hard.

"You're staying married." Karen frowned. "This is something to do with their mentor and the whole inheritance business?"

"Yeah. If I leave, Zach loses everything."

Karen cursed. "I know the guys think the world of Bruce, but the man is a bit of an asshole at times. Was an asshole? Apologies for speaking ill of the dead."

"Oh, I agree," Julia offered. "Was one, is one—and I don't like their lawyer very much, either."

"You two have the weirdest lives." Lisa shook her head and folded her arms over her chest. "Are you sure you want to do this, Julia?"

Julia shrugged. "It's not that bad. Zach and I were already going to pretend to be together for the next couple of months."

"Two months and twelve months are slightly different, in case you're not mathematically inclined," Karen pointed out.

"We'll figure it out." Jeez. Now she sounded like Zach. She gave both of them her best pitch. "We set down some ground rules, and I believe we'll get along quite comfortably. I think by the time we're done, we'll be good friends." She held a finger in the air. "But since I won't be leaving town, we need the rumours about me and Brad to die fast. People need to believe that Zach and I are really a couple."

Lisa was staring at the ceiling, thinking hard. "I wonder..."

"Whatever you decide to tell people, I think the less elaborate, the better." Karen swirled a finger around the room. "You're moving in with him, yes?"

Nodding felt strange. "Well, not moving in, but sharing a place. Yes. Which isn't a hardship, considering this place isn't very homey and he's got a cabin with two rooms."

"You'll need rings," Karen said.

A sharp zap ripped through Julia's gut. "Okay, I'll mention it to him. Something simple."

"Simple is fine," Karen assured her.

"Karen's right." Lisa's expression had turned downright gleeful. "Not just about the ring. I think the simpler and the closer to the truth you keep this, the better. No one will believe you two are so madly in love you spontaneously decided to get married. People *will* believe you went on a bender and, while under the influence, did something you secretly *wanted* to do. And now you've decided there's no reason to get a divorce since you were dating anyway."

"That's absurd."

"Yep." Lisa's grin grew wider. "Everybody everywhere will be talking about you and Zach, two wild and impulsive kids, accidentally tying themselves down and now being too stubborn, or too cheap, to bother getting a divorce."

Karen's eyes lit up. "Oh, that's good."

It was brilliant. "Everybody will be talking about *me and Zach*."

Which was exactly what Julia wanted. Exactly what was needed—because frankly, who cared what people said about her and Zach? As long as it was the two of them in the rumour mill.

Only one question remained. "You guys know the truth, and Zach will tell Finn and Josiah. But what do I tell Tamara?"

Confusion spilled into Karen's eyes. "That's up to you."

"I'm asking what you think is best," Julia insisted. "The three of you have been a unit for years. I don't want one of the first major things I do to be tossing a secret between you."

At that, Lisa marched across the room, grabbed her by the wrist and hauled her to her feet. The next moment a finger was shaking in her face. "Julia Blushing, not even sisters tell each other everything. This isn't some kind of a sorority we'll kick you out of because you didn't do the secret handshake right."

"If you want to tell Tamara that you're okay, and you'll come to her if you need advice, that's more than enough." Karen's shoulders rose then fell in a soft shrug. "It's all you need to tell any of us. Your secrets are your own. We just want you to be happy. Honestly."

She must've hesitated too long because the next thing she knew, Julia was wrapped in a two-person hug.

The tightness inside eased, and her voice came out muffled against Karen's shoulder. "You guys are good people."

"Oh, hey, a group hug."

"Can I get in on this?"

Two familiar masculine voices broke apart the impulsive support hug, but not before Lisa gave Julia's arm a final squeeze.

"Too late," Karen responded to Finn's question airily. "But I do see some furniture that's calling your name. Desperate to be cradled in your arms."

Zach snickered. "Desperate wood. That's depressing to hear from a newlywed."

"I thought that was the name of your new rock band, Zach," Julia quipped.

An amused hiss rose from Lisa and Karen, and then everybody headed back to their tasks, heaviness pushed aside, worry as well.

Julia folded the top of the nearest box and handed it to Zach the next time he entered the room. He hesitated for long enough that she caught his full-on smile. "You okay?" he asked.

"I'll explain the details later. I have very smart sisters," she informed him.

"Smart runs in your gene pool." He winked and slipped from the room.

It didn't take that long to empty her apartment, but by the time they were done, a crowd of interested onlookers had gathered. A few pretended to rest on the bench across the street. More peered out the windows of Connie's restaurant as Julia's belongings were stacked in the back of the trucks.

"I need to get my car from the fire hall," she told Zach after the final boxes were removed.

"I'll drop you off before I head back to the ranch." He made a face. "It'll take me a bit to get my things out of your way."

"Just stack my stuff on the porch or in one of the empty cabins for now," Julia suggested. "I have what I need for tonight in my suitcase. And I have some work clothes stashed in my car I'll grab for tomorrow."

"Sounds good."

A second later all the air shot from her lungs. He'd stepped in close. So close their torsos touched. But that didn't seem to be enough because suddenly his hand slipped around her, pressed to her lower back. Contact between them increased as he dipped his head.

Julia pressed her palms against his chest to pause his forward motion. "What are you doing?" she whispered.

"We have an audience," he whispered back. "Sorry."

His lips brushed hers. Whisper-soft. Barely there. Just enough of a tease to set her heart pounding.

Her fingers curled involuntarily, caught in the soft brushed cotton of his T-shirt. The hard planes of his muscular chest rose under her palms. His breath ghosted over her skin.

Zach swept in again, his tongue teasing her lips. Tracing their outline until she opened, and he took total advantage. Between them, heat rose, a fire unfurling in her belly. His taste slid in, overwhelming her senses and filling her head.

He adjusted position, easing their bodies until they clicked like two pieces of Lego lined up just right. His hardness pressed against her, and she was shocked to discover her hands had moved of their own accord. Fingers now gliding through his hair as she leaned in and hungrily participated in the kiss. In the contact.

In the...very public display of affection that was even now bringing the catcalls and whistles from their rapt audience.

Zach eased the pressure between them, but he didn't stop. Not right away. He took his damn time. So slow, in fact, that before his lips left hers, she felt them curl into a smile.

His pupils were dark and mesmerizing as he stared down, breathing heavily. "You good?"

"You're bad," she whispered.

"So are you," he teased. "But since the point is that we're supposed to be bad together, mission accomplished." He let her go only long enough to link their hands as he led her to the passenger door of the truck. "Come on. Let's get you home."

10

*Z*ach didn't push it when they both finally made it back to the ranch. In fact, he made sure to stay as out of the way as possible after helping move in the boxes Julia needed to organize her room.

She caught him up on the idea her sisters had shared regarding being too stubborn to get a divorce, which made it easier to share their news. It also meant he had a guaranteed one-year timeframe to work within, which all things considered, he wasn't going to complain about.

After she mentioned their need for rings and he promised to take care of it, it seemed appropriate to give her a little space to adjust to everything that had shaken down over the past forty-eight plus hours.

"Got some chores I need to do," he informed her. "There's leftover pizza in the freezer we can have for supper if that sounds okay."

She didn't pause her task of putting sheets on the bed. "I've got a bunch of stuff I rescued out of my fridge to make a salad. What time do you want to eat?"

"Six-thirty sound okay? I mean, I'll be back so I can get things started. We can eat a bit later."

"Okay. I might be organized by then, as well." She waved him off and dove into a stack of pillows.

He walked away slowly, the whole ordinariness of the situation striking him as extremely bizarre.

Outside, the air had grown cooler, the fall wind sliding in from the mountains to the west. Still, he didn't have much to complain about as he headed to the barn to track down Finn.

He found their foreman first. Cody Gabrielle did a double take, dropping the hoof he was cleaning to the ground before patting the mare on the back side and closing the pen door after himself. "Hey."

Zach offered a quick smile. "Have you seen Finn?"

Cody pointed farther into the barn. "I hear congratulations are in order."

News had spread fast. Zach decided to play dumb, just to see which particular part Cody was the most interested in. "For what?"

"Oh, come on, now." Cody's chin dipped disapprovingly. "If nothing else, you should have warned me off. I was considering making my own move on Julia," he confessed.

The flare of possessiveness that struck Zach—it wasn't good.

She's my wife...

Zach stopped in his tracks and let the actual words sweep over him. He had a wife. Julia was his *wife*.

Dear Lord, he was married, to Julia. Which made him a—

"Your face is priceless," Cody said dryly. "I don't know if I should hose you down or punch you in the gut for gloating."

Zach flashed a grin and pulled his act together. "Save the gut jabs. You should offer me a toast."

Cody nodded, but a trace of concern snuck in. "Cheers. But, damn, man. That's one hell of a dating method."

The casual shrug came easy. "When it's right, no use in waiting."

"Please." The man snorted. "Don't try to pretend you've fallen in love this fast. I mean, you two might fit like oil and vinegar, but it's still ridiculous. You're up to something."

Curiosity struck. Cody wasn't giving him grief over the "married in Vegas" deal. "Yeah? You figure out our deep, dark secret?"

Cody flashed him a grin. "Got to be money on the line, somehow."

That was an understatement. However, the least said, the better. "Weather's looking decent over the next few days."

That earned him a soft snicker and a wink. "In the meantime, you've got Julia in your bed—not a punishment, man. Not in the least."

Except for the damn *No Sex* rule. Zach kept his smile in place. "Watch how you talk about my woman," he warned.

The foreman laughed. "Anyway, we've got things to discuss. Come on. Work first, then you can get back to the honeymoon."

Didn't Zach just wish that were the truth?

Still, the hour spent with Cody going over the list of tasks to be completed on the dude ranch gave Zach a good chance to rest his brain.

He had a year. No use pushing too hard and fast and getting Julia's hackles up. Although he liked her when she was feisty just as much as he liked her sense of humour.

The only mood he didn't like was when fear rose in her eyes.

After saying goodbye to Cody a few minutes before six-thirty, Zach paced back toward the cabin, concern rising.

She'd mentioned the kidnapping business so casually, and yet it had to have been hell. Maybe still was. Crowding her was definitely off the agenda.

Luckily, he had all sorts of other options when it came to edging the fake into real.

He marched up the front steps of their cabin, noting with interest the small stack of boxes and random furniture gathered in a neat pile. One step farther, and he pushed through the door.

"Hi, honey, I'm home," he called cheekily.

The living room-slash-kitchen area was empty. Voices sounded from the back of the cabin, and he followed the noise, curiosity rising as Julia's laugh drifted over a deep masculine tone.

"You're probably right," Julia said as Zach cautiously poked his head through the open doorway to the guest room.

"Of course, I'm right." The voice seemed to rise out of nowhere before Zach noticed her phone propped up against a stack of books. "Oh, hello. You must be Zach."

Julia twisted on the edge of the bed, gesturing him closer. "Hey. I thought I'd be done by now. Come and meet Tony."

Zach settled beside her as ordered, hoping for a clue as to if this was a person to outright lie to or what. Should he kiss her? Ignore her?

He stuck with simple for now. "Hi, Tony."

Thank God, Julia offered a grin and put Zach out of his misery. "Tony's my therapist. He knows everything. Sorry, I should have asked first, but he called unexpectedly."

"It's both our secret. Also, therapists get a lot of slack," Zach offered even as he examined her face. She seemed a little calmer than usual. "You okay?"

She nodded, gesturing toward her phone. "With the

weekend excitement, I forgot to reschedule my next appointment. Tony called to see what was up."

On the teeny screen, the man was eyeing him hard. Decent-looking fellow, maybe late forties. "Hell of a situation, you two," Tony drawled.

"It is," Zach admitted readily. "But Julia's got lots of family here keeping an eye out for her, and I'm going to help her get through this as easily as possible."

"Good to know," Tony said. "She said you're trustworthy. Like to hear that. I'm also willing to chat with you anytime. Or the two of you. You know, as you deal with this setup over the next year."

Zach opened his mouth to deny he would ever be interested then hesitated. In terms of the whole doing whatever it took to make this work, why not? "If Julia wants, sure."

The man nodded approvingly, but his gaze stayed sharp and assessing before he turned back to Julia. His expression softened.

"I should go," Tony said. "Give me a shout in a week, and we'll catch up, okay?"

"Definitely," Julia said.

Tony raised a finger to stop her from slipping away. "Oh, and think about what I suggested."

For some reason, the comment made her cheeks flush red. "Goodbye, Tony."

"Bye, J."

She retrieved her phone, gaze skipping away from Zach's face a lot less comfortably than a moment earlier. "Sorry about that."

"No problem. Glad I got to meet him." Zach turned away to give her space, heading to the kitchen. "Shall I get supper started, or do you need help with anything first?"

Julia beat him to the fridge and began hauling out vegetables. "Supper first. I'm starving already." They worked in silence for all of thirty seconds before she spoke again. "Tony is pretty cool."

It was the biggest opening Zach was likely to get. "Seemed the easygoing type."

She paused in the middle of unwrapping a head of lettuce. "Yes and no. When he's trying to make a point, he's like a rat terrier with its teeth set. I started seeing him after the kidnapping mess with Dwayne. Talking to Tony helped."

"Good for you," Zach said sincerely as he laid frozen pizza slices on cookie sheets. "Nothing better than getting help to put our heads on straight."

Julia eyed him for a moment. "True, but that's not everyone believes. I mean, some people think you should just suck it up and deal. Or that talking with a buddy should be enough."

"If it's enough for them, great. What's wrong with having a trained friend who's a little smarter in a particular area point out a smoother path?"

He threw the two full trays in the oven and set the timer.

When he stood, she was looking at him as if he'd grown a third eye.

"What?"

She shook her head. "You want tomatoes in your salad?"

"Yes. Now, don't bullshit me, Jules. There a problem?"

Under her fingers, the knife moved swiftly through the tender flesh of the salad fixings. She hesitated twice before letting out a long, hard sigh. "You're saying all the right things, Zach. Like, don't worry, this year will be a breeze. Don't worry about your job or the fact we have to live together. And now you don't sound like the people who think having a therapist means I'm broken."

It was wrong, but he couldn't stop a chuckle from escaping.

"It won't be a breeze, but we can have fun. Worrying doesn't change things, actions do. Therapy is a tool to use when we need it—all things my mother has said many times over the years, by the way. If that makes me right, thanks. Glad you noticed."

He finally got a laugh out of her. "That's one healthy ego you've got there, Beau."

Zach shuddered. "Hey, I thought we agreed to use the far less offensive nickname *baby*."

A smile danced over her lips as she scooped salad into two bowls. "That's going to be fun in front of Karen and Finn."

"Have a ball," he encouraged.

A minute later they were seated at the table, digging into the salad while the pizza finished warming.

Julia did a slow, considered pause again, fork lifted in the air as if gathering her thoughts before pushing the words out. "Tony reminded me to warn you about my nightmares. Although you kind of already know."

Zach nodded, his mouth too full to respond otherwise.

She forged ahead. "I don't get them often anymore, honestly. They're just sort of once in a while, a lingering pain in the ass to deal with and an annoyance. The best thing to do is talk to me. You can turn on the lights or just tell me to wake up."

"Okay. I can do that."

"Sorry in advance for being a difficult roommate." Her nose wrinkled.

"Stop apologizing." Zach grabbed a deck of cards off the side counter. "The only real question now is how badly I can beat you at rummy."

"Gin or regular?" Stress slipped off her at the change in topic.

"I guess we have to try both. Or multiple variations thereof."

Cards were dealt, pizza devoured. By the time they'd washed the dishes, wrote up their schedules for the week, and posted the agenda on the fridge, Zach's cheeks were good-tired from his constant grin.

The contrast between his list and hers was night and day.

His—simple line by line in his happy-go-lucky scrawl, although he had managed to make it decipherable. Julia's perfect script was embellished with small stars and moons at the edge of the page, and she'd included two side sections, one with a space for meals and one for a grocery list.

As she finished rearranging the fridge magnets, Zach grabbed another blank page and took his best shot at creating a fancy-dancy formal title.

"What's that?" she asked, peering over his shoulder.

He held it out. *Fun Stuff Schedule.* "You know, the things to make time fly."

Between her shifts and the commitments on his calendar, it took a bit of juggling, but they finally nailed it down.

Julia's approval was clear as she pinned it beside the others. "Wednesday night riding, Thursday morning yoga, Saturday dancing, Sunday dinner."

"At least this week. Your shifts change constantly, right?"

"For the next couple of months, I'm on two days, two nights, four days off."

He nodded. Her job situation beyond the end of next month was on his to-do list for the next day. Not that he was telling her that.

A yawn escaped her, then she shook it off. "Sorry. It's been a big day."

"Big days," he agreed as she slid toward her room.

He paused to put away the dry dishes, surprised to see her

reflection in the window as he worked. Instead of vanishing, she lingered in the doorway. She stared at him, gaze drifting up and down as he moved. Assessing? Worried? Was being under one roof going to be too much?

Then her tongue slipped out, moisture painting her lips. His body hardened even as her expression turned hungry. He was one second away from turning and asking what else she wanted to add to their to-do list—he'd like to start with tasting that sweet mouth of hers all over again—when she shook her head and escaped into her room.

Damn it. Two steps forward, one step back. Zach debated grabbing a shower and dealing with his issue...

No debate. Lying in the room next to hers with a hard-on was his idea of torture.

One dirty shower, coming up.

MORNING DAWNED clear and bright as sunshine streaked across her bed and past the curtain Julia had failed to close the night before. The sunshine was a gift, but an even greater joy was the sense of peace stealing over her.

No thumping footsteps in the hall, no listening anxiously for someone to try her door.

She'd slept like a rock—which was a miracle in itself considering how tangled her brain had been the previous night when she hit the pillow. Every step in the process had been logical by itself, but looking back, it was all so impossible.

She was married and staying that way, for a year.

Nope. Still not possible.

Moving around her room continued to make both those emotions grow stronger. Gratefulness washed in at having a clean, great-smelling, and safe place to hang her hat.

Incredulous disbelief flooded in equally hard that she was *here*, and this was real.

No matter how easy the time had been with Zach the night before, discovering she had an empty kitchen to herself this morning let her relax once again as she dug in the fridge for breakfast. A quick glance at the schedule showed he'd been out of the cabin for a couple hours already. She hadn't heard a peep when he left. Considerate man—just like she'd told Tony the day before.

Julia caught herself growling. Damn him, anyway.

Tony, not Zach, because the current number one source of her whirling emotions was her therapist. Good man, total hard-ass when it came to making Julia admit difficult truths.

Falling asleep, Tony's voice had kept ringing in her head.

He'd asked how much she trusted Zach, and that question had been easier to answer than expected. They'd spent enough time together over the past months that he was comfortable to be around. With her sisters' added good opinions and the knowledge Finn would never let anything bad happen, Zach was safe.

It had been a great revelation, but then Tony had to go and push it one step further. His suggestions regarding sex and Zach...

Nope. Not even going to repeat those ideas to herself, considering that *thinking about* thinking about them made her cheeks heat.

And thinking about them in the night had made for some very interesting dreams.

Nope. *Roommates. Focus on that, Blushing, and stick to friends.*

Besides, Zach was the least of her worries for today. Back to work meant facing the firing squad. By the time she pulled her car to a stop outside the fire hall, Julia still didn't have her story set.

Time to fake it.

Of course, this would be one of the days the entire building seemed full to the brim with every damn volunteer in town. Which maybe was a good thing. She'd only have to do this once.

The cheering and laughter started the instant her feet hit the second floor of the hall. That's where the large kitchen was, and a table big enough to seat twenty spanned the length of the room.

There was no warm-up, just straight to the point.

"Vegas wedding? Really?" Alex, a local cowboy and one of the shift supervisors, stepped in front of her.

"You never heard of someone winning the jackpot in sin city?" Julia asked cheerfully, stepping around him and deciding to do this the biggest way possible.

She climbed on the nearest table and gave a sharp whistle.

Only once all eyes were on her did she continue. "I'm sure you've all heard by now, but yes, it's true. Zach and I have been seeing each other on the sly for a bit, and it appears that while under the influence of Jose Cuervo, we accidentally tied the knot. Being as we were already planning on moving in together, we've decided to just let it ride. I'll take questions from the peanut gallery now—"

A few hands shot into the air as some people called out dirty suggestions.

Julia eyed the rude ones with disapproval then pointed at the other volunteer supervisor, Ryan Zhao, who stood with fingers raised.

His dark eyes twinkled. "Jumping in with two feet—that's one way to do it. You want us to take up a divorce fund? Or start a baby pool?"

The nearest volunteer smacked him on the arm before raising her voice. "Congrats, Jules. Zach's a hottie."

"Agreed, Crystal. Also makes him an appropriate match for me, working at the fire hall and all." Julia's cheeks had to be beet red.

Because Zach was a hottie, and damn if Tony's suggestions didn't flood into her mind again, detailed and dirty.

"Blushing?"

Julia shook herself from her naughty daydream. "Yes?"

Alex again, with a snicker this time. "We noticed."

She rolled her eyes then folded her arms over her chest as she offered a mock glare. "Comedian. So, anyway, just to get the dirty truth out there. Yup, I'm married, yup, he's a hottie, and nope, you can't get any more details." Laughter rolled around the room, and suddenly a brilliant idea struck. She raised a hand one final time. "We'll be out at Rough Cut on Saturday night if any of you want to help us celebrate. No presents, but bring something for the food bank. We'll top up the collection as a reverse wedding gift to the community."

More cheers rang out. Julia crawled off the table as the crowd dissipated into groups for training and rest shifts.

Alex and Ryan waved farewell before heading out with their crews, which meant in a shockingly short time, she was alone in the room with her shift mates.

Which included Brad.

She'd avoided eye contact during her little impromptu speech, but there was no escaping the next few minutes.

Oscar winning acting engage now...

She marched forward and once again went for the bold approach. "Didn't see that one coming, did you?"

Brad didn't move from where he'd leaned against the kitchen counter, big arms folded over his chest. He didn't speak for a moment either, just looked her over with that assessing big-brother gaze she'd come to know so well over the past couple years.

The others in the room were busy at the table a few feet away, making this a totally public discussion. Yet his answer when it came was quiet enough to not be overheard.

"Didn't see the wedding part coming, nope." Brad's gaze stayed steady on her. She was about to make a smart-ass quip back when he spoke again. "Glad to know it happened, though."

It was Julia's turn to stay silent. Thoughts whirled as she struggled to keep her smile from twisting with shock. "Really?"

Brad nodded. "He's a good guy. You deserve someone who thinks the world of you—and he does."

This was getting interesting *and* weird. "Um, thank you?"

He laughed. "You thought you were going to shock me with this? I mean, the wedding was obviously an accident, but the two of you? I've had my suspicions for a while."

Another dose of weird, but at this moment, Julia would take it. "Can't get anything past you, I guess."

He grinned harder then lowered his voice more. "I'm happy for you. Both Hanna and I are. If we can ever help with anything, you just have to ask."

"Thanks. I will."

He straightened and headed to the table, leaving her slightly bemused at how simple it had been.

Except for the bit where he'd read more into her and Zach's pre-liquor Vegas relationship, it seemed she had the blessing of the one guy whose good opinion she needed the most.

She pulled out her phone and sent a quick update to Zach before heading into alert mode for her shift.

Julia: *the crew has been informed, and other than a few raunchy suggestions, they fell for it. Brad as well, so we're good.*

Julia: *also, I might have told them we're hosting a party on Saturday night at Rough Cut. Oops.*

Zach got back to her almost instantly: *party is a great idea. And hell, oops is how we're running this show. Will discuss details at supper. I'm cooking.*

That was it. There were enough whispers and sneaky glances over the remainder of the day to make it clear stories were flying, hard and fast, but they were all about her and Zach. Not a word about her and Brad.

Julia couldn't have been happier as she strode through her day, dealing with callouts to various seniors in the community and a kindergarten class where a boy had decided nap time was a great opportunity to shove a marble up his nose.

And if she happened to drift into remembering Tony's suggestions regarding Zach far too often, she'd blame it on the nonstop sexual teasing that went hand in hand with the successful deception.

She wasn't going to act on the ideas. No sir.

No matter how much the devil on her shoulder insisted she should at least consider it.

11

Zach wasn't even sure why he noticed, but he did. The toilet paper roll was on backwards.

Okay, he probably noticed because he wasn't an animal. He'd been well-trained by his sisters and mother that leaving an empty or even nearly empty roll was a punishable-by-death level of crime.

He'd used the last of the previous roll, so he'd replaced it. Simple.

Only it was now facing the opposite way to how it should, and instead of the tissue rolling out with ease at his first tug, he had to slap the roll a number of times to get the end to show up. And then when he did give it a tug, it broke off after only four squares.

Pain in the ass, no pun intended.

He hauled the holder off the wall, reversed the tissue, and replaced.

Satisfied by a job well done, he washed up then finished putting the final touches on dinner as he waited for Julia to get home.

Day three of being roommates, and so far, so good. He'd kept their interactions lighthearted and simple, and she'd done the same.

One truth was already clear—Julia was a neat freak. His haphazard approach to tossing his things over every surface as he entered the cabin had already been noted and eyed with disapproval.

Tough habit to break, though.

In fact, he spotted his discarded jean jacket draped over the arm of the couch, and the sweatshirt he wore in the afternoon on the knob of a kitchen chair. Guilt moved his feet, and a moment later, he'd hung them both on the hooks beside the door that had magically shown up the previous night while he'd been doing chores.

A firm knock echoed through the building.

"Come in."

An instant later, Finn was in the doorway, his expression the unreadable stone face he wore when he had evil plans.

Zach knew the warning signs far too well. Still, he didn't let it show, just let his friend pace past him into the cabin. "What's up?"

Finn paused by the table, eyeing the collection of packages scattered everywhere. "Running away from home?"

"Hardly. Picnic supper."

"With Julia?"

"No, with Dandelion Fluff. I figured Karen's cat would like to explore the trail system in style."

Finn held back all but a split second of amusement. "Update me. How's it going?"

"Your guess is as good as mine at this point," Zach admitted. "It's too soon for a breakthrough. I didn't expect Julia to fall into my bed the instant we got home."

His friend's grin flashed. "Too bad."

"I will hurt you," Zach warned. "Lucky bastard."

Finn winked then grew serious again. "Heads-up. Karen said there's something brewing in terms of a gathering next week."

"As long as it's not the weekend. I'll need Julia to come to Nelson with me."

"The gathering is for family." Finn paused for emphasis. "*Extended* family."

"Okay." The way Finn kept staring meant Zach was missing something important, but for the life of him he couldn't think of—

Oh.

Oh, *damn.*

"Family, as in Julia's dad will be here?"

"Correct."

Well, then. Nothing like an old-fashioned panic attack to get a man's heart pumping. "Did George Coleman mention he was bringing a shotgun? I figure Karen learned to shoot from someone, but I was hoping to avoid being a target again for a good long time."

Finn grinned. "You'll be fine. Just wanted to warn you so you can be prepared when Julia springs the news on you."

"You're the best." Zach held up a fist, and Finn bumped it firmly.

The door swung open, and Julia rushed in, talking as she moved. "Zach, you here? Sorry I'm—"

She full-on collided with his body.

He wrapped his arms around Julia to catch her before she bounced to the floor. "Steady there, gorgeous."

The weight of her in his arms was perfect in so many ways, but the instant she wiggled for freedom, he let her go.

"Sorry, again. Didn't mean to rush in like a pinball. Hey, Finn. You sticking around?"

"Hey, Julia. And nope. Karen and I have plans." Finn tilted his chin at Zach. "See you tomorrow."

The whirlwind continued. Julia's excitement had her nearly bouncing as she rushed off to change. "We eating before or after we ride?" she called over her shoulder.

"During," he responded. "Change first, details later."

Half an hour later, they were on the trail. Julia's grin stretched from ear to ear. She leaned forward and patted the dun-coloured gelding, Corncob, on the neck. "What a perfect way to end the day."

It was, although Zach could think of a dozen other things he'd also like to do with Julia that wouldn't involve leaving the cabin. "Trail rides are on the Fun Things list."

She straightened suddenly, examining him. "You do like riding, don't you?"

"Yup."

Julia sighed in relief. "Thank goodness. For a minute there, I thought I might be tormenting you instead of doing something we both enjoy."

"That's the yoga tomorrow." He said it with a wink but quickly reassured her. "I'm teasing. I don't mind trying it one bit. My sisters rave all the time about how much it's improved their flexibility and helped with concentration."

"It does," Julia agreed. She paused, and her tone went utterly casual. "Which of your five sisters?"

Talking about his family was a nice, safe topic. "At least half of them at any given moment. Don't try to memorize their names, because I'll remind you as needed. Lindsey, Mattie, Rachelle, and Quinn are older than me. Petra is younger."

"She's the one who pinkie swears," Julia said with a smile.

"She does. She also stole my toys, broke my bike, and once got us locked in the crawlspace of the house. She was my playmate growing up."

Which moved the conversation into stories of living with that many females under one roof. He talked, and she asked questions, the flow interrupted over and over when one of them spotted something in the field, or a hawk flew overhead, or when the trees in the distance moved to reveal a deer staring at them with interest and caution.

The fall evening was warm enough that when he spread the blanket on the ground by the river, Julia relaxed onto it with a contented sigh.

She rolled onto her back and stared skyward. "It's so peaceful and quiet. This is exactly what I needed."

Zach lowered himself beside her, the food basket off to one side. Her expression was pure contentment.

His gaze drifted over her curves with appreciation. "Me too."

Somehow the words didn't come out *too* lust-filled.

Julia took a deep breath, and for an instant their gazes met. He wanted to cover her slowly. Stretch his body over hers and take those pouting lips that she'd just licked in a kiss that would heat up the air around them to a spring day.

The moment vanished as Julia laughed, reaching for the picnic basket. "I'm starved."

Him too. Not just for food.

Zach pushed down his lust and forced a carefree smile. "Let's eat."

She steered the conversation back to his family, which meant by the time they'd eaten, she knew how many of his sisters were married (three), how many nieces and nephews he had (seven, with one on the way), and how often he saw them all (often, but in small doses).

They were riding back, and her chatterbox conversation had trickled to nothing. It didn't seem awkward, though. Just two people sharing a companionable silence, thinking their own thoughts.

His were about how right spending time with her was. Also, to be honest, more than a few thoughts focused on how soon he could convince her there was no use waiting to get intimate—

The heat between them was undeniable.

"I'm not used to having family around."

Her words interrupted a very steamy daydream. Zach blinked to attention. "What brought that up?"

She shrugged. "My sisters have had each other forever. You've had lots of people as well."

"The more to torment me, you mean."

Julia laughed. "Torment, tease, play with, bounce ideas off... It was only me and my mom forever. Sometimes it feels as if you're all speaking a foreign language I don't understand."

Interesting point. "You're right. Although, the best kind of family is the type you pick for yourself. Sometimes that means the one you're born into, and sometimes it means the people you choose to have in your life. Finn is my brother in every way except blood."

Her eyes brightened. "That's sweet."

"Don't tell him I said that," Zach insisted. "I don't need him hitting me up for a family loan."

She snickered. "Please. From the sounds of it, you two have all the money you need..."

Her words trailed off.

He didn't make her clarify. He felt it. The reason why they were going through with this whole farce was to keep the money intact. He wanted to rant that it was more than that already, but it was far too soon for those kinds of reassurances.

Instead, Zach grinned. "Enough money to have splurged

for dessert. There are two kinds of pie in the fridge. Since I didn't know your favourite."

"Pie is my favourite pie," she joked back, and the awkward moment vanished.

But it was a reminder that he had to work for this. The roots of a relationship were there, but it wasn't going to be a slam dunk moving forward.

He had to be very patient and deliberate to make it clear their relationship was of far more value than any bank bottom line.

IT WAS A NICE ENOUGH CABIN, and until now, Julia had considered it roomy. She had her space, he had his, and the shared bathroom between their rooms was massive and comfortable.

But even moving the coffee table aside hadn't created enough open space in the living room to allow them to stretch out on their yoga mats without being very close.

Intimately close, as in bumping limbs occasionally.

More annoying was the fact every breath he took echoed through her as if she had sonar and was picking up his frequency.

They'd only been at it for ten minutes, and she was already flushed.

She glanced to the side. Zach remained in the twisted seated position she'd guided them into. His eyes were shut, and while his flexibility wasn't anything to scream about, he was trying. Inhale. Exhale and twist farther, just the way she'd told him.

While he was occupied, it was too tempting to resist a leisurely look. He wore a loose pair of sweats and a grey T-shirt that stretched over his chest and biceps. As he twisted, the shirt rode up, coming untucked far enough to show a thin sliver of tanned skin.

Bare feet. *Nice* bare feet—which was a weird thing to notice, but she'd been around enough guys in shower houses and medical situations to know some people had good, solid, but ugly, support systems.

His feet were...sexy.

Dammit, brain, stop taking me there.

"Okay, let's move to the next thing." Julia tore her gaze off his body, toes and all, and stood.

Zach copied her. "So far, so good," he teased. "I haven't gotten stuck once."

She laughed. "No pretzel moves, I promise."

"You go right ahead. I don't mind watching." His gaze drifted over her, and she felt it like a caress. He adjusted position, feet braced on the mat. Those sweatpants didn't look nearly as loose anymore...

Shit. Staring at his junk and trying to figure out if he was really getting turned on from looking at her was not a good idea.

Stick to the program, Blushing. "We're going to do a basic move now, repeating it on both sides."

"Lead on," he murmured, copying her position at the top of the mat.

One move after another, she guided him through a sun salutation routine. He didn't tease or make any more comments. In fact, anytime she glanced his way, he seemed to be fully concentrated on keeping his balance.

She fell into the rhythm and ignored him as best she could. It was a strange exercise, considering how much space he took up. How close he seemed at every moment. How much less oxygen was available in the room than usual as she grew light-headed from having him beside her.

As she twisted into a new position, she could have sworn his gaze lingered on her body.

She'd pulled on a pair of yoga pants and a sports bra. Nothing fancy, but comfortable. Something she'd worn during training a million times around her workmates.

This felt...different. Hotter, more intimate.

Dangerous?

No, not that. Not with Zach.

Then why not give him a try? The little devil was back on her shoulder.

She dropped into her lunge position too vigorously, attempting to shake sense into herself. The too-quick move tipped her balance point and she fell sideways, contorting to try and catch herself.

"Got you." Zach's strong arms curled around her, pulling her close as they headed toward the floor. The landing was a lot softer than it could have been, yet still firm as she settled into his lap.

"Sorry." Julia remained motionless, not wanting to damage him in her rush to get away.

His grin said it all. "Nothing to be sorry for. I figured this was some new, interactive yoga move, and I'm one hundred percent on board."

Her shoulders were perpendicular to his, one hand pressed to his chest. One of his arms cradled her back, and other than embarrassment, heat was the fastest-growing sensation.

"You're terrible," she said as calmly as possible.

His gaze had fallen to her lips, blue eyes fixed in position. "I'd heard of hot yoga before, but never thought I'd get to experience it."

She snorted. "Dear God, that sounded like the start of a really bad *Penthouse* letter."

"Are there any really good *Penthouse* letters?" He was still staring, hunger on his face.

It was far too tempting to lean in and close the distance between them. Press their lips together and once again enjoy a taste of the man and his wonderful kisses.

But they had twelve damn months to get through, and this was not going to make it easier.

She was about to find a way to break away when he rolled. A squeal escaped her, and he laughed, continuing the motion to his feet and leaving her behind on the yoga mat.

He held a hand down, his sexy smolder replaced with jovial amusement. "Come on. I have an idea."

His idea involved slipping on their shoes, yoga mats under their arms as they paced to the next cabin over.

"Our own private yoga studio," he said with a flourish as he gestured her in the door.

The cabin was smaller than Zach's, but the living room and dining area lacked furniture, leaving an open hardwood floor for them to spread out with plenty of room to move.

Julia shook her head. "Great. Why didn't we start in here?"

"I forgot." He stepped into the middle of his mat and eyed her expectantly. "Ready when you are."

The quick shutdown of her libido was a good thing. At least that's what she tried to tell herself as they finished the session. All traces of sexy-talking Zach vanished, and when they headed back to their shared living space, it was as if she'd imagined the entire thing.

"Great yoga session," Zach told her, hand raised in the air until she connected with his palm in a firm high five. "Dibs on the shower, though. I've got to meet with Cody in half an hour."

"No problem."

He vanished into his room, and she was left with a jumble of thoughts that made her want to squirm.

Imagining Zach in the shower, strong hands moving over his torso. Down his body...

Over his firm—

Nope. There be dragons.

THE NEXT TWO days passed in a blur as she transitioned into her two night shifts in a row. Working six p.m. to eight a.m. meant she left the house before Zach was back from whatever he was working on that day, falling into bed without seeing him the next morning.

She was grateful for the soft bed and the safe room to come home to. No denying that.

Saturday morning, though, when she stumbled back to the cabin after a heavier number of callouts than usual, she discovered Zach waiting for her.

"Hey. You headed out?" She barely covered her mouth before blasting a yawn in his face.

He chuckled. "Nope. Day off."

"Me too. After I sleep. Shower. Shower first." She sniffed then groaned. "Don't come near. Mr. Heller decided to walk off the edge of his hayloft."

"Sounds exciting. And dangerous."

"Luckily, he landed in the manure pile he's been building right outside the barn." Zach had taken her coat off and...her shoes? "Unfortunately, he landed in the manure pile. Not the nicest place to sit with a broken leg."

"It'll make a great story," Zach assured her.

They were standing in the bathroom. When had that happened? "Shower."

She tugged off her shirt, focused on getting clean enough to collapse onto her bed.

A soft groan echoed in the space, but the water was pouring down, calling her name. She shoved off her pants and undies, ditched her bra, and eased under the heavenly downpour.

Julia woke six hours later with no memory of leaving the shower, just the dire need to pee like a racehorse and her stomach growling as if she'd fasted for days instead of hours.

She finished her business as soon as possible then made a beeline for food.

Inside the fridge was a covered plate and a note.

I made lasagna last night. Saved you a piece. Remember we're at Rough Cut tonight for our wedding party. Should be a blast.

Julia had the lasagna in the microwave in three seconds flat, the scent as it warmed making her drool.

The party tonight was going to be something, although *blast* wasn't necessarily her choice of words. Still, it was another nail in the rumour coffin, and it wasn't going to hurt to enjoy some dancing and time with her sisters.

A valid excuse to be in Zach's arms won't suck, either. The damn devil on her shoulder got the words out before vanishing.

Yeah. There were far too many good reasons to stick with the status quo, but the temptation to open that side door continued to grow. Julia dug into the food with a determined focus, because at least while she was eating, she wouldn't be planning big mistakes.

The rest of the hours stretching forward would be enough trouble to manage.

ach pulled into an open space outside Rough Cut and turned to Julia with a smile. "It's party time. Ready?"

She glared momentarily. "You don't have to sound so happy."

"What?" he demanded, slightly confused. "We're going to dance and have a few drinks and raise a little for the food bank. Plenty to be happy about."

Her nose wrinkled. "I guess. Only, no tequila, agreed?"

Zach solemnly drew an X over his heart.

Julia's concerned expression wavered. "You're impossible," she complained. "I'm trying to be borderline serious before we head in there, and you're still all fluff and nonsense."

He shrugged. "No use in pretending this is more than it is. People are probably hoping we tie one on too hard again and give up some juicy details. I figure the best response to that is to smile lots and baffle them with bullshit."

After the damn yoga session that had sent him into cold-shower mode, and the innocent striptease Julia had given him that morning, Zach had been one step away from simply reaching for what he wanted.

Yet the absolute trust she'd shown while ninety percent out of it wasn't a gift he could bear to throw away.

He'd given the question every bit of his waking hours, deliberating until coming to the conclusion there was only one way to win her over.

Make *her* ask for more.

This had to be all about her choices. While he could roll in and make demands as boldly as the next guy, she needed a delicate touch.

Which meant he'd say yes to absolutely everything she wanted from him. He'd back off and give her all the room she claimed to need. Instead of pushing, he'd do yoga, and take her on trail rides, and whatever else she requested, because spending time together would allow him to put part two of his plan in place.

The chemistry between them was combustible. Given enough time, the banked heat would flare, and she'd demand he—

"Kiss me."

Zach blinked, turning to Julia. Was his subconscious talking out loud now?

"Too slow," she complained. She crawled into his lap, curled a hand around his neck, and brought their lips together.

His brain was still catching up, but instinct kicked in. Zach cupped her hips, pulled her flush with his body, and took over, a hallelujah chorus ringing in his ears.

Her taste drilled through him—peppermint and pleasure. Her torso pressed warm against his, soft breasts waking hunger and need. He nipped at her lip, soaking in her gasp as—

A sharp clatter rang from the driver's side window. They

snapped apart, or at least broke the lip-lock. Zach maintained his grip on her hips.

He wasn't silly enough to let go prematurely.

"The party's inside." Josiah stepped away from the truck, heading to the top of the stairs with Lisa tucked under his arm.

Behind them, a duo of women sauntered past, tossing quick glances over their shoulders as they moved slowly so as not to miss a single second.

Zach grinned but spoke quietly to Julia. "I take it you saw something?"

"Two of the biggest gossips in town, according to Tamara. I bet they try to outdo each other spreading the word we can't keep our hands off each other."

Now there was a good lead-in for a very entertaining evening. "Anytime. We should hit the dance floor and give them other things to flap their gums about."

He lifted her off carefully—still a little worked up in spite of how brief the connection.

His friend and Julia's sister were grinning like fools as Zach led Julia up the stairs.

"You two seem to be getting along okay," Josiah murmured to Zach as the women slipped through the door ahead of them.

"Shut up," Zach retorted, but he smiled as well.

Yup, he was going to *yes, yes, yes* every single request Julia made. And if karma continued to be kind, there might be some very enjoyable results sooner than later.

The dark, wooden walls shone with golden spotlights, and the scent of beer and pub food floated on the air. Music blared, but louder still were the voices calling out greetings and cheerful good wishes.

Zach hurried to Julia's side, slipping their hands together.

She jerked in surprise for a second before deliberately leaning in closer as she waved at friends.

Her head tilted back, lips brushing his ear. "Straight to the dance floor? We can avoid questions for a while that way."

No arguments from him. He helped her with her coat, shrugged out of his jean jacket, and hung them both on a hook at the side of the dance floor.

He tucked her fingers into his and led her into the fray. A moment later, she was in his arms, and the world clicked a notch to the right.

This was perfect.

Her face tilted toward him, broad smile shining up. "You're a goof," she said.

He pulled her tighter, twirling her away from the masses around them. "Not going to argue, but you got a specific theme for that comment?"

She broke the contact between their front hands so she could tap his chest. "You wore your GROOM shirt."

"I'm proud of this shirt," he insisted. "Even while drunk, I managed to get out of the wedding chapel without you turning me into a GROO, or a ROOM, or the worst possible, a G OO."

Laughter danced loudly at that, amusement written clear through down to her toes. "Good point. And I'll have you know, I did consider wearing my RIDE shirt, but I decided I didn't have the stamina to put up with the ongoing teasing that would trigger from the fire hall teams."

She'd pulled on a pale-yellow blouse that shimmered under the dance lights, paired with a jean skirt that ended above her knees. "I like what you've got on. It's cute."

And sexy. *Definitely* sexy with the long line of her toned legs visible every time she moved, but in the interest of seeing her expression continue to shine like he'd just handed her a trophy, he'd keep the *good enough to eat* comments to himself.

He contented himself with pulling her against him and twirling hard. Julia clung close, tucked in tight as possible as she allowed him to take control. Her hands were strong, and her warm breath fanned over his skin.

It wasn't just the dancing that made his heart race.

When the music finally changed tempo, dropping to a slow ballad, Zach was more than eager to switch his grip. He pressed one palm against Julia's back, their other fingers tangled together at chest level. Holding hands, swaying back and forth as her eyes shone.

Yup. He could take this, and much, much more.

Her gaze flickered away then back, a secret poised on her lips.

Zach pressed their cheeks together. "What?"

She slid her hands up his chest, curling them around his neck. Her voice rose barely loud enough for his ears. "We have a lot of whispering and gawking going on."

"It's my dance moves." Zach arched her back, cradling her over his arm. Hips together, legs intertwined.

Julia rolled her eyes as he pulled her to vertical. "Well, of course. That has to be it."

"Shhh. Don't mess up my concentration." Cheek to cheek again, Zach rocked and enjoyed the contact between their bodies far more than was wise. "I have to focus on my *Dancing with the Stars* moves or we'll be in trouble."

Julia breathed deep, relaxing into him. Heat and fire licked up his spine, and the temptation to turn his face and nuzzle her lips grew stronger.

The fact she moved against him in a wholly sensual way would have to be enough for now, no matter how much more he wanted.

The song ended, and Julia curled into his side, pulling him toward the chairs at the side of the dance floor. "Come on. I need to hydrate."

Her sisters were there. All three of them, which meant

Tamara Stone as well. Her sharp gaze snapped over Zach in a way that said she wasn't certain if she should shake his hand or kick out his knees.

Julia had no qualms, rushing into her sister's embrace for a quick hug. "Sorry I didn't make it over to Silver Stone this week to talk to you. I'm glad you and Caleb could make it tonight."

"Of course, we could make it. It's not every day we get to celebrate someone in the family getting married." Her gaze darted up to Zach. "I mean, *two* new brothers in one weekend. That's special."

She looked dangerous. Zach was happy to allow Julia to tug him farther away from Tamara and her oversized husband, Caleb.

The small table had barely room for eight, especially since enough glasses for them all waited on the surface.

Finn caught hold of a glass and raised it in the air. "Never dreamed I'd be doing this so soon after my own wedding, but when fate speaks, we listen. To Julia and Zach. It's not what's in the past that matters, but the future. May you enjoy the coming days. Find a path that's right for you and follow where it leads."

Caleb lifted his glass. "And if I can add, you got family beside you all the way. Don't ever think you're alone."

Zach glanced at Julia. She'd picked up a glass as well, but her eyes were suspiciously bright. He tucked his arm around her and cradled her close. "On behalf of Julia and myself, thank you. That means everything."

Julia cleared her throat, but her voice was still shaky when she spoke. "To the future."

The entire table raised their glasses in a toast. "To the future!"

The cheer echoed across the room, followed hard by screams of laughter.

Julia's gaze slipped past him toward the front door. An instant later she slapped a hand over her mouth.

Lisa turned to check the action, and her eyes widened. "Oh. My. God."

One slow twist later, as he made sure to keep Julia in his arms, the source of everyone's amusement grew clear.

His surprise had arrived.

THE MAN ENTERING the bar was dressed from head to toe in shiny metallic fabric. His dark hair was elaborately combed back in a style that was far too familiar.

Elvis was in the building.

He went straight toward their table, light glistening off the sequins on his broad lapels.

Inside, the laughter welled up hard and fast until Julia was gasping so hard she found it difficult to breathe. With one arm draped around Zach's neck, she leaned in close and rubbed her knuckles against his head. "You are an absolute goofball."

He flashed a grin. "Hey, you were very upset I didn't get him to our wedding. I figured this was the next best thing."

It had been the strangest of evenings already, but just when the solemnness of it had been about to overwhelm her, Zach had played a winning card.

Elvis stood in front of them, bowing formally in greeting. "I hear there's a couple of newlyweds who need a little serenading."

Zach caught her by the hand and pulled her back onto the dance floor.

In the background, the regular music faded as Elvis got his guitar into position and strummed a couple of wild chords.

Music started from the overhead speakers, and a second

later the performer in front of them joined in, smashing out "Blue Suede Shoes" on his guitar and singing loudly—and quite well—as the entire crowd in the Rough Cut pub joined in.

Zach twirled her out and then back into his arms, his smile beyond pleased.

The moment with her family had been almost too much. Karen and Lisa might've known part of the truth, but keeping a big part of why she and Zach were sticking together a secret from them *and* the whole thing a mystery from Tamara and Caleb—

They'd still offered unconditional support.

That kind of connection wasn't easy to accept. Not with her previous lack of family. Not with the unsettled guilt simmering in her gut over being angry at the only family member she'd had.

Family was a damn complicated thing. She never expected that.

Which was why the bit of impossible happening right now made it easier to continue and not feel as if the weight of the world was on her shoulders.

"Earth to Julia." Zach tilted his head to bring her gaze in line with his. "Got a favourite request for Elvis?"

The performer did all the classics, or at least all the upbeat and happy ones. And while she did have a favourite love song or two, she wasn't about to request them.

The level of temptation had been growing over the past week, and Julia was very close to caving in and opening up an interesting conversation with the man currently holding her in his arms.

But she wasn't about to pretend this thing between them was about anything more than friendship and heat.

Still, it was rather appropriate to be dancing with Zach as the words to "Fever" filled the pub halls.

They danced, and drank, and then danced some more. Everyone exchanged partners for at least one song.

It seemed all of Zach's friends were determined to give her advice.

"I know he seems easygoing," Finn offered, "but he has a tender heart. I think it has something to do with growing up around so many girls."

"You mean he's got cooties?" Julia asked with the cheeriest expression she could pull off.

Finn's lips twitched the barest bit. "Something like that."

Josiah waited until almost the end of the dance before he switched his lighthearted conversation to a more serious track. "I know I've only met Zach fairly recently, but one thing I can tell you is that the man knows how to work. It seems as if he's playing all the time, but he's getting a shit ton done in the meanwhile. That's something I respect."

"Good work ethic?" Julia asked with curiosity.

"More the part where he's not looking for a pat on the back. If it needs to be done, he's going to do it." Josiah winked then whirled her into Zach's arms.

"I take it they're all talking about me?" Zach moved them gracefully around the dance floor. "The reason I'm saying that is because I've been getting an earful about *you* from all your sisters."

"What are they saying?" Julia asked with honest curiosity.

Zach paused for a moment. "Well, there were the usual threats against my person if I do anything to hurt you."

Her jaw dropped, but she managed to pull it back into line. "Get out."

"Dead serious, but I kind of expected that." He twirled her close for an instant before moving far enough back so she could see his face clearly. "They all told me how much they wanted you to be happy, and how that was now my responsibility."

She couldn't help it. She rolled her eyes. "Well, that's a load of bullshit."

He blinked in surprise. "I'm not supposed to make you happy?"

"Well, I'd really appreciate it if you didn't make me sad. But as for it being your *responsibility*? Hell no. We're both grown-ass adults. We're going to do our best to get along and have some fun, but if I'm being a shithead and grumbly about stuff? That's not your fault. I expect you to tell me to get my shit together."

Zach nodded briskly. "Exactly what I thought. Don't worry, none of them actually threatened me with *immediate* death. Although, you tell me. Does Tamara strike you as a little more bloodthirsty than the other two? And that's saying something, considering I saw Karen shoot a man without blinking."

Julia made her own assessment regarding Tamara and had to agree. "I think it has something to do with being a mom. Protective and all."

Pain rolled through her, unexpected and unwelcome. Moms were supposed to be protective and well...while that had proven to be true, Julia was now learning there was such a thing as *over*protective.

Her own mother—the only bit of family she'd ever known—had kept Julia's origins a secret. Back in the day, it hadn't been something she'd ever pushed to find out more about. Mom loved her, wanted her. End of story.

Only with the proof of what having an extended family was like slapping her in the face every damn day...

Once again, Julia pushed away the hurt. Now was not the time to poke at the ball of discomfort in her belly. At some point, though, she needed to spill her frustration and anger on Tony and talk it through.

A few more dances, and slowly the party broke up. She

laughed the entire way home to their small cabin as Zach regaled her with a dramatic review of the evening.

When they hit the front door and slipped into the warmth of the living room, Julia teetered on the edge.

It was only the lingering uneasiness from thinking about her mom that made her choose to hold off for yet another day. She had no idea what was going to happen between her and Zach, but it wasn't going to start when she was stewing in her brain about uncomfortable family choices. About things in her past that annoyed her immensely.

Still, something had to be said.

She turned to Zach and stepped close enough to be able to rest her hands on his chest.

He went motionless.

Julia stared up at his face. At his kind and eager expression. "Thank you for making this evening a lot more fun than expected."

"You're welcome."

Before she lost her nerve, she shifted closer and pressed a quick kiss to his cheek, retreating before he could tangle his arms around her or tangle up the evening with more complications.

"Good night." Julia escaped to her bedroom. There was no other way to phrase it.

Heck, she'd probably been one step shy of a sprint, but at the same time, as she pulled off her party clothes and got ready for bed, it was with the strangest and most wonderful sensation surrounding her. Like a warm blanket around her shoulders.

Like something hovered on the horizon with the potential to be wonderful and good.

Curling up in her own bed, close to but not with Zach, increased her sense of anticipation in a good way. Like looking forward to a holiday or the presents waiting under a Christmas tree.

Some wonderful gifts that could be unwrapped very, very soon.

Waking the next morning to the scent of bacon just added to that delicious anticipation.

The dinner bell rang, and Zach called out cheerfully, "Breakfast time, sleepyhead."

"I'm up," she returned, shoving back the quilt. She pulled on a robe and slippers and joined him in the wonderful-smelling kitchen.

He'd made breakfast consisting of four different types of protein accompanied by a stack of perfectly buttered toast.

"You are a god," Julia informed him, stacking bacon on a piece of bread and slathering the pile with mustard. "Thank you."

"You are a heathen," he retorted with a grin. "That's supposed to be ketchup. But you're welcome."

She waited until her mouth was empty, savouring the flavours as she eyed him closely. "What're you doing today?"

"Not much. Finn is taking the whole slowdown of getting the dude ranch running seriously. Since we don't need things up and at 'um until the spring, both of us have time to deal with other tasks."

"I never did understand why you guys switched from going hell-bent for leather to a Sunday stroll."

Which is how, for the next umpteen minutes, Zach went over the details of what had happened regarding Red Boot ranch. About the challenge for Finn and Zach that turned out not to have been a challenge in the end.

It all seemed very far-fetched, or at least it did until Julia considered their own strange predicament.

"Now I understand better why Karen said your mentor

isn't necessarily her best friend." Julia stacked their empty plates and took them to the counter, preparing to do the dishes and cleanup.

"Bruce meant well," Zach offered. "He was an amazing man, but he definitely didn't do things by the book." He glanced at her. "I am sorry again that you got caught up in his wrangling. I'll do everything I can to make the time go as smoothly as possible."

Julia nodded, dipping her hands into the hot water and getting started. "I think we're getting along okay—so far, so good." She ignored the big topic that would need to be discussed at some point soon but not when she was elbow-deep in bacon grease. "We need to talk about my employment possibilities. What are the chances you're willing to move farther north for a while?"

It appeared she'd managed to shock him. He gaped at her. "Why do you want to move away from your family?"

"Because my internship is done at the end of October. There's a job available in High River, but I'd hate to have to drive two hours every day for my shifts."

Zach moved to her side to dry and put away the dishes. "Now that you brought it up, I kind of have a job for you already."

It was her turn to freeze. "What kind of job?"

"Medical officer here at Red Boot ranch." Zach lifted a hand. "Hear me out. This is not me making up a job out of charity because of the situation we're in. This is an honest-to-goodness position that needs to be filled. I can even show you—it's been on the books since day one."

"You want me to be the medical officer for a dude ranch." Julia heard herself say the words, but it didn't seem possible.

There was that word again. It seemed *possible* might not mean what she thought it meant...

"We'll have to go over the exact requirements, and of course the salary needs to be set—"

"I accept. Oh, hell *yes*, I accept." She threw her arms around him, ignoring the wet spots she left behind as she squeezed him tight. "I have wanted to work on a dude ranch since the minute I left. I adored growing up on one, and hated that I had to leave to go to school. And I know this is a real position—you *have* to have somebody, and I would be perfect for it, I swear."

Zach patted her back gently. "I've already offered you the job. You don't need to show me your resume."

She was grinning from ear to ear. It was irregular in some ways, but the entire situation they were in was—yeah, not typical. "I'm sure we can work out the details, but *thank you*. That is a load off my mind."

He winked. "You're welcome."

They'd just finished cleanup, and Julia was about to head to the bathroom to get ready for the day when loud knocking shook the front door.

Zach rolled his eyes. "This is what happens when Finn says he's going to take the day off." He marched to the front door, speaking loudly as he went as if hoping Finn would hear. "Wouldn't hurt if you spent one day on your ass and let the rest of us do the same."

He jerked the door open.

It wasn't Finn. It was Julia's father, George Coleman, standing there larger than life with a very unwelcoming expression on his face as he stared Zach down.

"Don't usually spend a lot of time on my ass, especially when one of my girls gets married without letting me know. There's a family dinner on Monday. Figured this might be a good time to come and get to know my new son-in-law a little better."

13

Unexpected was a mild word for it. Zach held his ground, even as Julia jerked her robe tighter around herself. She inched her way out of the center of the room.

"Hey," she said. "Give me a minute to get dressed, and I'll come say hi."

She slid out of sight, disappearing into the bathroom.

Being alone with her father set a twitch rolling at the back of Zach's neck. Still, he kept it together enough to gesture the man farther into the room. "Can I get you a coffee?"

George Coleman nodded briskly, slipping his boots off by the door and making his way across to the table. "I made better time than I expected. Figured it would take until at least midmorning to get here."

Zach worked the coffee machine. "You got somebody covering chores while you're gone?"

The other man settled in the hardback chair where a short time ago Zach had been happily staring across the table at a sleep-tousled Julia. In fact, he'd had all sorts of delicious plans for the day percolating through his brain.

And while the information about the job had snuck out a little sooner than planned, her impulsive hug had meant a lot.

He liked making her happy.

Zach put the coffeepot on the table along with a cup and cream and sugar. Settling into his chair made him realize the other man hadn't answered his question. He just sat there, glaring.

Zach raised a brow. "Something wrong?"

George folded his arms over his chest. "You think I'd come out here without having someone taking care of things back home?"

Dammit. Zach prided himself on being able to talk to just about anybody about anything. Usually he could sweet-talk them into profitable ventures for him and Finn to boot.

It seemed he had met his Achilles' heel.

He was about to launch into his defense, when Julia reappeared, slipping back into the kitchen area now dressed in jeans and a T-shirt.

Zach blinked. She'd reentered the room by walking out of *his* bedroom.

"Hey, Dad. This is an unexpected surprise." Julia snuck in close enough to give the older man a quick peck on the cheek before she settled in the chair closest to Zach.

When she tangled her fingers with his, Zach finally found his smile. A true smile, because she was putting them out there as a real couple.

It felt good.

George eyed them both before filling his cup and adding a dash of milk. He stared into the liquid as he stirred. "Tamara told me to come for dinner Monday night, but I figured I'd come a little early to spend some time with you." He lifted a finger toward Zach, not meeting his eyes. "I'd like to have a chat with this one."

Julia's expression tightened. "I hope you don't intend to try some 'what are your intentions with my daughter?' thing with Zach. Our relationship is *our* business."

George dipped his chin, seemingly fascinated with his cup of coffee. "So Tamara told me. Nothing wrong in a man wanting to make sure his girls are being treated right, though."

Beside him, Julia nearly vibrated. While Zach understood some of her frustration, he understood a whole hell of a lot more where George Coleman was coming from. "Of course you're concerned. But I assure you, Julia and I are doing just fine. We've got things figured out."

"Still be good to have some time to chat," George said briskly. He glanced at Julia. "The other girls told me you've got a spare room here in the cabin. Thought I'd bunk with you guys this trip. Make it easier to shoot the breeze while I'm here."

Zach's first response was the fervent wish he could swear out loud and profusely. Having a houseguest was going to complicate things. The second thing to race through his mind, though?

Having a houseguest could make things very interesting indeed.

Julia hesitated before managing a shaky smile. "Sure. Just have to give me a few minutes to tidy up. I've kind of spread out all over the place."

Utter bull hockey. The woman never left a single thing out of place, and her room looked like a military unit had bunked down with him. Still, Zach figured he knew what she was planning.

"Why don't I take your dad for a tour of the ranch while you deal with that, sweetie?" Zach squeezed the arm he'd wrapped around her waist.

Julia's expression as she stared up at him was halfway

between amusement and terror. "Sounds like a great idea, *baby.*"

He shoved down a snort of amusement, finishing the rest of his coffee before tilting his head at George. "Ready to go?"

It was rather surreal wandering Red Boot ranch with Julia's dad. The man asked a few generic questions, but mostly just marched at Zach's side, peering into nooks and crannies as if they were of vital interest.

They'd just entered the main barn where the horses were stabled when Finn appeared. Thank goodness for small mercies.

George's expression lightened the slightest bit. "Finn."

It seemed the arrival of their father-in-law—there was a strange realization. *Father-in-law!*—had also come as a shock to Zach's best friend.

Finn recovered quickly though, marching forward to offer his hand. "Didn't expect to see you here this early. Dinner's not till tomorrow night."

"Took some time off." George folded his arms over his chest again, glancing between Finn and Zach. "Now which one of you is going to tell me what the hell is up?"

Even as Zach prepared for battle, Finn chuckled, easing the tension.

His best friend had experience dealing with the older man. If Finn could find a way to make this go smoother, Zach would back his play all day long.

A gentle shift of Finn's shoulders followed. "Don't know if you've seen this in action yourself, but what I figure is this one here"—Finn jerked a thumb at Zach—"saw what a good thing Karen and I had going on and decided he was ready for it himself."

George's frown remained in place. "It's a little quick."

Zach followed Finn's lead. "Not really. Julia and I met last spring. It's true we didn't officially start dating until the summer, but as Finn said, there's a lot to like about Julia."

George Coleman's expression hardly budged. "Don't try tossing me a line, boy. Whatever's happening, it isn't because you're head over heels in love."

Lie, or go for the truth?

He never got a chance to decide which route to try because feminine laughter rang behind them. Karen and Julia appeared, as if they'd just happened to end up in the same place at the same time.

"Hey, Dad. Julia told me you'd shown up. Glad you made it early." Karen came and gave him a quick hug before stepping back with a seemingly excited smile. "In fact, this is perfect timing. Finn and I have been wanting to take you for a ride with some of the new stock we purchased."

George's expression grew conflicted. "Wanted to spend some time with Julia. And him." The flick of his finger was pretty much as if he was knocking an unwanted fly away.

Zach rubbed his hand across his lips to hide a smile.

Julia was at his side, hand slipping into his again. "We'd love to go for a ride. No reason why the five of us can't head out."

It seemed that was all it took. Finn gestured the older man farther into the barn. "Come on. I'll show you a couple to take your pick from."

The temptation was obviously too much. Julia's dad cracked a smile and paced after Finn. "Karen told me you've made some fine purchases."

At Zach's side, annoyance zinged across Julia's face. "Karen was the one who made those purchases," she murmured, leaning into him.

The expected error from her father wasn't the first thing on

Zach's mind. "I thought you were cleaning up your room so your dad can use it tonight."

"I started, but then realized no way I should leave you alone with him for any length of time. I called Karen, and we figured since we're here, we were the quickest rescue squad. Lisa is coming over. She'll sneak into the cabin and move my stuff into your room."

Teamwork at its finest. Zach nodded. "That means we don't have much to do except enjoy another horseback ride. Your dad's not gonna get out of line with Finn around. He respects him too much."

Which meant the next couple of hours passed in a comfortable haze. George Coleman was suitably entertained by Finn pointing out the latest developments around the ranch.

Also, Karen periodically asked her father's opinion about various animals. Advice she didn't need, but the questions stroked the man's ego just enough to keep him off-kilter.

Zach was forced to contrast this with his last interaction with his own parents. Zachary Senior and Pamela Sorenson did demand their children live up to their potential—but said potential was always based on what made each of them personally happy, not on kowtowing to parental expectations.

It seemed what he had was less common. His family had always been there for him. Even now he knew they would be supportive and help him reach his goals—once he got around to mentioning his current situation, however much he decided to share.

That wasn't the case with Finn. Zach had also caught bits and pieces over the past months that suggested the Whiskey Creek girls hadn't always felt supported.

Watching George Coleman move through the morning with his daughters and Finn—and admittedly a plus-one unexpected son-in-law—Zach wondered if the older man had the ability to change enough to be what Julia needed.

That old sensation of possessiveness struck, but this time with a twist. Zach didn't really care what the man thought about *him*, but he cared immensely how Julia felt at the end of the day.

It gave Zach an additional reason to be watchful. Perhaps his recent resolution had been to say *yes* to all of Julia's requests, spoken and unspoken, but it was equally important to say *no* to anything that would hurt her.

Somehow, he needed to do it in a way that made it clear she would be provided for but also listened to. If George Coleman had a problem with Zach being that person in her life, the sooner they found out, the better.

Family to the rescue.

Even the thought of that seemed strange, but also sweetly welcoming. Julia inched closer against Zach's side, partly as a pretence to stay out of the conversation on the other side of the fire where her father was regaling them all with a tale of something big and supposedly important.

While the official family dinner wasn't until tomorrow evening, Lisa had offered up an impromptu barbecue at her and Josiah's place.

Barbecue meant less time sitting at the table and more spent relaxing beside Zach.

Thinking of Zach—the entire day he'd been wonderful and terrible all at the same time. Always within reach, yet never overwhelming. When it was appropriate, he'd held her hand or draped an arm over her shoulders.

Julia had to face the truth. This pretend thing between

them wasn't enough anymore. Barely a week in, and she was ready to toss good sense to the wind. Which made her the worst possible fake girlfriend—oops, worst possible fake *wife* ever.

Because wanting more was just going to get them both in trouble.

As the night grew later and the sun dipped behind the Rocky Mountains, Julia decided she may as well take the chance. Zach could be trusted. He wasn't going to run off and spout her business to all and sundry.

Still didn't mean he would say yes to her proposition.

The fire crackled, and a yawn escaped her.

Zach took that as his cue to squeeze her waist. "Ready to head home?"

She glanced across at where her father was still involved in a vigorous conversation with Finn and Josiah. "He doesn't look ready to leave yet."

Zach shrugged. "He's got legs. If he insists on bunking with us, he can get a ride back with Finn and Karen, then march over to the cabin and let himself in."

On her other side, Lisa tapped a hand on her leg to get her attention. She crooked a finger, waiting until Julia leaned over far enough to hear her quietly spoken words.

"Go home. Dad surprised you in the first place, but we've got it under control. You'll spend all day tomorrow dealing with him." Her eyes widened, then mischief painted her features. "Although, I meant to remind you. You and I said we would meet at Buns and Roses at ten."

"We did?"

Lisa nodded solemnly.

Understanding flooded Julia. "Oh, *right*. We did."

Her sister's grin flashed brightly. "Bring him along. We'll divide and conquer."

Impulsively, Julia caught Lisa's fingers and squeezed them tight. "Thank you."

"You're welcome. For everything."

Julia wasn't exactly sure what that last bit meant, but as she pressed her shoulder against Zach's, Julia winked then raised her voice to be heard across the fire. "Zach and I are heading home. Do you want to come with us now, Dad? Or get a ride with Karen?"

George Coleman glanced toward them briefly before dipping his chin. "You kids go on ahead. Finn will take care of me."

Julia caught Karen's gaze for a moment. So much shared emotion passed between them. It took effort to pull herself back together to offer a lighthearted response. "Okay. We'll see you in the morning."

Escaping wasn't quite as simple as that. Everyone offered hugs, including her dad. Sort of. He laid a hand on both her shoulder and Zach's and squeezed. "Just leave the door open. I'll be sure to be quiet."

Slipping in the door of the cabin was like taking a deep inhalation. Trembling on the edge of a decision, Julia knew she had to make a choice. It was either time to move ahead or stop tormenting the two of them for good.

Zach turned in the middle of the kitchen area, giving her plenty of room as his expression turned apologetic. "I guess we're back to being literal roomies."

She nodded. "Don't try and give me some half-cocked idea about sleeping on the floor. Hardwood is nice, but not as a mattress."

He hesitated. "Well, why don't you get ready for bed? Hopefully you can find everything from where Lisa hid it."

"You go ahead," she insisted. "I need to make a few notes

for tomorrow while I remember." She picked up her journal and wiggled it in the air. "I won't be long."

He glanced at the book in her hands then turned obediently. "See you when you're ready."

The sound of water coming on in the bathroom mixed with her pen moving slowly across the page. If she was going to do this, she may as well make it official.

It took thirty seconds to write the actual words, but it seemed she'd barely finished when ten minutes later, Zach cracked open the bedroom door. "Bathroom is all yours."

Chin up, she stepped boldly across the room and across the threshold, closing the door firmly behind her.

At first glance, there weren't many of her things around the room. But then again, she didn't tend to have a lot of knickknacks to spread out.

Zach pointed at the dresser. "I'll say this for her, she's efficient. Lisa amalgamated my stuff into the drawers on the left. Your things are on the right."

She made a face. "Sorry. I didn't realize she would crash your privacy while helping me."

A snort escaped him. "I am devastated that she discovered I have mismatched socks in my sock drawer."

Julia folded her arms over her chest then stared at him.

His brow rose. "What?"

"You're being far too reasonable again."

"Reasonableness is my downfall," he confessed. "Sometime you'll have to take it up with my sisters. I'm sure it's their fault."

"I'm sure."

Still laughing, Julia grabbed what she needed from the drawers on the right then disappeared into the bathroom.

Five minutes later she gave herself a stern pep talk, staring into the mirror. "This is a *no harm, no foul* situation. Either he says yes or he says no, and either way, we'll know how to proceed."

A firm chin dip later, she opened the door and marched to the side of the bed.

Zach was tucked under the covers. He wore a pale-grey T-shirt, his broad shoulders and muscular chest visible as he sat upright, leaning on a stack of pillows. He had a reader in his hand, and—

Holy crap, that was sexy. "You wear glasses?"

The most adorable flush covered his cheeks. "Sometimes?"

She made sure her expression matched her approval. "I like them."

"I like them too, since they help me see and all." Still, he slipped them off, placing them on the side table. "They're special glasses with a tint to them. They help me track better on digital devices. I don't have much of a problem when it comes to paperwork, but screens are a different matter. My mom figured out that's why I was getting wicked headaches back in high school."

"Go, Mom." Julia took a deep breath and settled on top of the covers of what she guessed was her side of the bed. "Can we talk about something?"

His expression turned inquisitive, his full attention on her.

She held out her journal. "Since I figured we'll be all awkward sharing a bed because of not letting my dad find out the truth, I decided we may as well go for full-out embarrassment."

Zach took the notebook from her. "What's this?"

"I decided my third thing for us to do together." She said it as drily as possible.

His expression changed just the slightest bit. A hint of disappointment, which was brutally satisfying, considering what he was about to read.

He opened the book to the page she had bookmarked. His gaze skimmed the page, and she knew the moment he hit the addition.

Zach glanced up, his blue eyes wide. "You're kidding."

"Nope."

His expression remained hesitant for about three more seconds before his smile bloomed into sheer satisfaction. "Sweetheart, I have zero problems agreeing to your third request. It's a bit of a challenge, but it's one that I'm more than willing to make the sacrifice to achieve."

Julia laughed. "So glad you're willing to throw yourself on the altar of fooling around. But let's talk about that for a minute, before you get too excited."

He wiggled his brows. "Very funny."

Another jolt of amusement escaped her, but they still needed to discuss the matter. She leaned forward on her elbows. "We need to define fooling around."

14

If karma were an actual person with a home address, Zach would've mailed her an entire box of cream-filled doughnuts. Chocolate-coated, maybe with sprinkles as well.

This was not the way he'd expected the evening to end.

Oh, he'd been hopeful, considering the whole jammed-into-one-room situation, but not in his wildest dreams had he imagined Julia handing over her notebook with the request they start fooling around down there in black-and-white.

Although he wasn't as keen on having to define terms, he was willing. He patted the empty space closer to him. "Let's talk."

Julia's lips twisted wryly. "I think I'll stay here for now, thanks." Her head tilted as she examined him. "First off, I trust you. Which is why we're even having this discussion in the first place."

"Thank you." He folded his hands behind his head, getting comfortable for however long the process took.

Now that the evening would end with Julia not just in the

bed with him but in the bed *with* him, he suddenly found he had a bucketload of patience.

She opened and closed her mouth a couple times. Her nose wrinkled—damn, why did he find that so adorable?

Words poured out of her as if she had decided her confession had to happen in the shortest time possible. "I don't like sex. I mean the actual part where the guy's penis goes inside my vagina. I do like a bunch of other things. Kissing is great—kissing you was pretty spectacular the other day. And I like being naked and touching, but when it comes to actual... well, *coming*, one is better than two."

He'd been trying to keep up, but to be truthful, his brain had kind of stuttered to a stop as soon as she'd started speaking. "You might have to go through that a few times so I can catch all the nuances. You don't like sex?"

A decisive head shake. "Nope."

That was what he'd heard. Next— "But you do like kissing, and touching, and...that's where I get a little confused again."

Interestingly, she no longer looked at all embarrassed but a whole lot of determined and perhaps a touch angry. "I have no problem enjoying an orgasm when I masturbate. I rarely have one when someone else is involved."

"That sucks."

The words were the first thing that popped into his brain, so he said them. Only, by the expression on her face, maybe he should've been a little more diplomatic.

She stared him down for a moment then shrugged. "Sort of. Definitely frustrating, so I just want to make something clear. I'm not looking to be fixed or anything. I know exactly how to get myself off, but it is more fun getting worked up *with* a guy than without."

Zach's brain was going a million miles an hour, while the fact he'd grown hard just being part of the conversation made it clear even if she wasn't putting sex on the table right now, he was still interested.

"Okay. We'll need to discuss what this means as we go along, but I'm game."

Air rushed out of her as if he'd agree to keep some life-altering secret. "Thank you."

"So." May as well get some of the nitty-gritty details right out on the table. Or bed, even better. "You said touching is okay. Does that mean full-body contact? My mouth anywhere I want it? My fingers?"

A shiver shook her, which he really liked. "Yes, but within reason. There's nothing more annoying than a guy who is so insistent he can get me off, he keeps pushing. If you're having fun touching me, do it. But don't *keep* doing it just because you think that at some point, *bada boom, bada bing,* you'll manage to rock my universe."

The conversation was fascinating, but Zach had to wonder... "Not arguing with you, but can I ask? How many guys have you been with? Full-on sex, or otherwise?"

She raised a brow. "Are you gonna give me your sexual history as well?"

Zach shrugged. "If you want it. I've hard-core or otherwise fooled around with probably two dozen women over the years, give or take. Had actual full-on penetrative sex with four."

She blinked. Julia had obviously not expected him to take her literally and answer the question. "*Really?*"

He laughed. "Which part don't you believe?"

Her cheeks flushed. "OK, I've had sex with three guys. I've fooled around with about ten."

"And how many of the guys you fooled around with did you enjoy, instead of getting frustrated?"

She sighed heavily. "Three."

Damn. Probably the three she attempted actual sex with. "You're twenty-five, right?"

Her lips twitched. "Just like it said on our marriage certificate."

It was too easy to grin in return. "Okay, I promise I'm not trying to fix you, but at the same time, that's not a ton of experience. It's possible you might enjoy sex someday."

"It's possible, yes, but I'm not signing up for extra frustration right now. I do like fingers. The G-spot isn't a myth, but unless you can demonstrate you have a very unusual penis, you're not gonna hit that spot with it the same way that fingers can."

It was a good thing he wasn't drinking because he would've spewed everywhere. "A *very unusual penis?*"

Julia sniffed. "VUP for short, if you'd like."

He snorted. "I thought short penises were a problem."

Instead of laughing, she looked thoughtful. "Actually, the best part about any kind of touch down there is right at the start. So maybe a small, stubby penis would work better. The whole *bang, bang, bang* like a piston is a waste of energy on me. It's uncomfortable, to be honest."

The conversation shouldn't be so damn amusing, but it totally was. "Honest is best. No jackhammering for Jules, I got it."

"No sex for us," Julia reminded him. "That last part was an entirely fictitious conversation. I'm not broken, and I'm not looking for a magic penis."

"Fooling around only. Fine by me." Zach decided to go for absolute bluntness since that seemed to be what she wanted. "You have any objections with me jacking off at the appropriate moment?"

"Be my guest. Plus, I have zero objections to helping you sometimes."

This had to be the weirdest conversation he'd had in his entire life. Considering some of the doozies he'd been forced to face, between his nursing-trained mother and his oversharing sisters, that was saying something.

Julia sat motionless on her side of the bed, him on his, his e-reader still in his lap.

He picked it up and put it safely on the side table then twisted back. "Do we need to schedule your fooling around request on the Fun Stuff calendar, or are you okay with us kind of winging it?"

Some of her confidence faded, as her cheeks rose to a flush. "I think there's a connection between us that's pretty hot. I'm not wrong, am I?"

Holy shit. "On a scale of one to ten for your three requests, and my interest in them, yoga is a seven, riding is a ten, and fooling around is a solid twenty-nine."

She remained motionless, staring at him. Her oversize T-shirt lay flush against her body, rising over her breasts. She'd tangled a hand in the extra fabric over her belly and pulled the material taut.

It seemed the next move was up to him.

Zach crooked a finger. "You said you trusted me."

Her eyes were huge. She nodded.

"Then trust me with this as well."

He said it softly, but it seemed to be enough. Julia crawled across the bed to settle beside him, space between them, her expression bold one moment yet needy the next. Like a kitten that was not quite sure if it was safe to make the final approach.

Zach could work with this.

He scooped her up, ignoring her little gasp of surprise as he settled her in his lap. Her knees rested on either side of his hips, their noses level with each other.

He stared at her as he lifted a hand to stroke her cheek

gently, fingertips brushing forward until he could cradle her chin and tilt her face to the perfect angle.

Such soft skin. Such enormous eyes. Such trust, as if waiting for him to make magic.

With pleasure.

He slid his fingers around her nape and into her hair. The other hand went to her lower back, the position already as familiar as breathing. Bodies close, he moved in and pressed their lips together.

His intent was to tease for a bit. To stir up the ashes around the coals slowly enough so the connection between them would be undeniable.

It seemed Julia had other ideas. The instant their lips met, she ripped into high gear. Arching against him, pressing their mouths closer. Her tongue darted out to tangle with his, and he groaned with the perfection of it.

She caught his head, stroking her fingers through his hair as she kissed him eagerly. Hungrily. Hips moving as if possessed over his now very hard cock.

Christ, she was fire and heat and all sorts of trouble. Because right now they were on a trajectory course off into the stratosphere, which was not at all his objective for their first time.

He tightened his grip in her hair and tugged. The motion was sharp enough to draw a gasp from her as their lips separated.

Zach grinned, pleased at her response, yet desperately looking to get back in control.

At least of himself.

"Slow down, sweetheart. There's no need to rush. I promise the buffet table will be open all year."

She flushed and bit her lower lip. "Sorry."

Amusement rippled, escaping in a soft chuckle. "Not

looking for an apology. But back to the trusting thing—let's take our time and enjoy ourselves. We'll do the fast thing as well down the road, but I've been dreaming about touching you. Kissing you. It's not something I want to rush."

She blinked. "You've been dreaming about it?"

"Oh, hell yes. Daydreams, dirty dreams." He winked. "Wet dreams. Waking up with my cock in my hand and you on my mind has pretty much been the status quo for the last month."

The words were barely out of his mouth before he realized his mistake.

Her eyes widened. "I only kissed you in the bar ten days ago."

He shrugged. "Told you I was interested in dating you for real."

JULIA'S SENSES REELED. Knowing that Zach had been thinking dirty thoughts about her for longer than expected? Interesting twist.

But with need strumming through her, the information wasn't the most important thing.

"Kiss me," she demanded.

He looked far too amused. More than that, the grip he had on her hair didn't budge, which meant she had zero wiggle room. "Slow down," he repeated.

She bit off the growl that had escaped involuntarily, closing her eyes and picturing herself in the middle of a yoga session to try and find some control.

With the front of her body pressed against his, his hands slid further around until she was wrapped in a tight hug.

The big breath of air she'd taken escaped slowly as, one

vertebrae at a time, she relaxed against him. No use in fighting, not with the ironclad clasp he had around her.

To tell the truth, the immovable hug felt good.

Her cheek pressed against his, Julia allowed herself to embrace him as well. Bodies meshing tighter as she relaxed against his muscular torso.

He held on, and for the next however many minutes, she sat there. Her blood still pounded, tingling sensations zipped over delicate portions of her anatomy, but the largest sensation was—comfort.

Slowly, ever so slowly, the hug gentled. Julia remained relaxed, curious now for his next step.

Zach twisted his face the slightest bit, nuzzling against her neck. His lips moved against her skin in a teasing caress. Nibbling, nipping.

The shivers had returned, but this time instead of grabbing hold with both hands and trying to steer the boat, Julia allowed Zach to lead.

Which turned out to be a wonderful decision because those kisses she'd enjoyed from him before? They'd only been the beginning. Now that he had the go-ahead, he wasn't content with simply putting their lips together. He explored her jawline, teased and licked his way around her earlobe, and found a magical spot at the base of her neck that seemed to have a direct connection all the way down between her legs.

She let her hands roam where she wanted, matching the speed he'd set. Fingertips traced slowly over his shoulders and down his back. Palms circling over firm muscle as his biceps curled.

Reaching down his torso caused a thrill as his six-pack flexed against her exploring touch.

At some point she went airborne, and suddenly she was flat on her back on the bed, looking up into bright blue eyes.

His fingers teased along her collarbone. "You said naked was on the books."

Most definitely. "For you as well, I hope."

His teeth flashed white for a moment then he reached over his head. An instant later he'd peeled off his T-shirt and tossed it to the floor. "I'm all about equal opportunity."

When she would've helped him take off her own clothes, she found one hand pinned to the bed. He caught her by the other wrist then firmly planted her palm just over his right nipple.

Wordlessly, he slid his hand under the base of her shirt at her waist and spread his fingers over her belly button.

The flash of heat was instant. "You have big hands," she told him seriously.

Zach grinned. "Thanks."

Dear God. His reaction was off the charts. "Did I just make some sort of sexual reference I failed to understand? Like, are guys with big hands supposed to have big penises?"

His gaze was fixed on her breasts, but amusement crinkled the corners of his eyes. "Since we've established that very large penises are not necessarily better than small ones, no." His fingertips were in motion now, teasing her skin and slowly making her T-shirt ride higher, higher, until he exposed her breast. "Just warning you that I *do* have big hands, which includes big fingers, so if I do anything you don't like, let me know."

Those fingertips were now skimming in concentric circles that grew closer and closer to her nipple as it tightened into an aching peak. "Okay. I'll also let you know what I like."

"Please do."

His gaze rose to her lips, and he leaned in and kissed her again. His body pressed tight against hers, hand teasing along her rib cage before fluttering back to where she needed him.

The small tweaks he gave her nipple weren't enough, but it wasn't the same kind of frustration as when she knew somebody was trying to get her off and getting bored.

She glanced down, but nothing about him said anything except to reaffirm what seemed to be happening. Zach was one hundred percent enthralled with touching her.

Julia closed her eyes, tugging slightly to pull him over her. His weight pressed down, pinning her in place for barely a second. He was gone before any fear had time to kick in.

And then he was kissing her, and any thoughts about past traumas had no place in the here and now.

He shoved the fabric of her T-shirt up to her neck and lowered his mouth to suck and bite her breasts. One hand caressed even as his mouth teased.

She slid a hand between her legs and into her panties, barely touching her clit. A gentle wake-up call because everything else going on right now was so spectacular there was a good chance that when she did start teasing herself for real?

Tonight might be quick.

It was better to not think about it. It was better to just feel, and oh, there was so much to enjoy. So much to be distracted by.

Somewhere in the background she swore she heard a door open and close, but Zach was murmuring words against her skin. Swearing, actually. Also, groans and moans and a noise as if he'd just consumed something absolutely delicious.

Her T-shirt had vanished, her panties as well. Her fingers where she played between her legs were wet. Her own touch wasn't going to be enough, though.

"One minute." She rolled away. Zach grasped after her, cursing in dismay.

She went instantly to her underwear drawer, pulling out the bag where she kept her toys. Tonight wasn't about prolonging anything. Tonight was about getting down to business. She grabbed a straight, no-nonsense vibrator and rejoined him on the bed.

She wiggled under his body, refusing to feel embarrassed. "Sorry. Next time I'll be better prepared."

He had one brow raised in a fine Vulcan imitation. Zach held out a hand. "May I?"

She passed him the vibrator. "I'm going to drive tonight," she warned.

That got another soft chuckle even as he twisted the end of the device and set it rumbling. "Don't worry. I understand how possessive people can get with their toys. I don't let just anybody drive Delilah, either."

His classic convertible. Julia snorted. "Exactly the same thing."

Zach put the vibrator against his lips, licking slowly.

The pulse of heat that struck between her legs was on level with a mini orgasm. Then he lowered the toy between her legs, slipping his fingers out of the way as she took hold.

The instant she put the business end against her clit, a loud groan sounded from beside her. She glanced to the side to see Zach's face contorted as if he were in pain.

He was staring between her legs, his mouth hanging slightly open as he panted. "Fuck. That is so goddamn sexy."

He slid a hand into his boxer briefs and curled a fist around his cock.

Another shudder took her. "Let me see."

It seemed tonight would be one of the rare times she came quickly. It didn't happen often, but this was a good night for it. Julia rejoiced in the quick and dirty release barreling toward her at freight-train speed. Between the vibrator strategically placed where she needed it most, and Zach very willingly shoving down his briefs—

VIVIAN AREND

His knuckles had gone white, his grip tight as he pumped over his length. He was up on his knees, close enough he could drag the fingers of his unoccupied hand over her thigh. Knuckles stroking her belly and up to her breasts.

His gaze fixated on her fingers as she brought herself to the edge.

Tension coiled inside, and Julia ignored everything that was strange about the setup. Focused instead on the pleasure streaking in like lightning. She gasped, hips pulsing upward. Switching her gaze between his face and the steady beat of his hand.

Muscles tensed, his abs were a work of art, but it was the sight of his cock peeking out between his fingers over and over combined with the relentless pressure of the vibrator that sent her over. "Oh my God. *Zach.*"

Zach's rapid pace faltered. Curling tighter toward her, a steam-whistle type gasp of her name escaped his throat as he came. He was close enough the shot hit them both. Semen splashed in lines over her belly and his arm and fingers where they splayed against her skin.

He collapsed onto his back beside her, chest still heaving. They lay there silently for a few minutes.

That had been unexpectedly hot, and decidedly dirty. Exactly what she'd been hoping for.

Julia felt every inch of the smile stretching her face, and it was impossible to keep the gloating tone out of her voice. "Well. That was fun."

He twisted his head far enough she could see him wink. "I sure thought so."

Enough endorphins were floating in her system that Julia was tempted to just grab a sheet and pull it over her body, but that obviously wasn't going to happen. Not without some cleanup first.

Reluctantly, she rolled to a seated position, grabbed her toy and made a beeline for the bathroom. "Back in a minute."

"Hang on." Zach was on his feet and at the door before she could reach it. "Let me make sure it's safe."

Heat flashed on her cheeks. Oh. My. God. She hadn't given a single thought to the fact that her father was bunking down on the other side of the wall.

Standing there with semen dripping down her belly was *not* the most embarrassing thing about this current moment. Not when she considered the kind of noises they'd made as they came.

Zach finished checking the bathroom. He returned with a washcloth in his hand. "I locked the other bathroom door. You're safe."

Even standing there naked, dripping and all, she had to ask. "How loud were we?"

His lips twitched. "I'd like to lie and tell you we were as quiet as a mouse."

Oh, dear. She shook her head. "Great."

He snickered. "Well, on the bright side, it's pretty much a given your dad believes we're truly a couple now."

Julia vanished into the bathroom because there really was no answer to that. She took a brief shower, exiting the bathroom wrapped in a towel. She put away her now-clean vibrator and turned toward the bed.

Zach was waiting. His cleanup had taken less work than hers. He was bare-chested, leaning against the pillows again. "Just so you know I am wearing briefs. Whatever you're comfortable wearing, go for it. I am, however, hoping to do a little spooning. If you're agreeable."

Which told her what she needed. She pulled on a clean pair of panties and rescued his abandoned T-shirt off the floor.

"You really are a messy roommate," she informed him briskly as she climbed into the bed next to him.

He surrounded her. One strong arm pulled her back against his body, cradling her head on his other arm. "Yeah, sorry about the messy part."

He said it with such amusement, she wasn't sure he was talking about the T-shirt or the far more intimate mess. "Go to sleep, brat."

Zach hummed, burying his nose against her hair. He took a deep breath then sighed contentedly.

Julia's brain raced a million miles an hour for all of three minutes. Then the heat of his body and the even pace of his breath lulled her to sleep.

When she woke, he was no longer curled around her. Instead, they'd both rolled, and she was pressed against his back, arm tucked under his as if she were allowing him to give her a piggyback ride.

It was nowhere she had expected to be, but it was somehow the right place at the same time. It wasn't even awkward getting out of bed, although they both grinned far too much.

No way could she look her dad in the eye during coffee, though. Thank goodness for the excuse of a visit with Lisa that morning.

George Coleman was the one who brought it up. "Hear you're supposed to get together with your sister today."

"This morning," Julia agreed. "You're welcome to come."

Her father shook his head. "You go on without me. Josiah invited me to ride along on his veterinarian visits. He's picking me up in about forty-five minutes."

Once again, she'd been saved by family.

It wasn't until breakfast had been cleared away and Zach walked her to the door that she realized they'd turned a corner she hadn't expected. He helped her into her coat, keeping hold of the material to tug her in close. His gaze examined her closely, and he must've liked what he saw, because he nodded firmly.

"Have fun with your girls. Don't talk about me too much," he whispered right before pressing his lips to hers and sending her heart into acceleration mode.

She was out on the front porch, the door closed behind her when she realized—

What on earth was she going to tell her sisters?

15

Something weird was going on. Not that Zach wanted to complain, only considering George Coleman had expressly come out to Heart Falls early supposedly to give Zach what for—

Julia left the house and...nothing happened.

Zach cleared the table then ended up following the other man out the front door where he'd vanished.

It was tempting to stay hidden, but at some point Zach figured they had to get this out between them.

But instead of laying into him hard, Julia's dad seemed more interested in examining their surroundings. "It's a pretty piece of property Finn bought," George stated.

Finn *and* Zach, but pointing that out wasn't really necessary. "Finn's a good judge of ranch lands. I can see Red Boot ranch pulling a tidy profit in just a short time."

It was the perfect opportunity for George to start the grilling, and he finally took it. "You grow up on a ranch?"

"Grew up in rural Manitoba, but my parents rented the land out to other locals for crops and grazing. They wanted wide-open spaces for us kids to roam and enough room for my dad to work on his experiments without blowing up the neighbourhood."

The other man blinked for a second.

Zach was all ready to dive into an explanation, because that was normally what happened after he mentioned his father's work habits.

But it was as if the other man had zero curiosity about the bits that made most people wonder. Instead, George leaned back in the chair he'd settled in on the porch as they waited for Josiah to arrive. "Your parents still live there?"

Go with the flow. "Mom is retired from nursing, but Dad still tinkers. He said as long as he's got the shop and space to experiment, he'll always be entertained. And my sisters have all settled close by, so my parents get lots of time being grandma and grandpa."

"Never expected that bit to be so much fun," George confessed out of the blue. "Scary too. Never sure what those girls of Tamara's are going to get up to when I'm around. Emma decided to throw herself off the swing set at me the other day. My heart damn near burst out of my chest when I barely had time to catch her."

It was too easy to imagine it. Zach laughed softly. "I've seen those girls in action. I guess the good part is you successfully raised three girls while living on a ranch. All of them are smart and capable of anything they put their mind to. Julia as well."

The conversation paused for a second. Zach glanced up to discover George staring at him intently.

Zach should have held his tongue, but he simply couldn't resist. "Is this when you ask me what my intentions are?"

"Little late for that, considering you've already married her," George drawled. He leaned forward, elbows resting on his knees. "Like I said yesterday, I know something's going on that

VIVIAN AREND

neither of you are sharing. While I'd like to demand answers, I was reminded again last night I don't have that right. I still need to learn how to be Julia's dad. The only thing I know for sure is she deserves good people in her life."

Zach could agree with both parts of that, especially the bit about learning what Julia needed. "That's what I want to be to her. That's who I plan to be," he assured the other man.

Dust rose in the distance as Josiah's vehicle came closer.

George Coleman picked up his hat off the side table and put it in place, rising to his feet.

He turned toward Zach one more time. "Don't take this the wrong way, but I'm keeping an eye on you."

"No offense taken." Zach folded his arms over his chest. "I'm doing the same to you."

Julia's dad stiffened.

Zach had made sure to say it as politely as possible, but the truth was, this road went two ways.

The truck stopped in front of the porch and Josiah got out, offering a quick chin dip in greeting. His dog, Ollie, raced around the back of the truck and beelined for Zach, wagging her tail rapidly.

A pet for the dog, a wave for Josiah, then Zach stood there grinning as widely as possible as George Coleman glared out the window as if trying to light his hair on fire by thought alone.

Yep. Not a lot of cuddly feelings zinging back and forth between him and Papa Coleman. Zach did a quick run through of their conversation in his head but still didn't think he'd been out of line.

He didn't want George Coleman to hate his guts, but no matter that the man said he was trying, Zach didn't think he was trying hard enough. Julia had gone twenty-five years without a father, and he got the feeling that while she didn't mind some of the new family interactions she'd been tossed into, there was a fine line. She had opinions, and she had worries.

Finding out what made her tick on a more intimate level was something Zach was very much looking forward to exploring.

He got to work on a few tasks on his list even as his brain continued to problem-solve. Last night had been amazing in terms of getting physical, but they had a long way to go. He didn't just want her in his bed. He wanted a partner who talked to him, and shared goals and dreams, and all the things he'd watched play out in his parents' relationship over the many years.

When his phone rang not even an hour later, Zach had to grin. If he had instinctive good luck and often had that sense that it was time to take a leap, his parents had a different talent.

If he thought about them too hard, they would phone.

He opened up the call to discover his mom and dad grinning back at him, both of them on their own phones with different backgrounds behind them.

"How come you two aren't off making mischief?" Zach demanded.

His mom rolled her eyes. "Please. Your father is totally causing trouble. I, on the other hand, am a perfect saint as usual. I just finished making three batches of sugar cookies."

Amusement rumbled in Zach's gut, not only at her pleased grin but his father's ability to keep from laughing. "Let me guess. Quinn is coming over with the girls to visit you tonight."

"I told you he'd figure it out," Zachary Senior said with a little nod. "You want to tell us when you're coming over next so she can make *your* favourite cookies?"

"Since my favourite cookies are also your favourite cookies, I sense there's just a hint of self-interest in that request," Zach drawled.

His father winked.

His mom waved a hand at both of them. "Serious question, though. When are you coming for a visit?"

That was the question. "Soon. Maybe."

He definitely wanted to introduce Julia to his family, but he didn't want to push it too far, too fast. The last thing she needed was even more people being thrown in her direction.

Then he wondered what her favourite type of cookie was. She definitely had a sweet tooth, but in all the time they'd talked, had she ever mentioned a preference?

A little too slowly, he realized he'd been lost in his own thoughts and missed part of the conversation while he'd been daydreaming. That much was obvious, because as he glanced back at his screen, his parents both had brows raised and questioning expressions.

"What?"

His mom folded her arms over her chest. "Zachary Beauregard Damien. What are you not telling us?"

His dad pulled a face. "Wow, Pam. Triple naming him right off the bat?"

"He's keeping a secret," she insisted. "Don't you think he's keeping a secret?"

"Of course he's keeping a secret, which is why we called in the first place. But you're supposed to sneak up on these things, not charge right in."

"Pshaw. Upfront is the best way." Somehow it was clear her attention was now more on her husband than on her son. "We don't keep secrets in this family. Right?"

His father managed to look indignant and guilty at the same time. "The new contract I accepted wasn't a secret. I just hadn't gotten around to telling you yet."

The whole conversation was so exactly his parents, Zach couldn't stop from snickering. "I love you two."

They both stopped their conversation to beam at him. With perfect synchronization, they said back, "Ditto, kiddo."

To hell with it. "I'm seeing someone," he announced.

His father blinked, but a slow smile curled his lips.

His mom's eyes widened. "Julia," she pronounced sharply. "I approve. When do we get to meet her?"

They were impossible.

"How do you do that?" Zach demanded. "I should totally tell you that it's not Julia. That it's somebody I met last weekend in Vegas, and I've decided to run away with her and join the circus."

His father shrugged. "You already did the circus thing back when you were eight. Plus, Zach, you are not that subtle. Every time we've talked over the past four months, you've been telling us about what's going on out there in Heart Falls."

"And inevitably you talk about Julia. And Karen and Lisa, but considering they're both taken, Julia was a pretty safe bet," his mom pointed out.

"Fine. It's Julia." He was very tempted to spill the beans about being married, but since the whole idea was to try and break the news to them slowly, he resisted going for the shock value.

"Question still stands. When do we get to meet her?" His father leaned toward his phone. "Wait. If she's an EMT, her schedule must suck. You let us know what works, and if you want us to come out there instead, we'll make the time."

"And if you want us to hold off for a little while, we will." His mother made a face. "If we must."

"Right now, I think she's a little overwhelmed by family," Zach admitted. "And you're right, Dad, her schedule is pretty wild. But I'm enjoying spending time with her. There's something very comfortable about being with her, but not worn-out-couch comfortable. Like, interesting comfortable."

His parents beamed again, and his dad was just about to say something when all of a sudden, an explosion went off in the background, billows of smoke rising behind him.

Zachary Senior gave a quick wave goodbye, then his screen went blank.

Pamela Sorenson barely blinked, minor disasters being part and parcel of her husband's work over the years. "Well, I won't grill you too much more, but I'm glad to hear your news. I hope things go well for you and Julia."

"Me too. And I know, if I ever want to talk, *yada, yada, yada.*"

"Please," his mother rolled her eyes. "If you haven't figured out the sex thing by now, I'm not sure I even want to try—"

"Mom," Zach said with a complaining laugh.

She grinned. "You're so easy to tease. If you want to talk about gushy, emotional things, call your father. He's the romantic. But let us know if you need anything. We do love you."

"Give Quinn and her family a hug from me," he said before hanging up.

He was in his car and headed for town before he thought it through. There probably weren't too many more days to enjoy taking Delilah out. A little time driving on the gorgeous fall day, top-down and fresh air all around him, just affirmed what was already a solid part of this day.

He and Julia had something good going on. Maybe George Coleman wasn't a fan, but *Julia* had said she trusted him. That was enough to make the road forward a lot smoother.

He pulled into an empty parking space outside of the Buns and Roses coffee shop, whistling as he stepped in the doorway.

It was way too soon to be thinking thoughts like: How would he and Julia act forty years from now? But as he spotted her at the table, laughing with her sister, he couldn't stop the daydream from coming.

THE MORNING HAD BEEN a sweet bit of comfort, in more ways than one. Lisa had loaded Julia and Karen up with fancy coffees and some of the best baking in town, then they'd talked quietly about nothing.

It was a momentary bit of ordinary that Julia had desperately needed. It also helped tangle the threads of connection between her and the two women at the table even further. They understood that talking about calendars or hobbies or their favourite pair of sandals that they'd miss once the snow started to fly was important.

It wasn't until Lisa got up to chat with Tansy Fields at the counter that Karen laid a hand on Julia's arm. "How did it go having Dad around last night?"

Julia's cheeks probably flamed bright red, thinking about her and Zach being overheard while they fooled around. "Kind of forgot he was there," she confessed.

Her oldest sister's brows rose. "That's...good?"

No. Not really, but Julia wasn't ready to explain the change in her and Zach's physical relationship.

There was a different topic she wanted to touch on. "He's kind of oblivious at times, isn't he?"

"Dad?" Karen snorted, a very unladylike sound. "Um, yeah."

Julia took a big breath. "I'm sorry my presence means he's visiting more often. It seems as if it's tough for you to have him around."

Karen stared at her for a long time before letting out a sigh. "I don't want to mess up your relationship with him by dragging in my baggage. You need to figure out on your own what you want in *all* your interactions with the Coleman clan. I like spending time with you, and I want you to enjoy yourself. That's kind of where my thoughts begin and end."

"But you deliberately went out of your way yesterday to help make things go smoother. I saw that," Julia said softly. "And I know it wasn't easy. So, thank you."

"You're welcome." Karen winked. "One thing you need to understand is we girls in the Whiskey Creek clan learned the hard way we needed to support each other. It doesn't matter that I've only known about you for a short while, you *are* my sister. I will always be there for you."

Dammit. Tears were just around the corner. Julia had tangled thoughts regarding her mom and all the secrets that hadn't been shared over the years. Now there were also mixed-up emotions regarding George Coleman and his attempts at getting involved in her life.

Still, in spite of how confused her emotions were regarding her parents, one thing was crystal clear.

Julia caught Karen by the hand. "What you've got as sisters is strong and real. I feel as if I'm cheating, being allowed to step into the middle of it, but no way will I turn it down. I feel very lucky to be your sister."

Karen blinked hard, her eyes as watery as Julia's. When she scooted her chair over and wrapped Julia in a big hug, the sensation was amazing.

The squeeze lasted for a good minute. When they finally separated just far enough to give each other a faint smile, Karen spoke. "There are things about Dad I don't enjoy. I'm learning to be okay with that. I'm learning it's okay to be angry about the past, but also that I'm allowed to control my future. I want good things going forward. That's what Finn keeps reminding me."

Lisa returned to the chair on the other side of the table, glancing between the two of them with a knowing expression.

"You guys need more chocolate," she said decisively, placing a plate in front of them with three massive chocolate-covered, cream-filled doughnuts.

Karen raised a brow. "Thanks. Did you bring a knife to divide the third one?"

Instantly, Lisa claimed the extra doughnut. "Are you kidding? I need chocolate as well. Serious conversations linger on the air and can only be dissipated by the consumption of massive amounts of calories."

Julia couldn't agree more. Their laughter was still ringing as she sank her teeth into the gooey treat. Chocolate and sweet whipped custard exploded onto her tongue right as a hand landed on her shoulder.

Zach slipped into the chair beside her. "Looks delicious."

Her mouth was far too full to answer. He stared at her lips, which just made chewing and swallowing that much more difficult.

"You picking up stuff for the ranch?" Lisa asked when she finally had an empty mouth.

"Doubtful, considering Finn and Cody went to Calgary this morning," Karen said, licking chocolate off her fingers as she eyed him.

"Just looking out for my girls," Zach offered slyly. "Need me to buy you another round?"

"Maybe." Lisa leaned forward, mercenary smile in place. "None of us are silly enough to turn down extra chocolate doughnuts."

He stretched his arm along the back of Julia's chair. "Take your time. Maybe when you're done, I can take you for a ride."

That last bit had been directed at her. Julia finally emptied her mouth and licked her lips clean. "I drove into town."

He shrugged. "We'll come back and get your ride when we're done. It's a pretty day out there, and since Josiah's entertaining your dad until dinnertime, we should enjoy your time off."

"You could always go do some yoga," Lisa suggested.

Zach's grin flashed. "Maybe later. Hard to do a downward dog in Delilah."

By the time they'd finished the teasing and chatting, Lisa and Karen were both carrying boxes of doughnuts, with an extra one put aside to take to Tamara.

Julia tucked herself into the passenger seat of Zach's convertible, and a moment later, they were out on the highway, headed toward Highwood Pass.

With the top down on the custom Corvette, the air temperature was perfect. The breeze through her hair made Julia feel alive. They didn't talk or listen to the radio, just drove the highway as it rose and dipped, passing tall pine trees looming like towers, their dark-green needles contrasting against the blue sky.

Here and there larch trees were turning colours, the needles brightening to yellow and orange. A few of the deciduous trees had begun to change as well, the occasional flash of red a bright contrast against a sea of green.

Thirty minutes later Zach pulled into a lookout over the Rocky Mountains. Julia's heart pounded with sheer joy at being alive, and her cheeks were sore from smiling.

She twisted toward him. "It's gorgeous out here."

His gaze darted over her face, lingering on her mouth. "Totally gorgeous."

She flushed.

Her cheeks got even hotter when his thumb brushed the corner of her mouth. And when he leaned in whispering the word *chocolate*, she wasn't sure if her heart was pounding from the adrenaline of the ride or the knowledge he was about to kiss her.

His kisses were to die for. Shiver-inducing, tempting, and addictive.

There was so much to enjoy in that moment, as she twisted toward him and tangled her fingers in his hair. Mindful of the previous night, she didn't try to speed up, just enjoyed where they were right here and now.

He was the one who took it up a notch, hunger rising. One hand stroking the side of her neck until he cupped her breast intimately. Simply holding her while his lips moved, as if he were attempting to memorize every inch of her mouth.

When he separated them, she gasped for air, head spinning slightly.

Zach opened his door, reaching back to extend a hand to her. "Come on. Let's go for a walk."

He led her down a wide path, the sound of birds rising over their heads along with a low rush of wind in the treetops. Neither of them spoke, just enjoyed the views and the rising sound of rushing water.

Only five minutes later, they popped out of the trees. Over by the river, a small bench sat along the ridge, strategically placed behind a safety railing.

Julia leaned forward until the waterfall below them came into view. "I didn't know this was here."

Zach rested his elbows on the railing, gaze fixed ahead. "Most people in town head to Heart Falls instead of this one. This is just a little drop and tumble compared to how spectacular the falls are right by Silver Stone ranch."

"They are pretty amazing," Julia agreed. She took a deep breath, the faint mist of the water washing her senses with the rich scent of moss and moisture. "But I like this type of waterfall as well. It's wild and alive, dancing over the rocks."

Zach pointed upstream. "Definitely wild."

She followed the aim of his finger and watched with joy as a deer poked her head out of the trees. Sliding forward slowly, a pair of fawns followed cautiously.

Julia glanced back at Zach. "You think they were born this year?"

He dipped his chin, his gaze fixed on the trio as they made their way to the water to steal a drink. The happiness on his face was so clear, Julia was mesmerized.

She'd rarely seen guys so open with their emotions. Well, okay, they tended to show anger readily, or frustration. But with Zach, he seemed to have no problem letting others see that things were okay. That he was having a good day, and wouldn't you like to have a good day along with him?

Kind of Mister Rogers in a western setting. She snickered in amusement, unable to stop herself.

Zach bumped his shoulder into hers. "What?"

He probably wouldn't be pleased to know she was comparing him to the children's performer, but then again—

Maybe he would.

All she knew for certain was spending time with Zach was a whole lot easier than she'd ever expected.

They walked, and they drove, enjoying easy conversation, and the afternoon passed too quickly. He took her back to grab her car, and they headed over to Tamara and Caleb's for dinner.

The evening passed smoothly with all of her sisters working in unison, tag teaming on George Coleman when needed, but even that seemed natural. And it wasn't necessary very often, because Grandpa George, or Geegee, was in a great mood. He had stories to share about his day with Josiah, and the little girls ate it up.

With Zach at her side, and her sisters guiding the evening,

the only thing really on Julia's mind now was what would happen later when they got home.

As much as she wanted to fool around again, being far too aware that her dad was on the other side of the wall was a great deterrent to rushing forward.

When it was finally her and Zach in the bedroom, Julia found herself blushing madly. Folding her clothes as if putting them away as neatly as possible was vital before she joined him.

He was tucked in on his side of the bed already, book in hand, glasses in place. Julia snuck glance after glance his way before he snorted, gaze still fixed on his book.

"No matter how hard you look at me, I'm not going to disappear," he warned.

"Not sure if I want you to disappear, or my dad," she confessed.

Zach met her gaze, reaching over to pat the bed beside him. "Sweetheart, relax. Tonight is a cuddle night, nothing else."

She paused in the middle of pulling back the quilt. Frowned. "Oh, really?"

"Uh-huh." He flicked a finger at her journal resting on the side table. "Check your to-do list."

Confused, Julia settled, her back toward him. She flipped open her journal to where a brand-new bookmark had been inserted. It had a shiny surface, with a pastoral scene displaying a ranch and mountains and deer in the middle of a field. The shiny golden tassel pooled across her fingers.

She turned it over to see what was becoming a familiar messy font. Zach's handwriting.

One day at a time. Look for the special moments.

She was about to turn and thank him when she realized

he'd put the bookmark in on the RULES page. He'd made adjustments and added some notes.

The no sex rule had an asterisk beside it. Below, the note said *Unlimited hugs. Unlimited kisses.*

Her third point on the opposite page had two asterisks added, and the defining note below that said: **once a week until further notice.*

The hell? Julia twisted instantly. "What kind of rule is that?"

Zach glanced over the top of his glasses. "What's that?"

Suddenly aware she'd spoken rather loudly, she lowered to a whisper. "Once a week? I thought we said last night we didn't need to add fooling around to the schedule."

His expression remained bright, but a more serious undertone slipped into his eyes. "I was wrong."

16

Somewhere between the conversation with his parents and watching the entire Whiskey Creek clan band together to make the evening go smoother, Zach had come to an astonishing conclusion.

His decision to say *yes* to absolutely everything Julia wanted required an addendum.

The only way they could build something lasting was if they put down a firm foundation, and while the fire between them was damn hot, he wanted so much more. A little bit of anticipation would only make things better as far as he was concerned.

In the meantime, he needed to do his best to convince her they were together for far more reasons than to save his finances or because they were having fun in the bedroom.

Although last night had been fantastic, and he couldn't wait for round two, however and wherever that happened.

But now Julia was staring at him, two spots of red on her cheeks, a crease folded between her brows. "Go on."

He shrugged. "I got to thinking. While there are some

things that are fun to do every day—and yes, sex every day at some point in our relationship would be fun—right now I enjoy having something to look forward to. Also, we're going to be around each other a lot, especially once you start working on the ranch. We're still figuring out expectations and how to spend time together. Knowing pretty clearly that nothing will happen tonight means we can both relax and not start *what if* questions in our heads."

She twisted completely to face him, notebook abandoned. "Like, what if we get too noisy again tonight? Am I going to feel absolutely embarrassed, and then what if I want to tell you to stop, but then worry that you think I'm telling you to stop because I don't like what you're doing, and then what if that worry makes it so I can't have a good time?"

Wow. He blinked. "Okay, that was a far more on-the-nose description than I could've possibly come up with."

Julia smiled wryly. "Vivid imagination. I spend a lot of time wondering *what if.*"

He waited as she put aside the notebook, carefully arranging it to be even with the edge of her side table. She dragged a finger over the ribbon then crawled under the covers and twisted until she was looking up at him. Big brown eyes, hair loose against the pillow shining in the light from the side tables.

She wore another one of his T-shirts. Not the same one as the previous night, which meant she'd stolen into his drawers and taken what she wanted.

He smiled at her. "You headed straight to sleep?"

"I can't read before bed in case I get caught up in the story. I've spent far too many potential sleeping times reading. Not a good thing with my line of work."

Zach put his own book away, and his reading glasses, before

turning out his light. That left them bathed in the moonlight shining through the window.

He twisted to face her, reaching for her fingers where they rested on top of the covers. "Are you mad?"

"No." There was enough light to see her frown. "A little confused, but honestly? Mostly relieved. I was pretty embarrassed this morning and any time I remembered George Coleman probably overheard us last night."

"I hear you." He smiled. "Your situation is a bit different, but I will say my parents *live* to embarrass me and my sisters. I think they keep score, and at the end of each year, they compare notes to see who has managed to be the most obnoxious in each of our lives."

"Like what?"

"Let me think." Zach rolled slightly, hands under his head as he stared at the ceiling. His legs stretched all the way to the base of the bed, and as he adjusted position, he bumped knees with her.

Julia shifted, but instead of moving away, she curled around him a little tighter. She'd done it almost instinctively, but suddenly stilled. "Is this okay?"

No way was he letting her move from his side. Zach stretched one arm, lifting her slightly until her head rested on his chest and he could cradle her easier. "There. Now it's perfect."

Cuddled together, intimate and warm and yet completely chaste.

Definitely story time. "Oh, here's a good one. Older sister number two had a steady boyfriend in high school. Family rule was no entertaining the opposite sex in our bedrooms. Which simply meant when they wanted to neck, they had to do it in the TV room, which meant grossing out all of us other kids."

Julia snickered. "Even not having grown up around my older siblings, I imagine that was probably part of the fun."

"Definitely. But remember, this was the TV room, which meant if we wanted to watch something, that's where we had to stay. After a while we learned to ignore them. Only mom wandered in one day and decided for some reason it was a great time for an additional sex ed class. She pulled out a condom and a banana, and the next thing we knew, Mattie's boyfriend had vanished."

"Oh my God." The light danced in Julia's eyes. "That's terrible."

Zach shrugged. He liked the way the weight of her against his body felt. He liked the way she was tucked up tight, and he had no desire to escape to a new position. "I suppose in the end, it wasn't that bad. Ronan and Mattie have been married for over ten years now."

That got another laugh out of her. "I guess he knew what he was signing up for."

They lay quietly for a while. Julia trickled her fingers over his chest, almost as if she weren't aware she was doing it at first. Then a little more boldly. "This all right?"

He caught her fingers and brought them up to his lips. "You do whatever makes you happy. You take whatever you need to take."

"And what do you get out of this?" she asked, once again a note of disbelief in her tone.

Hopefully forever.

Zach hummed thoughtfully. "Unlimited kisses, unlimited hugs. That's not a bad place to start. And we *are* going to fool around a whole hell of a lot. Don't get me wrong, Julia. I didn't permanently turn off the sex button—"

He paused as she snickered.

"Okay, bad wording. We'll deal with the whole *whatever*

sex feels good thing as it comes, but everything else happened quickly as well."

"It really has," Julia agreed thoughtfully. "I'll admit today was the first day I've finally felt as if I was able to take a deep breath after racing through the past week and a half." She tilted her head and looked up at him, sliding one hand to brush her palm over the scruff on his chin and cheeks. "You are a very complicated individual, Zachary Beauregard Damien Sorenson."

He was about to deny it, but then remembered something from the years of watching his father the inventor. "Sometimes the simplest solution comes once you've removed all the complicated setup beneath the surface. I'm pretty much a *what you see is what you get* kinda guy, but I've learned a lot over the years to get to be at the point where I've peeled away what's not important to me."

"And taking our time is important?"

Another shrug. "It's more that *we're* important. What we need to make it through, here and now, isn't what we'll need next week, or next month, etcetera. No use rushing."

Julia stayed silent until her head rocked the slightest bit, as if she'd thought it through and was willing to acknowledge the truth.

She fell asleep in his arms not even five minutes later. A bundle of warmth and soft, feminine skin, the scent of her filling his nostrils. The feel of her in his arms soaked into his very core and changed him from the inside out.

That sensation in his gut that had told him this mix-up between them was right kept getting more and more certain.

He *would* build the foundation they needed, beginning with unlimited hugs and unlimited kisses plus whatever she asked for that would make them strong.

George Coleman took off in the morning with only a few

comments that could be construed as warnings. Julia missed most of them in the busyness of greeting Karen and Finn, who had come over to send off the older man.

Finn folded his arms over his chest as his father-in-law disappeared down the highway. *Their* father-in-law, Zach corrected himself.

"What're your plans for the week?" Finn asked.

Zach tilted his head toward where Karen and Julia were slipping into the nearest arena. A half dozen horses came forward, including Karen's rescued wild foal, Moonbeam.

Zach and Finn moved to join them. "Julia's shifts this week are Wednesday through Saturday. I figured I'd help with whatever you need around here during that time. Sunday, I'm taking her on a road trip to Nelson."

"She know that yet?"

"Nope," Zach confessed.

His best friend snickered before wiping at his mouth to hide his amusement. "Bit of advice. You might want to start involving Julia in your planning a little more. The whole *fly by the seat of your pants* thing you do is entertaining, but at some point, it's going to bite you."

Possibly. "Not all of us run our lives by having three layers deep of plans ready to implement."

"Nope," Finn echoed his word from moments earlier. He paused beside the gate before opening it to let Zach in. "You think Julia is more like me or more like you in this area?"

Drat. "I hate it when you're right," Zach complained.

As they joined the girls, it was clear that Karen had overheard his last comment. "Is Finn giving you advice?"

"Always," Zach said dryly. "Good thing I only occasionally need to listen."

Julia laughed, the sound turning into a squeal as Moonbeam put his nose in the middle of her back and pushed.

A moment later, she was in Zach's arms, pressed against his body as he caught her safely against him.

Julia draped her arms around him instinctively, and it felt easy to have her smiling up at him, amusement on her face and gratitude on her lips. "Thanks for catching me."

"No problem," he returned. "So, about this coming week..."

"Julia. Wait up."

She'd hit the time clock at the end of her final night shift and was now looking forward to a glorious four days in a row off that Zach had promised would involve good food, good beer, and a chance to fool around in private.

Getting home as soon as possible to start the madcap adventure was high on her priority list.

Still, she twisted back toward the fire hall and waited as Brad left his truck and made his way toward her. "Hey. Good morning. Didn't expect to see you before I headed home."

He stopped beside her car. "I came in early. Need to update you on something."

Julia hesitated. "Is there a problem?"

Brad made a face. "Not with your work or your internship. And congrats, by the way, on getting hired out at Red Boot ranch once you're done here. I'm only sorry we couldn't hire you on full-time past October."

"Thanks. I have to admit I'm pretty excited about the job. If I can't work for you, working at a dude ranch is pretty much my dream job."

He nodded, but concern had drifted in. "I know you're headed off for the next few days. Debated whether I should mention this now, but you have a right to know. Dwayne has been released from his halfway house."

An icy chill swept over her even though she'd known this was coming. The reaction was even more annoying because she truly wasn't worried about him coming after her or anything.

Her kidnapper clearly had mental issues, so instead of being incarcerated in the regular prison system, he'd rightly received therapy and guidance while being in custody. "That's right. I didn't have it on my calendar or anything, but I knew it was sometime soon."

She could tell from how closely Brad was watching her reaction that he hadn't been happy to share the update. Julia kept her spine straight and her expression as neutral as possible.

"The restraining order is still in place, so you should have nothing to worry about." Brad hesitated for a moment then sighed heavily. "He got in touch with me."

"What?" The word came out a whole lot sharper than intended. "Why would he do that? What did he want?"

Brad made a face. "He apologized to me again. Said that he'd tried to apologize to you, but you'd never responded."

"Because I didn't have to. It's not my job to try and make him feel better," Julia snapped before taking a deep breath. "Sorry, not your fault."

"No, I'm glad you said that," Brad insisted. "Even better, I'm glad you feel that way."

"Lots of therapy," Julia admitted dryly. "Tony finally got through to me that I don't have to forgive Dwayne for what he did to me."

"Good." Brad said it very decisively. He cleared his throat, slightly embarrassed. "I told him off. Also told him if he ever tried to make contact with you again, through me or any other source, there would be dire consequences."

Julia caught herself before she gave Brad a hug and nodded instead. "Thanks."

"You have a good getaway, and if you need anything, give me a shout." He made as if to turn away then stopped, meeting her gaze straight on. "You'll tell Zach about this, right?"

She opened her mouth to assure him she'd be all right and didn't need anyone babysitting her, when she realized she'd already planned on spilling her frustration on Zach as soon as possible.

That truth felt very strange.

She dipped her chin. "Don't worry. Zach's got my back."

"I'm glad." Brad offered a quick farewell wave before making his way into the fire hall.

The ride back to Red Boot ranch passed quickly enough as confusing thoughts and memories tangled together in Julia's brain. She slid into the cottage, prepping for bed and the nap she needed before she and Zach took off that afternoon as planned.

She'd gone back to sleeping in the guest room after her father had left. It had felt right to take that step of slowing down seriously. Plus, with Zach's plans to take them out of town for a getaway, she figured the fooling around part was coming soon enough.

Falling asleep as the morning progressed just got harder and harder, but at some point, she must have closed her eyes for long enough to ignore the tumbling memories, because suddenly she heard her name being repeated loudly.

"Julia. Wake up," Zach said, worry in his tone.

She shot upright in her bed, twisting toward his voice. Her heart pounded, and she stuck to the sheets as if she'd been sweating profusely.

She could still feel the heavy weight of being trapped. The icy cold of water dragging her down.

"Nightmare." The word whispered past her lips. "Zach?"

The bed tipped slightly as he sat beside her. "Right here, sugar."

A moment later, she'd latched onto him, curled up in his lap, arms knotted around his waist.

He held on tight, rubbing her back. Whispering soothing words. Her shaking slowed, until she finally got to the point she could take a deep breath and let it out in teeny increments.

Zach's lips pressed against her temple. "There we go. That's better."

She leaned back far enough to look into his face. "I fucking hate that nightmare."

"I know you do."

He didn't offer any pat words about how she'd get better someday. Or about how much better she was now than before. Which was good, because while she did feel so much stronger about her current reactions to the whole kidnapping situation, nightmares aside, Tony had been clear—the goal was not to be *over it*.

There were some things a person just never got over.

She managed a smile, patting Zach on the cheek. "I need a shower, and then I'll be ready to head out."

"Okay." Zach backed up slightly. "You need anything? Want me to pack a picnic lunch for when we're in the car?"

"You'd let me eat in Delilah?" Julia put as much astonishment into her tone as possible.

"Sure. What's a few crumbs between friends?" He paused. "I'm bringing the dustbuster. You can use it when you're done."

Julia giggled her way into the shower, totally distracted, just as Zach had intended.

The road trip between Heart Falls and Nelson took a total of four hours driving. It had been cool enough that Zach left the top up. Julia used Bluetooth to hook up her music list to the stereo, and time flew.

Once again conversation was easy. Zach had a list of great topics he introduced every time there was a lull, but it wasn't needed very often. They pretty much flowed naturally from one conversation to the next, words sometimes running on top of each other as each story they shared reminded the other person of something else they wanted to talk about.

The only thing Julia didn't bring up was the information Brad had shared that morning.

It wasn't that she was trying to avoid the discussion, but the story wasn't something she wanted to share with Zach while he was driving.

And then the closer they got to their destination, the less she felt as if she should bring up a big topic before what was supposed to be a fun and easy getaway.

The twisting road they'd been on for the last hour and a half unexpectedly opened into a wide parking space at the edge of an enormous lake.

Julia leaned forward with interest. "Where's the road?"

"We take a ferry at this point. There's another route to Nelson that goes over the pass, but I thought you'd enjoy going this direction first."

"Cool. How long is the ride?" Julia peered out the window toward the lake. "Ohhh. Is that the ferry there?"

Zach put Delilah into park, gesturing across the smooth surface of the water to where a strangely shaped barge approached slowly. "That's it. It's only a forty-five minute ride once we're on board. It's not like the massive ferries that go out to Vancouver Island, just a basic transport vehicle. We drive on board, then you can either sit in your car or walk to one of the observation decks."

Fifteen minutes later they were on the wide, flat-decked boat.

Zach caught her by the hand and tugged her toward the stairwell. "Come on. I'll show you my favourite view."

He led her to an area on the second floor with sturdy seating that let them stare out over the wide expanse of Kootenay Lake as the engines rumbled and steadily pushed them across to the other side.

The wind was crisp. Julia stared at the mountains rising all around the lake, some of them tipped with white. "It's colder here than in Heart Falls."

"There are glaciers in the area. The wind sweeping over them means the breezes are always crisp." He wrapped an arm around her, snuggling close to protect her with his body.

A forty-five-minute ride. Julia watched the water stream out in expanding waves behind the ship and considered her options. She didn't want to put a damper on his outing, not considering how excited Zach was about getting away.

But he'd said to be honest, and he'd said she should do what would make her happy, and while talking about the past wouldn't make her *happy*, per say, it would be good to get it out in the open.

Julia twisted toward him, sliding back far enough to grab his hands and meet his gaze straight on. "I have something I need to tell you."

His head tilted slightly, but he stayed silent.

"Just so you know, the reason I'm telling you this isn't because it's big and scary, or because it changes anything about what we're doing the next couple of days. We're going to Nelson to do research for your future brew thing magic. I still want to do that. That's important to me."

His grin wasn't quite as solid anymore. "Jules, if this opener is meant to be reassuring? You're missing the mark."

"Dammit. It's just... Brad told me this morning that the guy who kidnapped me got released. I knew it was coming, but I had kind of deliberately forgotten. It's not freaking me out, and I'm not worried about him, but I realized I needed to say something to you because—well, I think you need to know."

Zach nodded slowly. "That's why you were having a nightmare, wasn't it?"

Julia let out a huff of air. "Yeah. Someday I'll be able to mention what happened, or have somebody else bring it up, without having that reaction. But for now, Tony says physical manifestations to triggers are one of the things our brains do while dealing with unhappy memories. But since it's not hurting me, other than being a pain in the ass, I shouldn't worry about it."

"Okay." Zach looked a little uncomfortable. "I mean, *okay*, I hear you, but there's a part of me that's not okay with you having nightmares."

He was such a sweetie.

Julia cupped his face with her palms. "I know. But you were good help today, waking me up."

She pressed a quick kiss against his lips, partly to give her a moment to gather her thoughts before she sat back. The water around them reflected blue sky with white clouds. No one else was sitting outside, leaving them with more than enough privacy.

Also, telling Zach what had happened while here on the ferry meant she could talk about it and then walk away, which she really liked.

"It's not that long of a story. EMT training—I stayed on campus, and as usual, there was a group of us that kind of hung out together. I didn't date anybody. It was overwhelming enough to deal with school, living in a new city, and not being at home with Mom for the first time."

She adjusted the grip between their hands, Zach's big fingers giving her something solid to hang on to.

"We did lots in groups. Fun activities like movie nights, plus school activities that involved group projects. Dwayne and I were assigned into a group of four where one of our teammates quit and the other got sick. The two of us worked really hard to get everything accomplished without them. I was really proud that we handed in the assignment on time."

"Only Dwayne thought that you were more than just classmates?"

Julia shook her head. "That's the weird part. It wasn't about us being together, like romantically involved. Dwayne had some undiagnosed mental problems, and for some reason, he got it into his head that I was in danger."

Zach's hand squeezed around hers briefly. "Okay."

"He thought the other two people on our project had vanished because somebody had taken them out. He started talking about how we needed to be careful and stay safe."

She'd thought back over that time so often, she sometimes wondered where her memories failed and if she might have invented things to explain what had happened. It wasn't her fault for not having recognized that Dwayne's mental illness had flared to the danger level, but there were times she still wished she would've been able to do more.

"I tried to convince him that was just his imagination, and I thought I'd gotten through. I came out from buying groceries, and he was there. He offered me a ride home, which of course I took."

A soft swear word escaped Zach's lips. "He didn't take you home."

"Nope. He insisted he needed to keep me safe, so he took me to a cabin with a boathouse out on a nearby lake. I figured out pretty fast Dwayne wasn't thinking straight at that moment, but he was bigger than me, and stronger, and even though I tried to get away, I ended up tied to a chair."

An instant later, Julia was lifted off the bench and resettled in Zach's lap. He squeezed her tight, head buried against her neck, damn near vibrating under her fingers.

"Sorry. Give me a minute." His words came out tight and clipped.

She wasn't sure if patting Zach on the back was appropriate, so she just held on. She'd told the story a number of times now, but this was the first time anyone had reacted like this.

As if he'd been there the entire time and was even now experiencing exactly what she'd gone through.

17

Fury whipped through his veins even as Zach fought to control his anger. Losing his shit was not what Julia needed.

He was so damn proud she'd been willing to open up about this to him, which made his reaction that much more important. She did not need to know that right now, if he had Dwayne in front of him, he'd slowly turn the other man inside out.

It wasn't possessiveness. It wasn't because he thought Julia hadn't been able to take care of herself or that she hadn't done an amazing job of moving beyond what had happened to her.

But *goddammit*, he wanted to protect her from ever feeling that kind of fear again, whether in a nightmare or in real life.

He gave her a squeeze then let go, pushing back to meet her gaze again. "Okay."

Julia raised a brow. "We need to talk about your vocabulary problems. I don't think *okay* means what you think it means."

Involuntarily, he snorted. "You're right. I'm not using the

dictionary definition. More like *I've pulled myself together enough, please go on.*"

It was a good thing he had faked his control as well as he did. Because Julia went on to briefly describe being left in the cabin over the next four days. Each time Dwayne returned to give her food and water and a bathroom break before leaving her tied up tight.

Julia took a deep breath. "Dwayne started ranting about how we had to escape and that the safest thing would be to paddle out to an island he knew about." She stared down at where her fingers meshed with Zach's. "He would only be gone for a little while, he said. So, he tied me up again and carried me to the rowboat in the boathouse. He'd barely left when I realized the boat's keel was broken and the entire thing was slowly sinking."

No wonder she had nightmares. Hell, Zach was going to have nightmares just from thinking about her being helpless in that situation.

Julia squeezed his hands. "Brad showed up about half an hour after Dwayne left. I have never been so grateful to see anyone in my entire life."

Zach shook his head. "I don't even know what to say."

"You don't really have to say anything. I mean, it was terrible, I know that. But none of it was my fault. Dwayne is supposed to be better now that he got treatment, so I can't even really blame him because the guy who did it doesn't exist anymore." She made a face. "No. It *was* his fault, and it *was* his choice, but I also understand how mental illness means people do things they wouldn't do if they didn't have that chemical imbalance in the first place."

"You're far more understanding than I am." Zach slipped his fingers under her chin. "Thank you for sharing that with me. And if there is anything I can do, or anything you need me to follow up on, let me know."

"Thanks. I told Brad that I would let you know about Dwayne. About him being released and me getting the news."

Something inside him stilled. Zach examined her face carefully, fighting to keep the worry that had sprung up from showing.

Was Brad's influence the only reason she'd told him?

He wasn't used to the fingers of doubt shifting through his brain, but they were there, at least briefly, before he focused on the most important thing.

Zach shoved aside everything except making Julia know that she could rely on him, even when the ground under his feet felt shaky.

He lifted her hand and kissed her knuckles, meeting her gaze. Trying to figure out what needed to be said.

Julia took control, swinging across his lap so her knees rested on the metal bench under his hips. Straddling him, her ass warm on his thighs as she caught hold of his collar and meticulously straightened it. "Not to change the topic or anything, but it's time to change the topic. You said this was a research trip."

Amusement drifted in. Of course the woman would be not only strong enough to tell him what had happened, but strong enough to then push the events aside as if they weren't life-altering on so many levels.

Still, he took his cue from her. "It *is* a research trip," he agreed. "It's a double research trip. No, it's *triple* research."

Julia's lips curled upward. "Not quadruple? How disappointing."

"Sorry, couldn't find a fourth topic to dig into this go-round, but maybe the next time we go away." He rested his hands on her hips, thoroughly entertained as she groomed him back into a state of neatness. Adjusting his collar, stroking her fingers through his hair, patting the wrinkles out of his sleeves.

"Let me guess. First research topic is to do with beer. I did a Google search, and there is a really good brewery in Nelson. I assume we'll do some taste testing."

"Definitely. A couple of the restaurants put together menus with recommended local beverage pairings. We've got tapas and samples lined up from three different places."

"We should've asked Karen and Finn to join us. And Lisa and Josiah. They like trying new things."

It took everything in him to not gape at her in wonder. He forced himself to respond all cool and collected. "Good idea. We'll have to do that sometime."

"What's the second research? And the third?" The engines rumbled slightly, and they both glanced over the water. "We're getting close to the other side of the lake."

Zach helped her off his lap and brought her to the railing. He tucked his arm around her and held her against his side as they watched the ferry manoeuvre through the narrows toward the docking station. "Second research involves hitting one of the coffee shops tomorrow morning. Tansy wants me to bring back a selection of their baked goods. She heard good things about the place and wants to try to expand the repertoire at Buns and Roses."

Julia pressed against his side. "That's very nice of you to do that for her."

He laughed heartily. "Oh, yeah, it's totally a hardship to be asked to go to a bakery and bring back a dozen of everything sweet."

She twisted until he had to look at her. "See, that's the thing. You make it sound as if you're totally on the winning end of all these things you volunteer to do, but you're also putting yourself out." She leaned in closer, staring him in the eye. "I'm onto you, baby. I'm totally onto your tricks."

She tapped him on the nose, but before he could catch hold and tickle her, she ducked under his arm and scurried away.

He held out his hand and waited until she linked their fingers together so he could guide her back to Delilah. "Still say I'm getting the good end of that deal. The one that involves breakfast goodies."

Julia waited until they had disembarked from the ferry and were once again on the final stretch of highway before she asked, "Where are we staying?"

"An Airbnb. Not that we'll need the kitchen, but I like having enough room to spread out."

She nodded then played with her phone for a minute. He waited politely, except it was apparent she had mischief on her mind when the playlist that started up was all Elvis.

When she queued up "A Little Less Conversation," Zach outright laughed. He reached across the stick and caught her fingers in his. "What an interesting sentiment. Are you getting tired of talking to me?"

She winked. "Actually, no. Tell me another story about your sisters."

Which kept her entertained for the final half hour until they pulled into the driveway of the house in uphill Nelson.

Julia stared at the house in confusion. "Exactly how far do you need to spread out? Holy moly, this place is ginormous."

He hurried around to open her door. "It all depends how noisy your neighbours are."

"Maybe. But your neighbours could be a marching band and the symphony orchestra, and you probably still wouldn't hear them inside this monstrosity."

Zach pushed open the door and gestured her in. "Yeah, I suppose. But then, I don't think you've ever heard how noisy

Finn gets when he's involved in a rousing game of Pictionary."

Julia stuttered to a stop just inside the door. "What are you talking about Finn— *What?*"

"Surprise." Sprawled on the couch in the middle of the open living room, Karen and Lisa lifted glasses in the air.

Lisa waved hers a little. "I made Mojitos, but Josiah has taken over pouring. He seems to think I had a slight rum-to-mix ratio problem in the first batch."

Josiah drifted into view, a blender in one hand and a full glass in the other that he held toward the front door. "I hope you realize none of us qualify as a designated driver for this evening's outing."

"Good thing the food is being delivered," Zach told him, loving the expression dancing across Julia's face.

Surprise, yet delight, and when she whirled back toward him and threw herself into his arms to squeeze him so tight he could barely breathe, Zach figured he had probably done something right. "This okay?"

"Okay, as in the *I can't believe you pulled this off* and *hell yes, it's wonderful* definition of the word." Only when she pulled away, her cheeks were flushed.

Zach held on to her, loving the way it felt to have her body pressed against his. "What's that look mean?"

Julia's voice dropped to a mere whisper. "You're going to think I'm being silly, but having *them* overhear us fool around would be just as embarrassing as my dad."

Too funny.

He dropped his tone to match hers in volume. "Then we won't fool around until they leave. We have three nights, and I didn't invite them to stay the whole time."

They grinned at each other, an unspoken pact witnessed in that moment, before Julia turned and accepted the drink from

Josiah with grateful thanks before joining her sisters in the living room.

"What can I get you to drink?" Josiah asked as Finn wandered into the room, pausing to give his wife a kiss then striding across the room toward them.

Zach glanced around at his friends with growing contentment. "I should pour a drink for you. Happy belated birthday, by the way."

Josiah dipped his chin. "Thanks for setting up the impromptu party. Appreciate it."

"Thanks for having a birthday. Always good to have a reason to get together for a night or two."

But not three. That third night was just for him and Julia.

Because while he was an awesome friend, he was also smart enough to know there were some things that would be far more enjoyable once the family bonding time was over.

Two days later, Julia felt as if she had a permanent smile on her face.

They'd not only had the research dinner Zach had promised and the breakfast trip with multiple types of baking, they'd done it all over again the next day.

This morning they'd all gone paddling on the lake in tandem kayaks, followed by lunch out. The others were due to head home early afternoon, and Julia couldn't decide if she was sad that they were leaving or eager to discover what mischief Zach had planned for them after they had the house to themselves.

Sleeping in his arms had been a brutal form of torture. She'd considered reaching for him and turning up the heat, because she doubted her sisters would even notice anything going on in their far-off section of the house.

Yet Zach had been right last week when he said waiting had its perks. Anticipation now pumped through her veins as strongly as any drug.

Lust was tempered only by how full her stomach was.

She collapsed onto the couch, sinking into the lush leather. "I could not eat another bite."

"There are some chocolate eclairs left from dessert." Lisa appeared out of nowhere to stand over her, wiggling one of the million-calorie parcels of perfection in her fingers. "Oops, to be exact, there are three left. Considering there are six of us, you might want to move sooner than later."

Lisa popped the one she held into her mouth and moaned enthusiastically.

From where the guys were setting up to play one final card game at the kitchen table, Josiah swore.

"Excuse me, gentlemen." He pushed back from the table and strode over to Lisa, swinging her over his shoulder and ignoring her squeal of protest. "Sweetheart, you make that kind of noise, you're just asking to be removed from the room."

"Either that or she's auditioning for a porno flick. Either way," Karen said teasingly before warning, "we're leaving in an hour."

Lisa pushed up, arms braced on Josiah's back so she could offer a wink to the room as he carried her off. "Don't worry. We won't be late."

Josiah's laughter rumbled then shut off behind the door leading to their room. Julia's cheeks went red hot, and the need in her body jumped up another notch when she met Zach's gaze.

He was staring at her with all sorts of dirty intention in his eyes.

An hour later when their friends and family had finally left the house, Julia's entire body felt as if she'd been attached to a giant vibrator and teased for hours.

Zach's hands rested on her hips. He'd stood behind her as they waved goodbye, and he slid one palm over her belly as his lips dropped to her neck. "I'm glad they came, but I'm glad they're gone," he admitted.

She arched her neck to the side, goose bumps rising everywhere. "You know that whole anticipation thing?"

Pressed against her back, his muscular body wasn't the only thing that was hard. "Yeah?"

The word came out deep and breathless. Thank goodness, because she didn't want to be the only one feeling this way. "I am *extremely* filled with anticipation."

She twisted in his arms, stroking her palms up his chest. The soft cotton of his pale-green T-shirt tickled her skin. Tactile seduction, but it wasn't enough. Julia dipped her hands to his waist and untucked the fabric so she could slip her hands beneath the material and find bare skin.

His abs flexed against her fingers. "I need to warn you *my* anticipation is high enough my control is iffy. On the other hand, my recovery time will also be off the charts, so do your worst."

"Anything I want?" Julia hummed happily as she shoved his T-shirt upward. It turned into a contented sigh when he rapidly moved to help strip away the barrier. "I want lots of things."

"Yeah? Like what?" His smile shone down even as he groaned. "I really hope one of them is your hands on my cock. That would be a good thing to add to your list."

"Maybe." She leaned in close and pressed a kiss to his chest. Licking his skin and breathing in his sexy scent "*Hmmmm.*"

He stood motionless as she slowly drifted around him, teasing with her fingertips and her lips. She watched closely for every reaction because it was clear how much he was enjoying every second.

Here too he was honest. This was the part of being with a guy she'd missed. Not just being touched herself, but making another person feel wonderful.

And when she laid her fingers under the waistline of his jeans, she hit the jackpot. The muscles of his neck stood out in stark relief as his head fell backward and he moaned loudly.

The sound turned into a gasp when she wrapped her fingers around his rigid length. Julia stroked the best she could while trapped under the sturdy fabric.

Reading her mind, Zach rapidly undid his button and zipper, shoving the top of his jeans open—

The doorbell rang, and someone knocked vigorously.

They both cursed. Zach caught hold of her and twirled them toward the front door. He had her pressed against the sturdy wood an instant later before leaning to peer through the side window.

"For fuck's sake." He jerked the door open barely an inch. "What?"

"Sorry." Josiah sounded very apologetic, although also slightly amused. "Lisa forgot her purse."

There was nowhere to hide. Considering she wasn't the one half-naked, Julia wasn't sure why she was so flushed. Josiah strode over to the couch, grabbed Lisa's purse off the cushion, then hurried back toward where Zach stood holding the door wide open for a rapid escape.

He hadn't bothered to do up his jeans. Maybe as a warning to not bother with any small talk. It worked, because Josiah took off without another word. Although he did wink as he went past.

The instant Zach closed the door, the two of them pressed their noses against the side windows, watching intently until the truck vanished down the street.

Lisa and Karen waved from the back seat as if they knew they were being watched.

Julia snickered, and as Zach caught hold of her fingers and led her back toward their room, laughter swirled around them.

"Should've known they couldn't bear to leave without messing with us," Zach complained, but there was amusement in his tone.

"With friends like that, who needs enemies?" Julia drawled. She caught hold of the back belt loop on his jeans and tugged him to a stop. "Not so fast. I was doing something interesting."

Zach raised his hands out of her way, his eyelids growing heavy. "Okay."

"Which this time means *go ahead and have your wicked way with me*, yes?"

"*Hell* yes," he growled.

She learned from her mistake last time and dealt with his pants before moving ahead. She shoved his jeans and briefs all the way to his ankles before helping him step out of the fabric.

Rising to her feet, Julia took a deep breath as she admired the long muscular legs supporting the rest of his naked perfection. "Wow."

Zach flashed a smile even as he caught hold of her hands, pressing them against his torso. "*Wow* as much as you want but tell me you can do it while you're touching me."

"Touching is good. Kissing." She stepped against him, sliding her hands around to the small of his back. She tilted her head until their lips met, the kiss growing deeper and hotter by the second.

Her being fully clothed and him being completely naked

turned her on in an unexpected way. She felt powerful and utterly in control. She slipped one hand between their bodies to wrap her fingers around his erection.

"*Julia.*" Not a warning, but definitely a plea, and one she very much wanted to answer. She put her free hand against his chest and backed him up until he was against the wall. Then she took her time, stroking firmly, watching the thick head of his cock peek out between her fingers again and again. Glancing up to examine his face as pleasure drifted in.

When she bent over and licked, air hissed through his teeth. "*Jesus.*"

While there were a whole lot of things on her list, suddenly the most important one was to blow Zach's mind. Which now meant blowing something else entirely.

She laughed as she slid to her knees in front of him, fingers moving teasingly over his length as she got her mouth in position. She was no expert, but his excitement, the quivering in his legs, and the unsteady touch of his fingers as he dragged them through her hair were enough of an aphrodisiac that she couldn't resist.

Julia placed her mouth over the head of his cock then slowly sucked.

A stream of soft curses drifted from his lips, and the muscles under her fingers flexed where she clutched his thighs.

Zach's hips jerked toward her, his fingers in her hair tightening in warning. "Coming."

He instantly let go, and she could've backed away if she wanted, but she chose to stay where she was. She wanted to taste him, to continue to move around him as his cock jerked between her lips. Powerful? Undoubtedly. Happy? She swallowed then licked and smiled as he slapped his hands against the wall and fought to keep vertical.

"Holy fuck." Zach said it on an exhale, reaching down to

grab her arm and help her to her feet. Then he tugged her against him, blanketing his naked body with her clothed one. "Lean on me for a bit until my head stops spinning."

Julia found herself grinning. "Okay."

He snickered. "Cocky wench."

"One of us has to be. I think you've been de-cockified for a little bit."

Laughter bloomed, and he cradled her tighter against his body. "De-cockified? You've been hanging out around Lisa far too much."

"Hey, don't put down my sister's amazing talent for wordifying." She gasped as he swung her off her feet and carried her back toward their bedroom.

"You've still got enough energy to be sassy. I should do something about it."

"You totally should," she said encouragingly. Julia pointed at her duffel bag that sat on the nearest dresser. "Toys in the right pouch."

He laid her on the bed and crawled over her, ignoring her directions. "Toys later. Me first."

The statement would have set off warning buzzers in the past. Every guy she'd fooled around with seemed to think they had the magic touch.

But this was Zach, and as he stripped away her clothing, enough electric energy hung in the air she could've sworn there was already a vibrator strapped between her legs.

"Promise me you'll only do what makes you happy," Julia warned. "I want an orgasm, but I don't want to—"

He whispered "*shhhh*" against her skin, soft and reassuring. "Trust me."

She could do that this once, but the instant frustration began to slip in? She was totally nabbing her bag of tricks. "Okay, which this time means *touch me.*"

Zach was more than on board with that. He was also more than capable of setting her pulse pounding. Maybe it had something to do with that whole anticipation thing, but as he kissed and teased, her skin seemed to come alive.

He slid between her thighs, fingertips caressing from her ankles to her knees. His thumbs made small circles, moving ever closer to her core as he slowly pressed her knees into the air. Staring at her sex, hunger rising in his eyes. "Yes?"

The sooner the better.

Julia curled upright and caught him by the arms. "Touch me," she insisted as she tugged him closer. "Everywhere."

He willingly slid closer, fingers opening her, mouth covering her sex. His tongue teased, and his lips moved against her, a gentle touch but one she felt everywhere.

When his tongue hit her clit, her back involuntarily arched, pressing tighter to his mouth. Needing more. "I like that. You don't need to be gentle," she told him.

The words came out in a rush, because right now this felt good, and pressure was building, but there was no guarantee it would continue.

Zach was a quick learner. The gentle touch grew firmer. His tongue no longer teasing but flicking against her in a demanding rhythm that made her gasp. And when he closed his mouth and sucked, the hair on the back of her neck stood upright. "Oh. My. *God.*"

A soft chuckle sounded from between her legs, but he didn't stop. Suddenly fingers ghosted the edge of her sex. Teasing, slipping in no farther than maybe his second knuckle.

When he continued to tease at that same depth, the tension that had shot in that he would break her concentration vanished and she focused down on all the good things happening.

His fingers rocked in and out of her even as he upped the pressure on her clit, sucking hard.

She came. Unexpected, hard and fast. Pleasure broke over her, and she drove her heels into the bed, hips grinding against his face.

Zach chuckled, but kept going, at least until she tangled her fingers in his hair and jerked hard enough to break the seal of his mouth.

"Slowly," she gasped. "Slowly."

He hummed, sliding back to kiss her folds delicately. Easing his tongue against her swollen flesh as endorphins continued to scream through her body.

When she'd stopped jerking with aftershocks, he crawled up on the mattress next to her, wiping his mouth before offering a huge grin. "That was fun. Round two in a few minutes?"

Dear God. "That just might kill me," she warned him.

"We'll go slow. But you brought all sorts of toys that we haven't used yet. Plus, I bought you a new one. I can't wait to try it."

Julia jerked onto her elbows and stared at him in astonishment. Her previous boyfriends had all hated when she'd grabbed a vibrator. "You bought me a toy?"

He nodded, eagerness joining the happiness in his expression. "It's called a Womanizer, and it's supposed to be incredible. I need your take on it before I believe the advertising. Research is important, you know."

Amusement struck in a flash. "Really? Checking out sex toys is your third research topic?"

"Of course." He rolled over her, their naked bodies slicking with heat and the promise of some very fine memories. "I'm a thorough researcher," he warned. "I hope you took your vitamins this morning."

18

$\mathcal{J}$ulia was on her way out the door, headed to work, when Zach popped up beside her. "Here you go."

She took the envelope he extended toward her. "What's this?"

"My homework. I sent Alan an email to let him know that I have delivered the first of our monthly letters as required." He rolled his eyes dramatically, in a fair impression of an angsty teenager. "I'll give you his email so you can do the same later."

She'd nearly forgotten that part of the rules. "I don't have mine done yet."

Zach waved a hand. "We got married on the thirty-first, so it's not as if we're late. I figured it was easier to remember to do it by the end of the month rather than the start. Either way, there's mine."

Julia shook it. "How long is yours?"

He snickered.

It was her turn to eye roll. "You're such a goof. I meant the letter."

"I'm still laughing, darlin'. Doesn't matter how long mine is, your letter is your letter."

She pretended to pout. "Does that mean I'm not allowed to read yours first?"

"Do what makes you happy." He pressed a quick kiss to her cheek then took the stairs off the porch two at a time, whistling as he headed farther onto the ranch. "See you later. It's Cooking Adventures with Zach tonight. We'll attempt to not burn Asian noodle bowls."

"Sounds great."

She tossed the envelope on the dash where it haunted her the entire drive into town.

Pulling into the parking lot at the fire hall the same moment the doors went up on the fire engine exit meant everything vanished from her brain except joining the rest of her team as quickly as possible.

It wasn't until after lunch when they were finally back at the hall after putting out a bushfire that Julia had time to deal with her dilemma.

Do her homework first, or read Zach's to see how upfront and open he'd been?

She tapped the envelope on the table in front of her, the mental debate raging loudly before she sighed and dropped his letter, pulling one of her ever-present notepads toward herself. Truth was, she was in the very wonderful position of being able to have her cake and eat it too. She could write a note, then read Zach's, and if necessary, rewrite to match his tone. It was only kind of cheating.

Since she was going to rewrite no matter what, she didn't bother to make it fancy. Just tossed out what needed to be said.

September 30.

After falling into an impossible situation, I can look back on this first month and say it has not been terrible. I still can't believe that we ended up here, and just to be clear, tequila shooters are out of the question ever again.

This is the part of the letter where I'm rambling so that it's at least one page long. In case you couldn't tell.

Positive things: our to-do list has been entertaining. All three of my activities have been enjoyable.

Yoga is a solid eight for me, because it's physically challenging, but also entertaining to watch you. Thank you for being a good sport. If you want to start wearing tighter clothing, or less clothing, yoga might even make it up to a nine.

Riding on a regular basis has been so wonderful. I hadn't realized how much I'd missed it. Karen also said that she would let me help train Moonbeam when the time comes, so that's something to look forward to.

Fooling around— this has been far more interesting than I expected. That's about all I want to say about that topic for now. Yes, I'm blushing even as I write this.

She went on a little more, mentioning his three items, but when she was done rereading what she'd put down, it was more than a page and—to be honest—pretty dry.

What she'd shared was a very factual report with the tiniest touches of the truth dashed into the mix.

Did she want to say anything more? Did she want to talk about how the times they'd spent with his friends and her sisters had felt bigger than just random gatherings?

That somehow for the first time in her life she was beginning to understand a never-before experienced level of family. That it both thrilled and terrified her, and she wasn't sure why.

Julia pushed aside the trembling in her gut and decisively reached for Zach's letter. She all but ripped it from its envelope, slapped it out on the table in front of her and dove in.

Zach's familiar messy writing covered two sheets of paper.

September 30.

One month ago, minus a few days, you agreed to make a big sacrifice to save my butt. I'm very thankful.

I know this whole setup is a lot. You have to write a letter on top of putting up with my stupid ass on a daily basis. That's just evil —the letter part, I mean. My ass isn't evil, it's just annoying.

I was thinking about what to write. I figured you'd probably do a detailed analysis of our past month based on notes from your journal, maybe with numbers or bullet points. Therefore, this month, I'll try to speak your language.

THE RULES
• no further addendums at this time.

I do think you should still date that original page and make a new one that's a little less messy. Really, Julia, I don't know how you can keep track of things when you keep changing your mind :-)

(note—I am very glad you changed your mind.)

THE ACTIVITIES

• *Yoga: I would like to request a few less of those moves where we're on our stomach. Especially if you insist on wearing those pale-pink yoga pants. Ahem. Too blunt?*

• *Dancing: zero changes to our dance card.*

Wait—scratch that. I will warn you that if Trevor Daniels tries to cut in on me again, there will be hell to pay. It's not so much that I don't want you to ever dance with other guys, it's that he's absolute shit at it. Chances of you getting smashed into another couple go up exponentially every time the dickhead tries. Don't make me stage an intervention where I have to dive across the dance floor to save you.

• *Horseback riding: no changes.*

Getting a deeper appreciation of Red Boot ranch every time we go. Damn, it's pretty out here.

• *Cooking: sorry about the meatloaf. It was truly gross, but in my defense, the recipe called for oats. I didn't realize the package I had was peaches-and-cream flavoured.*

• *Research: heads-up. I'd like to go to the States at some point. You want to wait until November? Once you're done with your EMT shifts? Discuss. Other than that, I really appreciated having you along. You're good company, and your comments about the brew and food are helping.*

Regarding the other kind of research? Heh-heh. See next note.

• *Fooling around: definitely a complaint to register.*
I have yet to see the blue or the neon-yellow vibrator in action,
and frankly, that's a bit of a travesty.

Onward to October. I hope you enjoy the final month working
with the team down at the fire hall. Let me know if there's
anything I can do to make things easier for you, whether it's in
the transition for work or anything else.

You're a rockin' fake wife, and a really good egg.

Julia stared down at the paper then her own letter.

He'd hit the nail on the head with her making her comments in an orderly fashion, although he'd one-upped her by using actual bullet points.

She folded his letter small enough that it would fit in the expandable pouch at the back of her journal

Then she rewrote her own note simply to make it neater then reused his envelope. Only she hesitated, pulling out her coloured pens. She proceeded to decorate the outside with tiny little images and words.

When she was done, from a distance the entire surface looked as if it had brightly coloured confetti sprinkled on it. It was only from close-up that the tiny words in capitals became clear. YOGA and RIDING and the rest of them, including the one that made her giggle—RESEARCH.

And the images? Her yoga mats were clear, although some of her miniature horses looked like dogs. The tiny little vibrators, however, were perfectly identifiable.

Julia made sure to stay as casual as possible when she handed the envelope to him at the dinner table that night. "Back at you, baby."

Zach paused in the middle of picking up his soup spoon. He raised a brow but accepted the envelope, his smile growing wider as he brought the envelope in for a closer look. "That's hysterical."

She grinned back, focusing on the savoury broth and the bowl in front of her as he carefully brought out the paper and gave it a quick read.

With a quick nod of his head, he tucked the letter back in the envelope and rose, placing it carefully on top of the fridge before returning. "I'm having fun too. But obviously, you read that in my letter."

"I thought your bullet points were very well executed," Julia said primly.

"Why, thank you." He leaned forward, staring into her eyes with mischief written all over him. "I think your vibrators are a little bit disproportionate in size, though. Maybe our next research session we should break out a ruler and—"

"Oh my God," Julia said with a laugh. "What is it with guys and rulers and dicks? And that's not even really a rhetorical question, because you would not believe how many times down at the fire hall this topic comes up."

A hearty laugh burst from him. "I don't think I want to know."

Julia changed the topic, but only slightly. "Speaking of research..."

Zach's expression turned lusty.

She leaned forward as well, lowering her voice. "When's our next scheduled outing? I have a craving for some lager."

His chest rocked with silent laughter, and he shifted back to fold his arms over his chest. "Now that was just mean. Getting a guy's hopes up and then casting him off into a cruel vat of hops and mash."

"Sounds kinky. Also, messy. I think if we're going to fool around when there's liquid involved, it should be in the shower."

"Deal." He said it instantly, nabbing the barely started October calendar off the fridge and adding RESEARCH to the next Tuesday. Right between Monday's RIDING and Wednesday's YOGA. "You bring the toys, and I'll bring a ruler. We'll meet in the shower—don't be late."

It was easy to be with him. To enjoy a touch of silliness, even as she knew damn well waiting for Tuesday to roll around would be another opportunity for the whole anticipation thing to prove, once again, the right kind of tension did wonders for her libido.

One month down, eleven to go. It wasn't going to be boring.

By this point in the game, Zach no longer thought he was simply imagining things. Nope. Somewhere around the middle of October, it had become clear that no matter how often he fixed the toilet paper roll, it always ended up facing the opposite direction.

Considering the cabin occupants who would be messing with said toilet paper amounted to only two people, he knew exactly who his opponent was. Although why Julia had decided to wage war on this particular topic, he wasn't sure.

It was more fun not asking her the specifics, though, and blithely battling forward.

The last time he had adjusted the roll to face the proper direction, he'd used one of the really thick elastics off of a bunch of broccoli and lashed the edge of the holder in place so that when Julia went to turn it, it would take her more than a few moments.

The next time, he'd come back to discover she'd removed his elastic, flipped the roll, and somehow glued the center cardboard ring in position so there was no way he could flip it around without trashing the entire thing, which he was too cheap to do. So he left it and grumbled in amusement every time he had to face proof that she was currently ahead in the TP war standings.

It was a small amusement added to all the other positive things they were involved in. Not just their weekly activities, but when he went to put Delilah into storage, he had Julia help him. He brought her into the conversation regarding his future plans for the Brewster building in downtown Heart Falls. Picking her brain and getting her fresh ideas was a ton of fun.

Hopefulness rose that they were off to a good start, all things considered.

As the end of October approached, Zach began to plan his next letter. He figured every month he would slowly up the ante and share more about how he was feeling, although taking small steps still seemed important.

Plus, he had decided that this month he would decorate the edges of his letter with little pictures, just the way Julia did.

The house was quiet after supper, with Julia working for the night. Zach wandered outside, a warm jacket in place against the cool evening temperatures. This was one of the rare years that it hadn't snowed yet, although it was clear winter could arrive at any time.

Across the yard, Finn waved him over. His best friend looked amazingly content these days, as he and Karen continued to work together to build their home and prepare Red Boot ranch for next year's planned spring opening.

Zach took his time meandering across the yard, pleased to realize that in just a few days Julia would also be working full-time at the ranch. It would mean more opportunities to be together, and he was looking forward to it immensely.

"You look like a cat that's gotten into the cream," Finn offered dryly.

"Julia's farewell party is tomorrow evening. She's got only one more night shift before she's all mine." Zach paused. "I mean *ours*, since she'll be medic for the whole ranch starting next week."

His friend chuckled, tilting his head toward his truck. "I think you said it right the first time. You've definitely claimed ownership."

Zach matched Finn's pace without questioning until they were in the truck and headed into town. "Did you tell me where we're going?"

"Nope." Finn stared ahead at the road.

Zach hesitated. "Am I supposed to know where we're going?"

Finn snorted. "This time, nope. Your concentration has absolutely sucked for the last couple of months, but this time I can't blame your confusion on being Julia-obsessed."

Not much he could say in defense to that, so Zach sat back and enjoyed the ride, smiling as they pulled into the yard at Josiah's house. "Does he have a need for free labour?"

"Definitely. His sister sent a case of liquor from Ireland. I volunteered us to help sample."

Zach gave his friend's shoulder a squeeze before hopping out of the truck and joining him on the path up to the house. "Have I thanked you lately for being my second-best friend?"

"*Second?*"

Zach let them into Josiah's house without knocking then let out a loud whistle. "Hey, best buddy. Where are you? And where's the hooch?"

Laughter sounded a second before Finn smacked him in the arm with a fist. "Jerk."

They grinned at each other as Josiah called to them from the kitchen. "You two are trouble. Come on. We have some catching up to do. Not to mention some drinking."

Hours later the area around the fire pit was strewn with empty imported beer carcasses and a fine collection of open whiskey bottles.

"I'm not saying you should just straight-up tell her, but at the same time, why don't you just straight-up tell her?" Josiah swirled his most recent refill as he stared into the depths and repeated himself for the third or fourth time that evening.

A very dramatic sigh, even for him, escaped Zach. "I did tell her right at the start that I wanted to date her for real. Things just got a whole hell of a lot more complicated a whole hell of a lot faster than I expected."

"Uncomplicate them." Finn shook his head. "Never mind us. You're the one with the eerily accurate gut instinct. If you think slow and steady is still the way to go after two months of being married, then so be it."

"Slow and steady. Sounds like you're out in the field breaking pasture instead of spending every spare moment in and out of the bedroom convincing her you're a good deal." Josiah shook his head sadly.

Zach must've made a noise, or maybe he'd sighed again, because suddenly he was being stared at intently by both of the other men.

A very calculated expression narrowed Finn's gaze. "Every spare moment..."

"...in and out of the bedroom?" Josiah's jaw dropped. "You just cringed when I mentioned the bedroom. Please tell me you and Julia are not still sleeping in different rooms."

"We're not having this conversation," Zach said as firmly as

VIVIAN AREND

possible. A second later he reached down to find some random wood chips so he could throw one at each of his grinning friends. "Buzz off. I'm not talking about my sex life with you."

"Obviously, because you don't have one," Finn offered dryly. "I thought the idea was to be your usual irresistible self. How come you guys aren't hitting the sheets?"

"We're fooling around," Zach admitted. "We're having fun. Now drop it, unless you want me to discuss how often over the past five years I had to listen to you moon about Karen."

They were good enough friends that they listened, or at least pretended to for a moment.

Many hours later, Lisa and Karen, both clearly amused, appeared beside them at the fire.

Lisa laid a hand on Josiah's shoulder. "Hey, honey. You and the boys tying one on?"

Josiah waved his empty glass in the air before catching hold of her fingers and toppling her into his lap. "No rope involved. We could do something about that, if you'd like."

She pressed a finger over his lips, laughing as she chastised him. "Don't embarrass me in front of my big sister. She doesn't need to know what kinky games we play."

"And on that note, before somebody says something I'll regret hearing, let me take this tipsy one home. Or these tipsy two," Karen corrected herself as she tugged Finn to his feet and crooked a finger at Zach. "Come on, you wild men. I'll drive, and we'll pick up your truck later. You'd better get some sleep, Zach. Julia's going to want you in tip-top shape for her party tomorrow night."

"He doesn't get to party. He's partiless. Which is sadly not the same as pantie-less." Josiah's words were barely audible, his lips buried against Lisa's neck.

She giggled. "What?"

Zach considered slapping a hand over his friend's mouth

244

but decided he was just tipsy enough it was possible he would miss and give Josiah a black eye instead. It would probably hurt. Ha. Maybe it wasn't a bad idea after all.

Zach didn't remember the details, but he was still in bed when Julia made it home from her shift. That part was crystal clear because she came flying into his room and bounced excitedly on the mattress.

"I'm done. I'm done. I had a good time, and I'm glad I had the apprenticeship, but I am *so* looking forward to working at Red Boot ranch." She paused, perched on her hands and knees beside him as she examined him closer. Her amusement rose. "Do you have a hangover?"

"Don't be cruel," Zach whispered.

Sheer mischief flashed across her face. She knelt upright and pretended to hold a microphone to her mouth. "To a heart that's blue."

When she continued to sing Elvis at him, rather poorly and with increasing volume, Zach gave up. He enveloped her in an enormous hug and rolled her under him. Nibbling on her neck and tickling until she screamed with laughter.

He finally let her go, rolling away and pulling her to her feet. He kissed her forehead then turned her firmly toward the bathroom. "Congratulations on your final day. Now go get some sleep. I hear there's a party tonight in your honour."

It took a whole lot of coffee and a couple of Tylenols, but by the time he escorted Julia in the door of Rough Cut, Zach was back to one hundred percent.

It was a bit of a low-level party, with people generally showing up whenever it worked for them and coming to offer Julia a handshake or hug as appropriate.

In between, Zach and his friends took turns dancing with their ladies, music and energy rising as the evening wore on.

When Brad arrived with his wife, Hanna, Julia squeezed

Zach tight and hauled him across the floor to where they stood waiting.

"Good to see you guys," Zach offered. "Thanks for training my new employee of the month."

Hanna winked then turned to Julia. "I'm glad you'll still be nearby. It's my turn to host girls' night out next month. I wondered if you'd help me."

"That would be great. I'll get in touch this week," Julia said with a smile.

Brad offered his hand. "It's been a privilege working with you. And ditto, I'm glad you'll still be nearby." He shook her hand then offered a squeeze when Julia went in for a hug. He stared over her shoulder at Zach. "It's good to see you settling into the community."

"Heart Falls really feels like home," Julia said as she backed up.

Zach glanced around, but no one seemed to be paying any negative attention. Still, being proactive wasn't a bad thing.

He gave Brad his own hand clasp and hearty pat on the back. "Thanks for being such a good mentor to Julia. It's made a difference."

He wanted to say something about everything else he was thankful for, but it wasn't the place or time.

As Zach guided her back onto the dance floor, he realized he agreed completely with Julia. Any of the sacrifices they were making to keep Brad's reputation intact—it was worth it. On every single level.

Although it wasn't much of a sacrifice to have Julia in his arms.

They danced a quick two-step then ended up near the edge of the room when the music shifted to a slow ballad. Zach rearranged her in his arms, hand against her lower back so he could push their bodies together tight enough to be at the very edge of public decency.

"Somebody's feeling perky," Julia murmured, her hands linked around his neck. "I take it you're over your slight indisposition from this morning?"

He didn't answer. Just took a chance and stepped one leg between hers, nestling even closer. His thigh brushed her core with every step, and it didn't take long before her breathing went erratic.

Julia's cheeks glowed, and her eyes shone as if she were debating either murder or mayhem. "Zach. What are you doing?"

He whirled her in place then raised her up his body. The following slow glide down his thigh forced a moan from her lips. "If you can't tell what I'm doing, I'm not doing it very well."

Half a song later, her breath rushed against his cheek in rapid puffs. "You're killing me, baby."

He was doing a good job of torturing himself. Zach glanced around the room and spotted the service corridor that led toward the back storage rooms. He slow danced with her into the shadows and out of sight.

The music was still audible, so he kept up the pretense of the dance, but this was one dirty round that promised to have a spectacular finish.

Julia ground down harder against his leg, sounds sneaking from her lips that pushed him closer and closer to the edge. Zach gritted his teeth to keep from cursing. To keep from stripping them both down right there and then laying her out flat and thrusting into her hard.

She caught him by the ears, damn near ripping them off as she pulled their mouths together. She kissed him frantically, hips pulsing in a rhythm that said in no uncertain terms the end was near. He put all his focus on being there for her. Being what she needed. Tightening his grip on her ass so he could offer a little more leverage.

Her gasp rushed past his lips. He separated them far enough to stare into her wide eyes as her expression tightened and her lips opened in a perfect circle.

Her swaying rhythm faltered, but he kept her tight, dragging her higher.

That was it.

"*Zach*." She moaned his name before the word turned into a long drawn out quivering noise that released the cover on his safety latch. He came while staring into her face, loving how pleasure continued to grow until she relaxed bonelessly against him.

Relaxed a little bit too much, considering he had no blood left in any part of his body except his cock. His legs quivered, and he barely managed to rearrange them before sliding to the floor. Back braced against the wall, they landed with Julia in his lap, his legs stretched all the way out into the corridor.

Her breath quivered now, not just with passion as tiny chuckles slipped into the mix. "We're terrible," she whispered. "We're in public."

"At least it's not the middle of the dance floor," Zach pointed out.

She snorted, tapping her fingers against his chest. "At least it's not that."

The music played in the distance while they sat there in the shadows. Secret and yet not. Zach took a deep breath and pressed a kiss to her temple. "Happy retirement. Welcome to the ranch."

She laughed before slapping a hand over her mouth then staring back onto the dance floor as if certain somebody would spot them at any moment.

When she turned back to meet his gaze, she still looked far too amused. "Thank you. Now I think we'd better sneak out of my own party."

No arguments from him. And as uncomfortable as he was at that moment, he wouldn't change a thing about the evening.

19

*T*he snow arrived with a vengeance not even two days into November. Zach got a huge kick out of how excited Julia was as she peered out the cabin window, coffee cup in hand.

Her happiness lit up the room, and he stepped beside her to see what she was quivering on the spot about. "What's got you all perky?"

"It's just so pretty," she said. "This is why I love being in Alberta. Winter means pristine fields of white as far as the eye can see instead of grey skies and rain."

"I love it too, but remember there's a price to pay. We'll have a cold snap at some point. And they're already talking about El Niño, which means a huge snowfall around Christmas."

Julia shook her head decisively. "Nope. You can't harsh my buzz on this one. In fact..." She put her coffee cup down and stole his from his fingers, grabbing his empty hand and pulling him toward where their boots and coats hung neatly by the door. "Come on. Let's go for a walk."

Her excitement was not only contagious, it was delicious. The urge to grab hold of her fingers while they walked was nearly impossible to ignore. Instead, he shoved his hands in his pockets and strolled at her side as they wandered into the crisp morning air.

She pointed toward the building that was earmarked as the general gathering point for the ranch. "As part of my first official week here at the ranch, I'll be setting up the first-aid station. Cody said there's already a bunch of boxes waiting. You want to help me later today?"

Zach thought through his to-do list and trashed the ones that would have interfered with being able to help. "Love to. You're pretty excited about getting started."

"Hopefully the job stays pretty boring, even after the paying guests arrive, but yeah." She kicked up some of the snow underfoot, laughing as the horses in the arena beside them hurried over, hoping for treats.

"Boring is good. I hope you're not going to be too underworked."

Julia paused, resting her arms on the railing and looking over the horses. "The thing is, I know the work's not the same as being on an emergency callout. What I remember from growing up on a dude ranch was our medic focused more on the whole person for the full-time staff. She kept an eye on everyone, and made sure they were healthy and happy, which is different than simply dealing with dangerous cuts or broken legs."

Zach nodded. "That's a big, important responsibility."

"I've got a lot of resources to help me," Julia pointed out. "Including Tony, if it comes down to that." She grinned, twisting to the side. "I'm also on the emergency backup list with the fire hall still. If there is a disaster in the community, I'll be called out."

"I didn't know that. Good for you. If anything needs to be adjusted for your job here at Heart Falls to make that happen, let me know." Zach watched as she stepped a couple of paces away from the railing.

"Everything should be good. Although there is one thing I should warn you about." Her expression went solemn.

"What?"

Icy cold snow smacked into the side of his face, showering down on him as shock zipped up his spine.

Julia laughed as she ducked away. "Incoming snowball."

Zach twisted barely in time to duck away from a second volley of snowballs, flying through the air from where Finn and Karen peeked up behind the truck bed.

It was the first of many snowball fights over the coming weeks. Julia got her medic station set up. They continued to enjoy their horseback rides and yoga sessions, and all the other things on their to-do list.

Mid-November, Julia came back from her girls' night out looking as if she desperately wanted to tell him something but couldn't.

A few days later, when he kept catching her staring at him, a little smirk on her lips, he'd finally had enough. "What the hell are you up to?"

Julia shrugged. Only a noise somewhere between a giggle and a snort escaped her, and she rubbed a hand over her lips as if trying to hide her smile.

It was now cold enough for them to use the wood-burning stove in the cabin, and the comfortable chairs he'd bought were placed strategically in front of it for them to relax by the warmth.

Zach closed the distance between them, catching her by the hand and pulling her out of the chair. An instant later he'd settled in her place, dragging her into his lap. "You have gotten into mischief of some sort," he accused.

"Uh-huh." This time she met his gaze, only along with the laughter, there was heat in her eyes. "Want to know my secret?"

Her expression alone was enough to make him agree to anything. "Yes. Is it a good secret? Is it a dirty secret?"

"Very good." She stared at his mouth, her tongue slipping out for an instant, leaving her lips wet. "Dirty? Not so much as fun."

"Go on."

"You know the other day when I was with my friends and sisters? We have a tradition during girls' night out, taking turns organizing the evening."

Zach rubbed his hand against her thigh, the soft cotton pyjama pants she wore teasing his palm. "*Ohhhh*, do I get to hear girls' night out stories?"

"Sort of? This time there were only married ladies in attendance, and Lisa, because she said she and Josiah are officially permanently shacked up, which is as good as being married. And what Hanna wanted to set up with my help was a boudoir shoot."

"A who done what?" Memory filtered in before she could answer. "Oh, hang on. My sisters did something like that once. Like a glamour shoot? All dressed up and sexy—although not my sisters. Not the sexy part. The sexy part I meant about *you*. Also not your sisters."

Julia laughed. "Yes. A glamour shoot. It was all about loving ourselves and feeling good about how we look, and it was fun. I also heard about this interesting website, but more on that in a minute. It was good to spend time with them, plus, we talked about you guys while we were together."

Zach put his fingers over his mouth as if he were shocked. "Say it ain't so."

She tapped him with the edge of her fist. "But here's my point—and I do have one." Her expression went serious. "All of them were talking about things that made their guys happy. And I got to thinking that while we're not a real couple, we've become really good friends. And I think there's something we could do that would make you extra happy."

His brain had stalled out on her statement about them not being a real couple. Dammit. It seemed she was still moving the opposite direction he wanted this to go.

Her fingers touched his face and pulled him back from his thoughts. "Zach?"

Time to focus. "Just going to repeat what I've always said. You need to do what makes you happy."

Decisively, she nodded then reached beside her chair for something that she pressed into his palm.

He glanced down. She'd handed him a soft rubber contraption in the shape of a squished C. "Thank you. It's what I've always wanted." He gave her a wink. "What is it?"

"It's a vibrator we can use during sex. Because I want to have sex. With you," she clarified as if the first part hadn't been enough to make him blink in surprise.

Holy shit. Zach told his body to behave even as he tried to find the right way to respond. "*Ummmm...*"

"I know I told you I don't really like sex, but I have *really* liked fooling around with you. And that website I mentioned? It's called WowYes, and it's all about orgasms and sexuality. We can look at it sometime if you'd like, but there were a few good ideas, like this vibrator. I got to thinking, considering everything else we've done, and all the toys we've used, I should be willing to experiment. So I ordered that. And it arrived today."

Everything in him wanted to jump up and down, but he

stuck to his guns. "I don't want you doing anything you don't want."

Julia trickled her fingers down the front of his body. "Hear my words. I *want*. To have *sex*. With *you*."

"Okay." He grinned. "Which this time means *hell yes, but you have to tell me if something isn't working because we have been having sex and it's all been fucking fantastic and*—"

She covered his mouth with hers and stopped his rambling. Which totally worked.

It wasn't as if getting the green light for *sex* sex was that much of a deal changer. He hadn't lied. Every time he'd gotten to touch her and be with her had fulfilled something inside him. She needed to know that.

But as she kissed him, fingers drifting over his chest and teasing his sides, Zach figured that was a conversation for another time.

He picked her up and carried her blindly back to the bedroom, kissing the entire way. He only bounced off the kitchen counter. And the doorframe into the room.

Julia had wrapped her legs around his hips, clinging tight. He squeezed the fingers cupping her ass, sliding her against him and firing up every neuron in his body.

Lowering her to the bed made him that much hotter.

His fingers damn near trembled as he worked to take off her clothes. Pausing when each new section of skin was revealed, he used his lips and his tongue and his teeth until her nipples were pebbled tight and she was squirming.

And then he did it some more because Julia moaning as he brought her pleasure? Was the sexiest fucking thing on the planet.

She caught his arm. "More. I want more."

He handed her the new vibrator. "Let's see how this works."

She showed him where the on-off button was, and together they clicked through the first couple settings on the remote control.

"Looks like fun. Shall we try it?" He slipped the flatter part of the C into her sex, which meant the top rounded portion landed squarely over her clit. "Oh, yeah. This is going to be epic."

Julia gasped as he flipped through different settings. When the rhythm slowed to a vibration that pulsed higher then lower, she clutched his wrist. "That one."

Zach leaned in and used his tongue. Listening to her hums and moans as she got closer to the edge made him harder and harder in anticipation. His grip on her hips let him feel when the trembling began, and that's when he eased between her thighs, his condom-covered cock lined up with her sex.

Teasing into her made tingles start at the back of his spine. Easing the head of his cock between her folds pressed his sweet spot against her body over and over. It also meant the vibrator on the other side moved against him in a bizarrely erotic fashion.

He caught her gaze, cupping her cheek. "Yes?"

She swallowed hard, but her chin dipped rapidly. "You?"

"Hell yes." Still watching, he slid deeper. Slowly, pausing to check if anything caused a problem.

Her eyes damn near rolled back in her head. "Oh my *God*."

"Good?" *Please say it's good*, because he felt fan-fucking-tastic.

She clutched his shoulders and dragged their bodies together. "Kiss me."

He took that as a go-ahead to start a steady rhythm. Even as their lips tangled, he alternated between dragging his hips back and pressing forward. Slowly at first, their tongues dancing in the same rhythm. At least until she lifted her legs and jammed her heels into the small of his back. Strong thigh muscles drove their bodies together with an increasingly hard rhythm. She scratched her fingernails down his back, and every inch of him was fully alive and so damn happy.

"Oh my God, *yes.*"

The leglock around his hips combined with the tight pressure around his cock that signaled her orgasm jerked a response from him. There was no more holding back as pressure exploded from the base of his spine in a rush of pleasure that left stars bouncing in front of his eyes. Maybe it was the addition of the vibrator that sent his experience into outer space as well.

Somehow he had the presence of mind to remember that post-orgasm, Julia grew more sensitive. He twisted his hips and sadly pulled free, reaching down to nab the vibrator and shut it off.

He collapsed halfway on her, one elbow barely keeping his weight from squishing her into the mattress.

She pressed a kiss to his neck, his cheek, her rapid exhalations puffing past his sweaty skin but doing nothing to cool him.

Before they ended up with a mess to clean up, Zach slipped away to deal with the condom. When he came back and wrapped her in his arms, Julia snuggled in tight, tangling around him again, completely unashamed.

When he glanced down, her lips were curled in a contented smile.

Her head shifted from side to side on the pillow in disbelief. "I had no idea."

"Fun, right?"

"Better than I *ever* remember," she admitted wryly. "Does this mean you do have a magic penis?"

Zach laughed boldly before leaning down to kiss the tip of

her nose. "It means you like a lot of clitoral stimulation. It doesn't have anything to do with my cock being magic."

Only she looked thoughtful. "But sex isn't just about our bodies, Zach. It's about our brains. You've never seemed to mind us using toys, and that's made it easier. Thanks. I really enjoyed that."

"I really look forward to doing it again," Zach said. "And exploring your website." A yawn escaped. "Shit. Sorry."

She laughed, resting her forehead against his chest as she took a deep breath and yawned back.

AFTER WORKING shifts for so long, Julia found the transition to being ranch medic fascinating. Part of it was as she'd shared with Zach—she wanted a different kind of vibe to her daily routine. Getting to know all of the regular crew on the ranch meant some of her work involved sitting down with different groups and drinking too much coffee while shooting the breeze.

Not a bad gig.

In early December, Karen stopped by with a heads-up.

She brushed off the snow that had accumulated on her shoulders during the short trip between her house and their cabin then hung up her coat and joined Julia by the fire. "Thanks for inviting me over."

"Want a drink, Karen?" Zach asked from where he was on dish duty that night. "With or without a kick, your choice."

"Hot chocolate?" Karen suggested. "Without a kick, though. We're heading into the holiday season, and heaven knows there will be enough opportunities to drink."

"Two hot chocolates, coming right up."

Karen winked at Julia. "I notice he didn't bother asking you if you wanted some."

"You invoked the word *chocolate*. There's never a time I say no to that," Julia confessed.

Karen leaned forward in her chair and held her hands toward the glowing fireplace. "Holiday planning. Since this is the first year none of us girls are in Rocky, we've been talking about what we want to set up for traditions. The Coleman clans usually gather in their family units on Christmas Day and then have a massive free-for-all on Boxing Day."

It was an unexpected topic, but one that she should've seen coming. "I've got nothing, so lay it on me."

Her sister nodded, glancing toward the kitchen briefly but then focusing back on Julia's face immediately. "Tamara has rightly said she wants to keep up what they do in the Stone family. Finn and I have talked, and we want to have Christmas Eve for ourselves, but Christmas Day could be for more extended family. Lisa says at some point she and Josiah might be travelling during the holidays, so what it comes down to, is if we want to visit the family from Rocky, we've got to do it early."

A trickle of guilt slithered in. "Does that mean Dad will be alone on Christmas Day?"

Karen shook her head. "Tamara said he's always welcome at Silver Stone. Dad's also told Finn that my uncles have invited him to join them, and so have a bunch of the guys he hangs out with on a regular basis. The ones who don't have kids in the area anymore either."

Unfortunately, it was pretty much the answer she'd expected. The uneasiness in her gut continued, and Julia hesitated. "This Christmas is going to be really weird," she said. "I mean with the whole situation between me and Zach. I don't know that I want to go to a big Coleman thing."

The noises from the kitchen vanished. Suddenly, Zach was there, handing over two cups of hot cocoa piled a mile high with whipped cream.

He cleared his throat. "Sorry for eavesdropping, but I have to admit I have a holiday situation we need to discuss as well."

Again, Julia should've seen this one coming. "Shoot. Do your parents expect you to join them in Manitoba?"

Zach looked astonishingly like a little kid caught with his hand in the cookie jar. "Sort of? If you change that to my parents are expecting *us* to join them, and then change Manitoba to Hawaii. Yeah."

Karen snickered. "*Awww.* Julia, what a sacrifice. A trip to palm trees and sand instead of snowy fields forever?"

"Are you kidding me?" Julia finally found words, staring at Zach in disbelief.

"Sorry. I kept meaning to bring it up, but it kind of slipped my mind."

More laughter from Karen. "Well, you two can discuss that teeny oversight once I'm gone, but here's the plan. The Whiskey Creek girls and partners plan to head to Rocky next weekend. If you want to join us, you're welcome. Drive out Friday, return on Sunday."

"We'll talk about it," Julia promised before the conversation slipped to gift ideas for Tamara and Caleb's children.

Sitting in the quiet by the fire once Karen was gone, a million thoughts raced in Julia's mind.

Zach joined her, adjusting his chair until he could give her hand a squeeze. "You okay?"

She nodded, smiling as best she could. "Tell me more about the get-together in Hawaii."

"Finn is going to laugh his ass off because he warned me to tell you this sooner. My parents have a house in Hawaii. Everybody gets to use it whenever they want to, but for about ten days around the holidays, my parents open up the place and everybody tries to join them."

The idea was staggering. "Five sisters, four brothers-in-law, two parents, and seven kids. And they just *happen* to have a place that can fit that many people?"

"You remember the bit where my dad's an inventor?"

"What did he invent? A money press?" But there were more important questions to focus on. "I thought you didn't tell your parents that we got married."

"I didn't. I—" He jerked to a stop so fast she thought he'd choked on his tongue. He looked downright embarrassed before meeting her gaze again. "I told them we were dating."

Butterflies lit in her belly for some strange reason. Julia paused for a moment and got her head on straight.

She could deal with this. It was only right that if he had to go to Rocky with her and deal with everyone who thought they were married, she could go to Hawaii, suffer through sand and sun, and pretend to be his girlfriend.

She nodded decisively, deciding to deal with the simpler problem first. "Yes, I'll go with you. Not just because it's Hawaii, but because I think I'd like to meet them. *And* because it's Hawaii," she admitted.

His grin flashed, familiar happiness filling his eyes. "Thank goodness, because I already booked our flights."

She threw a pillow at him.

Then she stared at the fire and pondered the other problem for a while until Zach poked her gently. "I don't think you're here."

"I'm not." She was lost in a swirl of anger and regret.

"You want to talk about it?" he offered.

"Not sure I can explain the maze I've gotten myself into." She turned toward him, curling her arms around her legs. "I've met bits and pieces of the extended Coleman clan before. I'm very grateful that I found my sisters. I'm learning more about my dad, and that's sometimes good and sometimes bad. But the whole family thing gets overwhelming."

Zach made a face. "And then I threw all of my family at you as well, which I'm sure didn't make it any easier. I'm sorry."

Julia blinked. "You know what? Honestly, when I think about meeting your family, it doesn't fill me with the same sense of— I don't know. That's—that's where I get stuck. It's as if something dark and negative is hovering over one side of that equation that's not there on the other, so it's not just about the unknown people."

He considered for a minute before going into solution mode. "Tossing out ideas. Do you want to go by yourself? Do you want to go a different weekend and not bother with the big Coleman event? Do you want to just go for a single day?"

"That one," Julia said. "But not by myself. Will you come with me?"

"Of course I will. There's no reason why we can't head out in the morning, spend the day in Rocky Mountain House, and then come home."

The sheer and utter relief that washed in told her that was the right decision. The peace she felt while sharing when she talked with Tony the next time confirmed it again.

Which was why early Saturday morning, she woke with a lighter heart than expected. Something still nagged at her that she couldn't put a finger on, but with Zach's entertaining stories to distract her on the drive, Julia pushed the worries aside.

They made it into Rocky Mountain House shortly after sunrise, driving a little distance farther into the country to where the Whiskey Creek ranch sat.

Her father came out to greet them wearing a huge smile, offering Julia a big hug.

He shook Zach's hand and gave him a quick pat on the shoulder. "Want a tour of the place?"

"Breakfast first, Dad," Tamara said firmly from the front porch, waving for them to come into the house.

The little girls rushed forward to grab Julia by the hand. "We got to have a sleepover," little Emma informed her seriously. "Do you want to see our rooms or the kittens first?"

Tamara laughed, herding everyone toward the table. "Breakfast first," she repeated.

Julia settled at the old farm table, a mixed collection of chairs assembled around the sturdy surface. Plenty of food, including lots of bacon, appeared on the table, and with Zach by her side, the room was comfortable and warm.

That's where she kept him for the rest of the morning. Zach didn't say anything, but she caught him hiding his smile a few times as she kept hold of his hand and refused to let him be dragged away by her father.

When Zach took to wrapping an arm around her shoulders and affectionately pressing kisses to her temples every time her dad looked, Julia found herself hiding her own amusement.

Lisa stared harder than usual, though.

In a brief moment when Zach had taken off to help Sasha and Emma capture a mama cat, her sister took the opportunity to bump their shoulders together. "You and Zach are looking pretty cozy."

A warm sensation bloomed inside. "He's running interference," Julia confessed. "He's a good friend."

"Friend. Well, that's good. I guess." Lisa nodded sagely then vanished before Julia could poke her for being mysterious.

After lunch, the Whiskey Creek clan made their way to the main gathering, which turned out to be split between the two houses on the original homestead. The men disappeared into what was called the Peter's house, while the women gathered in what was currently Jaxi and Blake's home. Children were divvied up like packages between the two groups.

Julia instantly felt the loss of Zach by her side. She was

certain the Colemans were good people, but there were just so *many* of them.

She stuck close to Lisa and let her sister run interference.

After a while, though, a few members of the massive crowd slipped over, pulling her into conversations in a way that Julia appreciated very much. Beth and Becky especially, one older and one younger. Becky was just noticeably pregnant, one hand resting on the soft swell of her belly as she spoke to Julia. Both women wore a quiet dignity that made it easy to relax in their company.

The ringleaders of the current generation were clearly Jaxi and Dare. Although...

Julia glanced at Lisa and the way she almost invisibly guided the conversation when necessary. Her sister, Julia decided, was a dangerous force of nature, and she was very glad to have her on her side.

For the rest, it was a little like dropping in on season seven of a TV show. The hours she spent with them offered hints of people's characters and made Julia wonder what the individual stories were that had brought them to this place.

But they were good people, and in spite of not knowing more than that, Julia enjoyed herself.

That lingering sensation remained. The one Julia couldn't put a name to. Which meant when Zach came to get her to take her home, she took the quick escape eagerly.

20

*Z*ach had to catch Julia by the hand and tug her in the right direction to keep her feet moving. "Walk and gawk," he teased.

"There are palm trees in the parking lot," she said excitedly. She took a deep breath and nearly squealed. "The air tastes tropical."

He herded her toward their rental car. "It doesn't suck."

When he stopped beside the vehicle waiting in the preferred customer pickup area, he got an appreciative grin and then a smirk out of her. "A Jeep. I totally would've expected you to book us a convertible."

"And cheat on Delilah? Never." He lifted their suitcases into the back then opened the door for her. "Besides, some of my favourite beaches require a little off-roading to access."

The half-hour drive to his parents' house north of the airport passed quickly with Julia all but hanging out the window as she commented nonstop on the passing scenery.

Zach poked her in the arm with a water bottle. "Rehydrate. You're going to fall over if you don't take a breath soon."

She leaned forward far enough to catch his eye, delight dancing over her features. "Thank you for bringing me to Hawaii for Christmas. I'm very excited."

"You're welcome. And I hadn't noticed," he deadpanned.

The final approach to the house included a pause at the large security gate.

Julia whistled as the massive wrought-iron feature slowly swung back. "That is beautiful. It's an entire underwater scene. Fish and coral and dolphins. Wow."

"This is walking distance from the house. We can come back and take a closer look. It really is spectacular—there's a ton of things hidden in the details."

"I definitely want to do that. And I want to walk on the beach. And I want to explore tidal pools." Her jaw dropped. "Zach. These are really big houses."

"It's not the size that counts, remember?"

Her snicker seemed to knock her back into balance. She pulled one foot onto the seat and wrapped an arm around her knee. "I'm just a tiny bit impressed—holy *shit*."

Yeah. That was pretty much what he'd said the first time he'd seen the place. "Come on. I'll show you around, and then we'll come back for suitcases."

He'd parked in the middle of the driveway since no one else was supposed to show up for a few days. He'd deliberately gotten Julia out of town early enough so she could settle in and maybe get over her shell shock before his family arrived.

She waited hesitantly at the path leading behind the tall lava stone wall that surrounded the housing complex. Her nose wrinkled—damn, adorable to the core.

He wrapped his arms around her and squeezed tight until the tension in her began to fade.

Zach tucked his lips against her cheek and nuzzled against her softly. "Feel better?"

"Still a little nervous," she confessed. "Please tell me there's nothing hugely valuable that I might accidentally break."

He curled his arm around her, keeping her tight against his side as he went toward the main doors. "Remember I said my parents have the entire family here over the holidays? That includes children from toddlers to age nine, and the house is very childproof. I promise there's nothing you can break that I haven't broken at least once before."

Punching in the security code for the front door, he pushed it open then gestured her ahead of him.

Julia stepped inside slowly, a quivering *wow* escaping her lips.

There was no getting around the fact the place was impressive. The open-area family and living rooms stretched the length of the main house. Two kitchens, a main one that faced toward the island and the second for the bar closer to the pool and ocean.

"Those windows are incredible." She gasped and twirled toward him. "They slide, don't they?"

"Come and help me. You may as well get the full effect."

It took about fifteen minutes to unlock and slide all of the floor to ceiling partitions aside. With the front door wide open, and the windows facing the water parted, the entire house felt one step off the beach.

Julia poked her head around corners but came back to him, shyly slipping their hands together. She smiled. "I am very overwhelmed, but to hell with it. Lisa told me before to pretend I'd walked in on some kind of fairy tale, and that's exactly what I'm doing."

"Good for you." Zach pointed toward the section she hadn't yet explored. "Those two hallways lead to the north and east wing of the house. My parents' master bedroom is down one, plus there are a couple of two-bedroom suites with bathrooms that my sisters' families take over. Yes, it's a big house, but it's very nice that when so many people get together, everybody has their own space."

She nodded, then to his surprise, she stepped into him and wrapped her hands around his waist. "Does that mean we have space to ourselves?"

"Right now? The entire house. And I always stay in the guest house. This way." He walked them past the edge of the swimming pool, headed toward the cabana that was quite a bit smaller than the cabin they shared in Heart Falls. "There's no kitchen, and the bathroom's tiny," he warned. "But there's nothing wrong with that view."

He turned to take in Julia's expression as she stepped into the place for the first time. The sense of awe was there, but the biggest thing he saw in her expression was happiness.

"Oh my God." She pulled him through the door and to the opposite wall of the cabana. "These open, don't they?"

"Just like the house," he agreed.

Minutes later the entire front of the cabana was open. A low-level wall that provided privacy without blocking their view divided the property from the public walking path. Beyond that lay lava rocks and a coral reef, the ocean waves rolling in a steady rhythm as if Mother Nature herself were breathing peace into the room.

Julia quivered on the spot then threw herself into his arms, kissing his face. She crawled up him, as if desperate to hug him even tighter. "I love it. It's *gorgeous*."

His heart pounded, and that gut feeling that something wonderful was very close by struck all over again. "Bonus, for the next ten days, you don't have to worry about it snowing."

She pressed her lips to his, softer now. Running her fingers through his hair. "I feel very spoiled."

"Good." He nibbled on her bottom lip. "Hungry?"

Julia shook her head. "I want to go for a walk on the beach. And hop in the swimming pool. If you can wait."

"Whatever makes you happy."

She slipped on her swimsuit in the bathroom, but before she could cover up with shorts and a T-shirt, Zach crooked a finger. "You need sunscreen."

Which led to Zach being both very happy and very turned on. Teasing his fingers along the edge of her bikini top and sliding over her belly as he pulled her back against his front.

Board shorts did nothing to hide his body's reaction to having her mostly naked in his arms.

She wiggled away, winking mischievously. "We can add that to the to-do list, but...beach first?"

Enjoy paradise now, and later—exactly what he'd hoped for.

Dinner was at a restaurant a few minutes' walk down the beach. Zach twisted his chair so it sat directly beside Julia's, with both of them looking over the sand and water toward the setting sun. He settled his arm on the edge of the chair and tangled their fingers together.

Comfortable. Natural. *Dear God, please let her feel the enormity of this thing between us.*

Julia lifted her wineglass in the air, touching it lightly to his. "To wonderful memories."

Their glasses clinked. The toast was exactly what Zach wanted. Memories that they would look back on years from now, together.

He ordered a half dozen different appetizers so she could try a bit of everything. Every time she moaned in appreciation at one of the different flavours, he cursed his brilliant idea.

"This is my favourite." She scooped up some of the crab dip and offered it to him.

Zach took the bite, catching hold of her fingers and licking them clean.

The setting sun lit her face with rose and gold, enhancing the colour on her cheeks. But the heat—

That was all them.

As the sun headed toward the horizon, Julia grew quieter. The sound of Hawaiian music drifted on the air along with the scent of kerosene from the tiki torches.

She'd curled up beside him in the loveseat, fingers clasped together as she leaned into his side while staring over the water. "I've been to the ocean before, but never like this."

"Me too." Because even though he'd visited the island many times, and even sat in that exact chair before, he'd never watched the sun set with a woman he loved.

Damn.

Zach held on to the thought for a moment. Savoured it the way they'd allowed the flavour of the wine and the good food to fill their senses before sharing the experience.

He loved her. It wasn't just a possibility anymore. It wasn't a good thing that might happen someday.

He honest-to-God loved her.

As colours filled the sky from the horizon to the heavens, Zach curled his arms around Julia and held on tight.

Somehow, over the next few days in paradise, he needed to find a way to let her know.

HE WOKE HER EARLY, the sunlight pouring into the cabana an extra encouragement to get the day started on time. And when his kisses and caresses moved into something more heated, Julia was right on board.

Although she laughed when he took a small bag from his

suitcase and shook it out onto the bed, three brand-new vibrators bouncing on the surface.

"I was a little worried one of them would turn on while we were going through TSA," Zach confessed.

"I took the batteries out of the one I brought."

He grinned as he held one in the air and wiggled it, a low buzz emitting from the device. "Rechargeable."

Zach then proceeded to give them both what they needed to start the day off very relaxed.

Sex was followed by beach time, pool time, food, and more fooling around. Julia was totally immersed in the experience. By the afternoon of day two, she wasn't sure she'd be able to leave when the trip was over.

Her phone went off, and she reached lazily across the side table. When she discovered it was a FaceTime call from her sisters, she nabbed it eagerly. "Hey."

Lisa and Karen popped up in different boxes.

"Are you naked?" Lisa attempted to sound scandalized, but she was laughing too hard for it to work.

"Oh, please. That's not a question we need answered, as long as she keeps the phone angled the right way," Karen said dryly. "Hey, chica. Tell me you're drinking something sweet and sitting by a pool."

"Zach went in to make margaritas, and I can definitely give you the pool." She twisted so her back was toward the pool with the ocean shining behind it. Her sisters' response was highly entertaining. Julia turned the camera back on herself, propping it up on the side table so she could recline with her hands behind her head. "I'm pretty sure this is all a dream, but nobody's doing any pinching because I'm enjoying myself far too much."

"I hope so. This is our view." Karen flipped the camera and held it toward the mountains. "I mean, still beautiful, but considering this is a break in the storm, there's probably a whole lot more snow where that came from."

The Rocky Mountains were not just clad in white, they were buried in it. Even looking through a phone screen, the icy coldness and the vast loneliness of winter fields rang out loud and clear.

Karen twisted the phone to offer an exaggeratedly pouty face. "I would take a beach right now. And the pool."

"And the margarita, although I'd like to bring my own man. Sexy as yours is and all." Lisa ducked as something flew past her head. "Hey, I was defending you."

Josiah's answer was garbled, but whatever he said made her laugh.

Karen rolled her eyes then focused on Julia. "We won't keep you long, but we wanted you to know we had a big snowstorm. Don't feel guilty about having abandoned your sisters to the return of an Ice Age."

A glass appeared on Julia's left. She took it gratefully, smiling up at Zach. "Thank you, baby."

He leaned in and kissed her. She didn't think anything of it, responding in kind. A brief but intense interaction that left her heart pounding.

When he pulled back, it was to offer her a wink before heading to his own recliner and stretching out.

Damn the man was fine. All muscly and lean and already turning a delicious golden colour from the sun.

A soft cough brought her back from her ogling.

Shit.

She snapped her head toward where she'd propped up her phone. "Nothing to see here," she murmured innocently.

Karen pressed a finger to her lips, but she snickered.

Lisa just grinned.

It had to be done. Julia stuck out her tongue and then hung up to the sound of her older sisters' laughter.

The third day, the hoard—as Zach affectionately called them—arrived.

Julia had expected to feel at least some level of discomfort, but from the minute Pamela and Zachary Senior walked in the door, there was too much chaos to feel anything except amusement.

"Zach, sweetheart. Help your father. I have no idea why he insisted on bringing all those things, because this is supposed to be a holiday," she called the final words over her shoulder at the silver-haired gentleman struggling to pull oversize suitcases out of the back of an SUV. "You must be Julia. Come, if you're a hugger, give me a hug. If you're not—high fives."

A second later, Julia found herself enveloped by two sturdy arms that squeezed briefly then set her free.

Pamela immediately filled Julia's hands with packages to be carried to the kitchen or the coffee table or to be stacked in hallway one or two for when the rest of the family arrived.

Once his parents' vehicle was empty, the next set of family arrived. Mattie and Ronan with their six-, seven-, and nine-year-old boys were followed by Quinn and her husband, Drew.

By lunchtime, every room in the house had been filled with Zach's sisters, brothers-in-law, and nieces and nephews.

Julia got placed in the lineup slicing cheese for grilled sandwich production. To her left, seven-year-old Rita was explaining surfing rules as she carefully spread mayonnaise on an unending stack of bread slices.

On the other side, Zach's sister Petra was cutting up mango for an enormous fruit salad.

"Do you want to go surfing after lunch, Miss Julia?" Rita asked eagerly.

"I don't know how to surf," Julia confessed. "Somebody will have to teach me."

Rita nodded decisively. "Uncle Zach will lend you his surfboard. Auntie Petra, do you want to surf?"

"Maybe, short stuff. We have to check with your mom first, remember?" Petra offered Julia a secret wink. "Beach rules in effect. Nobody goes out alone without an adult, and nobody goes out without checking with mom and dad."

With a very firm grip on the bottom of Julia's T-shirt, Rita tugged. "You're an adult."

"I am. But your Auntie Petra's right. Family rules—check with your mom. If it's okay, maybe your auntie and I can come with you, and you can show me a few tricks."

All but bouncing, Rita went back to her task, her tongue continuing to move a million miles an hour.

The entire family gathered at the massive table. Petra rose and held a bag in the air before reaching in and pulling out a stone. She glanced at the name written on the surface. "Jason. You get to start."

The nine-year-old pushed back his chair and stood, cheeks flushed as he glanced down the table toward Julia. But he refocused across the table on his dad and spoke clearly. "I'm thankful for being here where it's nice and warm. I'm happy to see my cousins. I hope we get to see turtles."

He sat down instantly, but there was firm applause and appreciation as the food moved down the table.

Zach pressed his fingers onto Julia's thigh. "Our version of saying grace. Everybody's name is in the bag. When it's your turn, you say something you're thankful for, happy about, and a hope. Pretty simple."

Pretty sweet, Julia thought. "That's a beautiful tradition."

Across the table, Petra helped herself to the bowl of fruit salad before passing it to Julia.

"Do you want to try surfing this afternoon?" the woman asked.

"If that works, I'd love to."

Petra pointed a little ways from the house. "We don't have to go far, and it's a pretty good spot for beginners."

The crowd of them hit the beach, umbrellas and lawn chairs set up strategically to keep the littlest ones out of the full sun.

Zach leaned in close to whisper in her ear. "You okay if I abandon you? Or do you want me to give you lessons?"

Petra put both hands on him and shoved him toward where the brothers-in-law were waiting. "Go away. I'm teaching her."

It was too easy to laugh. Julia wiggled her fingers at Zach then gestured him off. "I already have two expert teachers," she pointed out, because Rita was bouncing up and down beside them, eager to begin. "Go play with the boys."

He winked and strode off with his surfboard tucked under his arm. Legs flexing with each step, board shorts nicely hugging his body.

Damn. That was one fine ass—

A snort sounded from beside her. "Okay, Rita. Once Julia is done drooling, we can teach her how to stand up on the board."

Julia blushed but took the teasing in stride.

As the afternoon passed, it was clear there was some kind of magic involved in the day. Zach's family welcomed her in as easily and comfortably as she could've hoped for. Beach time and surfing lessons slid into dinner preparation, which involved salads and carbs and preparing a whole lot of meat for the barbecue.

Everything paused right before six, though, when three-year-old Beau was handed a dinner bell that he shook vigorously. His eyes widened at the loud sound ringing from his fingertips, but he didn't let go.

Zach caught Julia by the hand and tugged her onto the deck. "Sunset. We don't have a lot of rituals, but this one is sacred."

The entire family gathered, sitting in little clusters with drinks in their hands as the sun moved steadily toward the horizon. A ship with triangular sails drifted toward the giant ball of light, and even the kids seem to find stillness in that moment.

She leaned into Zach's side. "This is astonishing."

He stared down, the laughter in his eyes turning serious. "I'm really glad you're here. Glad you're having fun."

She was having a wonderful time, and yet...

Something wasn't right. Because as they moved back into the house and finished dinner prep, the scent of barbecue burgers and honey-glazed salmon making her mouth water, there should've been nothing but joy in this moment.

This time she was placed farther down the table. The closest people to her were Quinn and Mattie, and while the conversation was enjoyable, her uneasiness grew the longer the meal went on.

"Once the dude ranch is operational, where are you and Zach going to live?" Quinn scooped a little more macaroni onto her daughter's plate before turning her attention back on Julia.

"For now, we'll just stay in the cabin." She glanced down the table to where Zach was laughing with his father and his oldest nephews.

"There's land coming up for sale in the spring on the other side of our property," Mattie said. "Zach always talked about wanting to build. I can tell them to get in touch if you'd like to check it out ahead of time."

The sense of dread grew stronger. "I'll mention it to Zach."

Julia kept it together until the meal was over, but the

instant plates began to be gathered, she couldn't take it anymore.

She sprinted across the room and caught hold of Zach, tugging him with her toward their cabana. "We'll be back in a minute."

Zach went willingly, deep concern on his face as she closed the door behind them. "What happened? What's wrong?"

"Everything," Julia said. "Nothing. Oh my God, your family is wonderful. And your sisters are trying to help us buy property so we can build a house next to them."

His brow rose, but he waited patiently. "And...?"

"And we're *lying* to them." She barely got the words out.

Everything snapped into crystal clarity. What she wanted was to sit down and have a really good cry, but that wouldn't change anything.

The only thing that could fix this was the truth.

Julia took a deep breath and went for it. "When we went to Whiskey Creek, I enjoyed seeing the ranch. And the Colemans are good people, really kind and caring. I couldn't understand why I was so glad to get out of there. Why the entire time we were driving home, I was so angry inside."

Zach closed the distance between them, wrapping her up in a hug and holding her against his body. "I had no idea."

"They hadn't done anything wrong. In fact, *they* did everything right. It wasn't them I was angry at." She pushed back far enough so she could look into his face. "I'm so angry at my mom. I love her immensely for everything she did for me over the years and all the sacrifices she made. But she deliberately chose to keep the truth from me—and it was wrong."

"Oh, Jules. I'm sorry."

Emotions continued to flood in, understanding rising. Julia

needed to put into words why this was so important, here and now.

"Mom didn't just keep the truth from me, she kept it from my dad. She kept it from my sisters. I'm not pretending that we would've all had some magical happily ever after, because we don't know if she and dad could've made it as a couple.

"But she stole a future where I would've gotten to know my sisters. Where my dad could've had a chance to have different people in his world, and the trickle-down to that would've been huge for the Whiskey Creek girls."

She rested her head against Zach's chest, listening to his heartbeat under her ear.

He rubbed her back slowly. "You're right. And I'm sorry," he repeated.

The next thing had to be said. "She lied, and I really wish she hadn't. I have to do better."

Zach went still. "Go on."

"I don't want us to lie anymore." She wiped at her eyes but stepped back, standing firmly as she met his gaze. "Okay, that doesn't mean I want to share every detail, but I really think we need to tell your family part of what's going on."

He swallowed hard. "And what's going on, Julia?"

"That we accidentally got married. That we've agreed as friends to make this work." She frowned. "Does your family know about Bruce?"

Zach's lips twitched. "Yes. Bruce was one of my dad's best friends, so they pretty much understand he was a wild card."

The tight knot in her chest began to ease. "Are you okay if we do this? I feel as if I need to take charge of at least one little corner of my world. And while it doesn't change what my mom did, or how it affected the Whiskey Creek world, it means *your* family won't be imagining things that aren't real."

He smiled, although his eyes didn't light up the same as

usual. "If it makes you happy, of course we can go tell them. Although I think we may want to continue to call what we're doing dating. I don't think Mom and Dad would be comfortable with the concept of friends with benefits."

Damn. She hadn't thought of that. Julia supposed there were layers to truth-telling.

"As long as it slows them down from making wedding plans for us in the spring." Even with the dating twist added, her sense of relief continued to grow. "Can we start with your parents? And not do a big general announcement?"

Zach curled his arms around her, squeezing tight before pushing her toward the bathroom with a pat on the butt. "My parents will be suitably shocked, amused, and horrified on our behalf. And my sisters as well, once we tell them. I'll grab Mom and Dad and light the fire pit. You wash up, and I'll meet you there."

Which is how, not even fifteen minutes later, she and Zach sat across the fire pit from his very curious parents.

Julia caught Zach's hand in a death grip as she stiffened her spine and took a deep breath before admitting the truth. "We accidentally got married this past fall."

21

*J*ulia's words triggered a response in Zach's parents that was pretty much what he'd expected. Shock, naturally, followed immediately by amusement mixed with equal parts of concern.

"Interesting. Care to elaborate?" His mother leaned back in her chair, gaze darting between him and Julia. "Wait. First, Julia? Are you okay, sweetheart?"

A little gasp escaped Julia's lips at the obvious concern in Pamela's tone, but she nodded. "Just a little nervous."

"There's no need to be. Since I doubt this was a secret from Zach, and he brought you here, it means he trusts you. Which means *we* trust you," Zachary Senior insisted. He eased in close enough to pat his son on the shoulder. "Although I do admit I always figured Petra would be the one to do something like this."

"Just wait," Zach offered. "This means she gets to do something even more off-the-wall."

"Heaven forbid. Okay, tell us the details." His mother sipped her mai tai as if she didn't have a care in the world.

Zach kept the explanation simple, skipping the parts that involved nudity and playing down the drunken bit as much as possible.

Julia sat quietly, fingers squeezing his as he spoke.

When he hit the kicker about the financial obligation to stay married for a year, his father let out an exasperated groan. "That was Bruce for you. He could never resist interfering."

Pamela shook her head then focused once again on Julia. She opened her mouth and then closed it. A second time she started, but this time spinning her attention to Zach. "Well. All right, then. You can move into the spare room off the house, and Julia can have the cabana to herself."

Shit. As expected. "It's okay, Mom. We're dating *now*." Zach leapt in, hoping Julia wouldn't change her mind and cave to the suggestion.

"We just didn't want you to get the idea that this is anything—" Julia hesitated. Tried again. "Zach and I *are* friends. But..." She sighed, an enormous tired sound. "It's complicated."

Zachary Senior nodded slowly before clapping his hands together and looking at them brightly. "Well, as long as things are okay with you, then things are okay with us. But for heaven's sake. If you need someone to talk to—"

"That's okay," Zach hurried to assure him, because while he and his father could have this discussion, he did not need his mother getting involved. His mother would somehow make the conversation revolve around sex, and that was utterly out of the question. "We've got it covered."

Zach gave Julia a break and gathered his sisters together for a quick and dirty rundown of the situation. He did *not* offer any of them the code to their wedding ceremony video.

Petra was the first to haul Julia into a hug, and when the rest of them followed suit, smiles and support obvious in their actions, Zach took the opportunity to slip out of the house and head to the beach.

His soul hurt.

His brisk walk faded to a shuffle then to nothing at all as he stared at the lights shining off the water from the houses bending around the bay.

Zach found a rock to settle on, stretching his legs in front of him as he tried to find his internal balance.

Julia wanted to tell the truth. He had honoured that request in the same way he'd tried to for the past months of doing what made her happy.

But the fact she didn't see them as more than friends yet cut him to the core. Because *that* was the truth he wanted. The truth he needed desperately.

He picked up rocks, mindlessly tossing them into the waves.

Behind him, stone clinking on stone warned of someone's approach. When his father settled beside him, Zach wasn't too surprised.

Still, he tried to deflect. "Nice night for stargazing."

Zachary Senior laughed. "You are a shitty liar, son."

"I'm a very good liar," Zach insisted before sighing out a complaint. "You just happen to have all my same tells, so you get to cheat and see what I'm trying to hide."

"Yeah, well. Sorry about that." His dad matched his position, staring up and nodding. "It is a good night for stargazing. Might even spot the ISS later."

They sat for another few minutes before his father spoke again. "You really like this woman, don't you?"

"Yup."

A warm hand landed on his shoulder. "Bruce messed things up for you, didn't he?"

"Maybe. Maybe this time with Julia is the best thing I've

got going for me." Zach glanced sideways. "I'm not that terrible a bet. This means I've got time to prove it."

"Have you told her how you feel?"

"How can I?" The complaint snapped out. Zach shoved to his feet and started pacing again. "She's trapped, Dad. Can you just imagine how terrible it would be for me to announce that I'm in love with her when she can't escape for another nine months? And I can't complain because she's doing this to save me. And to save..."

He slammed his lips shut before he gave away the detail about the impact on Finn as well.

It didn't work. Either his father could read him like a book, or he knew his former friend too well. "Bruce did something else, didn't he?"

Zach sighed. "It's not just my finances but the entire corporation that will be affected."

"Ahh." His dad stood as well, staring over the water with his problem-solving face on. He turned to Zach with a grin. "So. What are you going to do about it?"

Zach shrugged. "Nothing to do. Wait, and try to convince Julia to fall in love over the upcoming months."

"Great plan A. What's plan B?"

He eyed his father. "This isn't an experiment where you try twelve dozen different ways to invent a gizmo."

"No, it's your life, and if there's a chance you can be happy tomorrow instead of waiting nine months, I think a little experimentation is a valuable thing." Zachary Senior clicked his tongue disappointedly. "You're better at brainstorming than this. You've been discombobulated by the woman, that's for certain."

"Thanks, Dad. I take it that's the official verdict for me not knowing what the hell to do?"

His father shrugged. "She's a nice girl. You're a nice boy. I like symmetry in my world."

Amusement drifted in despite his frustration. "Love you, Dad. I'll think about other plans, but please, don't interfere. And do me a favour and don't let Mom start lecturing us on safe sex."

Zachary Senior pulled a face. "You might want to get to your bathroom before Julia does. I think your mother mentioned she planned to leave a box of condoms on the counter with some literature about the best ways for Julia to avoid urinary tract infections."

"*Dad.*" Dear God. Zach headed back to the house in hopes he could cut that one off at the pass.

"Sorry, but you'll discover the good part about loving a strong woman is they have a mind of their own. You never can tell what they're going to do next. Other than try to embarrass their children. That's a given."

Christmas Eve arrived, then Christmas Day. Holidays in Hawaii meant the sound of the ocean mixed with Christmas carols. With his family involved, there was always someone around to chat with.

Julia bloomed. It was the only way to describe it.

She played with his nieces and nephews, chatted with his sisters, and teased his brothers-in-law. Together they beat his parents so badly at cribbage, they'd refused to play anymore.

Surrounding their time together was laughter. The delight shining out of her filled every available space until she was damn near glowing with it.

Zach held on to every precious memory as if they were diamonds pulled from the hidden depths of a mine. Every day he thought about his father's question of what could be done to make happiness arrive today instead of months from now.

He hadn't found the answer yet, but he was getting closer.

In the meantime, getting to watch Julia shine, getting to hold her in his arms at night, getting to see her find her place in his family—because that was totally what she was doing—filled him with peace.

Sunset on Christmas Day, she curled up at his side, rested her head on his shoulder, and sighed contentedly.

It was impossible to resist. He pressed a kiss to her temple and curled his arm around her tighter. "Hawaii looks good on you."

"It's been an amazing experience." Her fingers traced lines on his thigh almost unconsciously. "I can't believe we still have another five days."

"That might give them time to dig everything out in Heart Falls," he teased. "Finn says the next time we take off for a long period of time at Christmas, he's going to take it as a warning that another snow-pocalypse is nigh."

She laughed then fell silent. The contentment pouring off her was easy to sense. Her gaze stayed fixed on the sunset as she spoke. "I'm glad you got to talk to Finn."

He was as well. They'd had a long overdue conversation that would be discussed in more detail in a couple days. Once Finn and Karen had a chance to discuss matters. "How was Christmas for your sisters?"

Julia smiled. "Ollie got a new squeaky toy, and Dandelion Fluff stole it. Karen said she and Lisa wandered into the kitchen an hour later and discovered the cat and the dog curled up together in the dog bed, each with one paw around the stuffed sheep."

"*Awww*. Besties."

"Yup." She glanced up at him, staring at his lips as she tangled her fingers around the blue larimar necklace he'd bought her a couple days earlier at the wharf. "Merry

Christmas. It's been another good day. Thank you for my present."

"You're welcome." He took the opening she was clearly offering and kissed her.

Then he directed his attention back to the sunset, and his family, and the plans B, C, and D that he'd begun to put in place. Mostly to keep from grabbing the matching blue larimar ring he had also bought, dropping to one knee, and asking her to make it real.

His time was coming. Not yet, but soon...

Very soon.

FOR THE FIRST time since they'd arrived in Hawaii, the sky was grey in the morning. Julia's walk along the shore that day was with Mattie and Quinn, both of them trying to outdo each other with stories about Zach growing up that made her laugh.

She reentered the house with them, and three tall, handsome men broke off from where they'd been taking care of children and breakfast prep to offer their women a hug and a kiss.

The six- and seven-year-olds groaned and rolled their eyes, but the nine-year-old offered a kissy noise in his parents' direction. Ronan growled then sprinted after him, and the room burst into laughter and screams and family connection.

Zach's arm around her tightened, but it was the motion of his chest revealing his laughter that made her lean in and turn to cup his face. "You're a goof, but I see now it runs in the family."

"Yup." He tapped her nose. "The kids want to make giant sandcastles this morning. Want to come or hang out with my sisters?"

Quinn wandered past, speaking softly. "Ahem. No kid time. The guys have them *allllll* morning, and we're having a ladies-only pool party."

Across the room, Petra mock whispered. "We have really good C-H-O-C-O-L-A-T-E stashed away."

Julia turned toward Zach and fluttered her lashes. "Thank you for the invite, but I think I need to stay and supervise. Act as lifeguard and make sure no one has a melting incident."

He laughed, leaning in to speak for her ears only "You're getting along with everyone?"

"They're lovely. Go. Have fun."

He waggled his brows. "I'll need help washing off the sand later. Just a heads-up."

Her cheeks heated, but with the fresh tan she'd been building, maybe no one noticed.

The noise of grown men herding children faded in the distance. Grandma and Grandpa had gone along to help, and suddenly it was Julia with Zach's five sisters.

Petra lifted her hands in the air and did some crazy dance moves. "Okay, girls. I'm bartender. Name your poison. If I remember from last year, though, two drinks off the top, then we'll switch to fruity cocktails." She glanced at Julia. "The kids might be gone, but they'll be back. We don't tend to tie one on too hard when children are liable to start screaming at any moment."

"Good plan," Julia said with a nod. "I'll help you serve. Everyone else, go relax."

It wasn't too much later that they were all floating in the pool or sprawled in reclining lounges, telling stories about the kids, sharing memories from growing up, and enjoying the sunshine that had arrived as the sky cleared.

Maybe the past months of spending ample time with her own sisters had changed things. Julia felt not just comfortable but welcome in their midst. The same way that Lisa, Karen, and Tamara had opened their hearts and homes to her.

Just like Zach, even from that first moment.

Mattie had just finished a story about Ronan coming to her defense in high school, and she turned an inquisitive gaze on Julia. "You look ready to burst. What did our brother save you from?"

"What's that?"

Quinn pointed a finger. "Your turn to dish. Come on. We never get to hear how well our little brother turned out. That's really not fair after we spent so much time and energy training him."

"Exactly," Mattie said. "You're welcome for him never leaving the toilet seat up."

Which *was* something to be thankful for, although Julia smirked at the memory of the other little battle they were still engaging in over the toilet paper roll.

"Zach's a great guy." She considered how to phrase this, her newfound determination to stick to the truth battling with the knowledge that not everything needed to be said. "He's also bossy. The first time he saw the bachelor pad where I was living, he refused to let me stay there any longer. He found me another place where it was safer."

"Was it that bad?" Quinn asked.

"Maybe worse. I was grateful to have one less thing to worry about." Although it was interesting how fast things had escalated after that point. She never had left his cabin.

Mattie nodded thoughtfully. "He is protective. Learned it from Dad, I imagine."

"Definitely," Quinn agreed. "Dad somehow found the balance between letting us explore the world and yet always being there the instant we needed backup."

Thinking back, it was easy for Julia to see that trait in Zach. "It's nice to have someone who's got your back without mowing you down at the same time." She thought of something amusing to share. "He's sneaky bossy, but in a totally sweet way. Like, he let me drive his car *once*—the day we put it into storage for the winter. Then he made me ride shotgun in my own car on the way home."

The pool area went utterly still at her laughing comment. Five sets of jaws dropped.

Petra blinked. "He let you drive *Delilah?*"

"Once," Julia pointed out with a laugh. Thinking back to how sweet it had been to handle the classic car made her smile, though. "Short lived success, I guess."

Another story followed, and the feeling of connection continued to grow. The older women got caught up in a discussion about kids' activities for the new year. Julia found her recliner floating farther from them toward the opposite side of the pool.

Petra laughed, letting go of the rope she'd used to bring Julia to her side. "I'm so glad you're here. When they start in on the mom talk, my eyes start to cross after the first hour."

"I think it's pretty natural when you get a big group together. With my sisters, only one has kids so far. The kid focus tends to be a sprinkling instead of an onslaught."

"Good description," Petra said dryly. "Tell me more about your job. I work in IT, where it's all desk jockeys and keyboards. What exactly do you do at the ranch?"

Getting to talk about one of her favourite things was no hardship. Although it was telling to notice how often Zach's name came up during their conversation. Julia kept mentioning him and everything that he'd done over the past months while they'd spent time together.

His little sister began smiling every time Julia said his

name. Finally, she outright laughed. "Are you sure he's not working in the office with you?"

Guilty. "We do end up around each other a lot. I hadn't realized how much until now," Julia admitted. "I like him. He's a pretty special guy."

"He is. I approve of him as a big brother." Petra glanced slyly at Julia. "I know you guys explained about the whole accidentally-married thing, but it seems as if there's more to the story."

The parts they were keeping secret were going to stay that way, as far as Julia was concerned.

She shrugged. "I guess you can say that we're good friends now. Zach's always doing things for his friends. I like being able to do things in return for him."

The other woman eyed her, curiosity rising. "Friends. Well, that's good. I guess."

Julia laughed. "You sound like my sister, Lisa."

"She's a very smart woman." Petra leaned forward on her elbows, the inflatable chair under her rocking slightly from side to side. "Just so you know? I've seen my brother with his friends. And yes, he's a very giving man, but I've never heard of him letting anyone drive Delilah other than his bestie. I've never seen Zach *look* at another woman the way he looks at you."

"Probably because nobody else has ever had the power to take away everything he's worked for." Julia tried to say it as if it were a joke, but her throat had grown tight.

When Petra just stared at her steadily for a moment, that knot slid into her chest and grew tighter.

Finally, Petra shook her head. "Honey, you might need to do a reassessment. Because I don't think my brother's worried about his pocketbook. If you want to talk about having the power to take something away, you might start by focusing on something in this area." She tapped a hand against her chest.

Julia wanted to protest. She wanted to explain how important it was for not just Zach but the rest of her family for them to survive this year. How if it was only the two of them on the line, maybe they would've been able to give up by now, but not when Finn and Karen would also be affected.

The rest of the family returned as lunchtime approached. The quiet conversation was over, but Petra's words kept drilling through her brain.

He's never looked at another woman the way he looks at you.

That night, as Zach caught her fingers in his and tugged her toward the edge of the deck so they could get into prime sunset viewing position, Julia couldn't keep the truth hidden from herself anymore.

She didn't want Zach to have to act as if she were important to him just to keep her family from being rightly upset at the tangled mess they were in. She didn't want this to be pretend. She wanted the kisses and the cuddles to mean something. She wanted the time that they spent in bed exploring new ways to make each other happy to be the beginning of forever, not a short-term, temporary distraction.

Beside her, Zach adjusted position so he could curl his arm around her. His lips pressed briefly to her temple, a tender move that nevertheless drove a stake into her soul.

She wanted this to be real. Because for her, it already was.

Julia Blushing had fallen in love with her husband, and that realization just might break her.

The sun took its time gathering colours this evening. Feminine laughter swirled around them along with childish voices.

Little Beau came stumbling over on his sturdy toddler legs,

eyes blinking hard as if desperately trying to stay awake even as he held pudgy fingers up to his uncle.

As easy as breathing, Zach leaned over and picked up his nephew, settling the little guy in his lap with one arm wrapped around him to keep him in place before he reached back for Julia's fingers and held on tight.

She caught herself staring at the sunlight reflected over the little boy and the man at her side. Beau rested his cheek on Zach's chest, thumb in his mouth as he stared back, eyes drooping in spite of his determination.

This. She wanted *this* as well—a family. From the interfering parental units to the sisters on both sides who would never stop asking the hard questions or making her see what was right there in front of her face. She wanted children with Zach's blue eyes, and she wanted to be able to see him guide them with laughter and kindness and truth.

No lies. Nothing but a firm foundation and a home built on love.

Her breath caught in her throat, because for one moment she had a perfect vision of what she wanted, and what could be—

Except that foundation could tumble away at any moment because it wasn't built on truth. It was built on Zach and her trying to do the right thing for others, and that's where the whole thing was going to tip over and break into a million pieces.

That's where her mom had gone wrong. Making a decision that forced others' hands and didn't let them decide for themselves. She couldn't do it.

Zach glanced at her, concern slipping in. "You okay?"

She forced a smile. Fortunately, before she had to say something that would be an outright lie or to explain that in this case *okay* meant *one step away from breaking apart because everything in my world is no longer real,* Beau jolted halfway awake, his arms flailing.

It took a second for Zach to soothe him, adjusting position so the toddler lay cradled against his chest. Long enough for Julia to slide her worries into a box and seal it up firmly to be dealt with in the morning.

She wanted one more night before facing the truth that in this fairy tale, the happily ever after wasn't real.

Much, much later, after dinner and games and family time were done, starlight glittered overhead as the final good-nights of the evening were said. She and Zach were the last ones left outside, sitting on the edge of the pool with their feet dangling in the water.

Zach's hand reached around her, fingers gently cupping her hip as he pressed his lips to the back of her neck. "I like it when you wear your hair up. I get to touch all the sweet, soft parts of you."

She tilted her head to expose more skin. "We could take this to our cabana. I wouldn't mind finding some sweet, soft spots either."

"Hard. There's an awful lot of hard spots you might need to discover first," Zach growled.

Stealing away as if someone was about to stop them, they slid into the room, hands reaching for each other. Touching, stroking.

Memorizing. This might be the last time, and it wasn't about how well they had fit together or all the things that she'd learned about physical pleasure from him.

No. As he pressed his lips against her skin, teasing each intimate spot that he found, as she stroked her fingers down the muscular lines of his torso. As they kissed deeply, bodies meshing together—

It wasn't just physical.

Moonlight and starshine poured over the bed, shining in the open doors facing the ocean. Zach rolled her under him, his hips pulsing slowly as he pushed his cock deep into her sex, the sound of the ocean filling the small room.

There was magic, Julia could've sworn there was. But just like the fairy tales where in the morning everything was back to normal, this too was fleeting.

It was perfect. It was broken.

Zach caught their fingers together, pinning their hands to the mattress. Julia stared into his face, at the pleasure there, the sweet caring and understanding.

Her body betrayed her, and for once in her life an orgasm rushed in far too quickly when she would've liked this to have gone on forever.

"Julia." Zach stilled over her, hips pulsing as he came.

She cupped his cheek and kept her smile in place. Let the physical satisfaction be enough, even though inside, her heart was breaking.

An hour later, after they'd cleaned up and returned to the bed, Zach wrapped his arms around her and almost instantly fell asleep. She wasn't so lucky.

She lay there, examining his features. Wishing desperately she'd been brave enough to tell *him* the truth. But as he breathed evenly, chest rising and falling, the faintest hint of a smile still curling his lips, it was all she could do to stay in one place and not shout it out to the heavens.

"I love you." The words were a bare whisper off her lips, but they shouted so loud inside her that it felt as if her entire body vibrated with the echo. "I love you so much."

It was the truth, rising from the core of her being.

Which was why she had to let him go.

22

*Z*ach had been hoping for an early-morning birthday present, but when he rolled over, Julia wasn't in the bed. The sliding doors were still open to the ocean, though, and contentment pooled in his limbs as he stretched then made his way to vertical.

She'd gotten into the habit of walking the beach every morning. He couldn't blame her, and considering he hoped today would end up being extra special, he could give her the space to wander and enjoy her time off.

Last night had been spectacular, and he could only hope that today would be even better.

He went to grab some coffee from the kitchen. His mom rose from where she'd been settled at the table to come and give him a hug and a kiss. "Happy birthday, little man."

"Mom," he complained, squeezing her extra hard before stepping out of her embrace. "Please."

She smiled smugly. "Sorry, darling. You're always going to be my little man."

"Be thankful your nickname wasn't something dreadful like

snookums." Petra appeared to offer her own rib-rattling hug. "Happy birthday, big brother."

"Hopefully," he said with a wink.

That earned him a massive eye roll. "Is your better half sleeping in?"

"Think she hit the beach already," Zach said as he filled a cup and headed toward the deck, debating if he should pour a second one for her and have it ready when she returned.

His father drifted into the room, papers in his hand that he was staring at with utter confusion. "Zach? Can I see you for a minute?"

Zach glanced at his mom to make sure she hadn't noticed. He put an arm around his father and guided him from the room. "If Mom sees you working, there'll be hell to pay," he said.

Zachary Senior looked up and blinked. "I'm not working. These came through on the fax. They're for you, but they make no sense."

"For me?"

His father tugged the papers out of his reach. "Put your coffee down."

Shit. Zach all but threw his cup at the nearest side table. "I don't like the sounds of this," he warned.

His father held the papers forward. "I don't think you're going to like how it reads, either."

Zach glanced at the cover page only for long enough to read the *from* part. Alan Cwedwick.

Why would his lawyer be sending three full pages of a small enough print to require a magnifying glass? Zach peered at the opening paragraphs to find tons of legalese. "I wonder if my birthday triggered something in Bruce's files."

His dad pushed aside the papers so he could point to the

last page. "I'm not sure, but this part seems pretty easy to interpret."

Still legalese, but part of the sentence *was* easy to interpret.

—granting divorce proceedings to terminate the marriage—

What? *What?*

His gaze snapped up to meet his father's. "These are divorce papers. For me and Julia?"

"That's how I read it. Umm, apologies for reading your mail, but I didn't—"

Zach marched away from his father, all but sprinting back to the cabana to grab his phone. Waiting for the call to go through to Alan was painful.

"Good morning. How's the birthday boy today?"

Zach was all but vibrating, but shouting obscenities at the other man wouldn't get him answers. "You sent me divorce papers."

"Oh. You got them already." Alan clicked his tongue a couple of times. "I suppose you want an explanation."

"You think?" Zach stepped out onto the small porch, glancing up and down the path to see if he could spot Julia anywhere. "Did Finn talk to you? Does this mean—"

"Finn? No, I haven't heard from him recently." It was Alan's turn to sound confused. "Julia got in touch with me this morning."

Everything inside Zach went still. "Julia did."

"Yes. She wanted to double-check again if there was some way that you could be released from the one-year requirement. We worked something out."

Over the past forty-eight hours, Zach had finally triggered plans that he thought would break the stalemate between them.

Finally move him and Julia toward the relationship he'd always wanted.

Inside, hope died. "This is real. We're not married anymore."

"It's real. You and Julia are no longer married."

He looked down to discover his fingers trembling as he held the papers. "And you haven't talked to Finn. Or Karen."

"Just Julia. And now you." Alan's voice turned soothing. "Breathe, Zach. Trust me."

The urge to burst into hysterical laughter was so damn high. Only he spotted Julia's flame-tinted hair in the distance. "Don't do me any more favours for a while," he warned. "I need to go."

"Talk to Julia," was the last thing Zach heard as he hung up.

He was out on the path an instant later, marching toward her. Jumbled emotions bounced with every step. He was so angry. So sad. So confused, and frustrated, and *furious.*

Zach stepped off the path into a small clearing where the more rugged rocks had been levelled to leave a big enough space to place lawn chairs or tripods for viewing the sunsets. That gave him a place to stand as Julia made her way closer.

Her gaze was down, watching her footing, and it gave him time to just stare at her, the long length of her legs and her strong arms kissed golden by the sun over the past days. Her hair hung loose around her shoulders, the highlights all but sparkling.

The papers in his hand couldn't be real.

She glanced up and spotted him. She smiled briefly before her expression faded, and she hurried forward, concern rising. "What's wrong?"

He opened his mouth, but nothing came out.

Julia stood before him, gripping his arms and all but shaking him. "Zach. Are you okay?"

He shoved the papers at her. "Alan sent these."

She froze. "Oh. Already?"

Zach stood there with his hand stretched out. He shook them. "Is this what you wanted? Because I've been telling you all along that you needed to do what makes you happy. Is this what you want?"

She peeled the papers from his grasp. "I don't know what these say. I called Alan this morning—"

"So I heard. And that's what he sent."

She lifted them, squinting at the small print. "What—"

His patience was at an end. Truth was, he didn't care what the papers said.

"I contacted Finn on Christmas Day," Zach admitted. "Told him the whole thing about us having to be together for a year wasn't just about me losing the company but him too."

Julia stiffened, the papers in her hand forgotten. "We agreed we wouldn't tell them."

Zach shook his head. "I agreed I wouldn't tell Karen, but you reminded me that the truth makes a difference. While it's not fair our actions could impact them, they have the right to know. They have the right to make their own choices and have their thoughts heard."

He stepped closer, catching hold of her fingers.

Her eyes were wide as her gaze snapped up to his.

"Just like your mom should've told *you* the truth. It would've been hard, and it would've been messy, but a different kind of relationship would've come after you'd dealt the messy. I realized that, even while I kept my promise to you. I told Finn and left it up to him what he wanted to do about telling Karen."

She wiggled the papers in the air. "Did you lose everything?"

Only the most important thing ever. Her.

Except, Julia wasn't acting like somebody who had been desperate to get divorced. Zach took a deep breath and decided to lay it all out.

"It's never been about the money. I want *you*. I've always wanted you, and the money can go to hell. I'd rather work a minimum wage nine-to-five somewhere with you beside me than have all the money in the bank."

She blinked as if he were speaking a foreign language and she had to translate. "But you had no choice."

"About what part? The bit where you kissed me and asked for me to be your pretend boyfriend? The part where I refused to let you stay somewhere unsafe? The part where I did yoga every fucking week? Julia, I've always had a choice. Even in the *have to stay married for one year or else* bullshit—if it hadn't been something I wanted to do, I damn well wouldn't have done it."

Her cheeks had grown rosy and her fingers tightened around the papers, clutching them hard enough that they would be impossible to lay out flat.

"Why?" The word came out soft and broken. She straightened her shoulders and took a deep breath, meeting his gaze straight on, and this time when she spoke, it was a demand. "*Why?*"

"The reason I let it stand is because I thought it would give me time to convince you to choose me for yourself."

A hint of a smile curled her lips. "Choose you for what?"

For fuck's sake. He pretty much shouted the words. "Your husband, dammit. Your partner. Your lover and your forever."

The furrow between her brows wasn't the same as usual. This time it looked as if her expression was being contorted between contrasting emotions. Not even the hint of moisture gathering in her eyes was enough to make him stop.

"So, choose, Julia Gigi Blushing, because this is it. What the hell is going to make you happy?"

She jerked her hand from his, and for a split second—

"You." Julia threw herself at him, wrapping her arms around his neck and squeezing like an octopus. "I want *you*."

JULIA's HEART was ready to burst from her chest. The papers he'd passed her had escaped her grip and were now being consumed by the ocean.

She'd spent the past forty-five minutes alternating between despair and hope, and the last five in utter confusion all the way up until Zach had gotten angry.

She held on tight, his grip around her body an ironclad reminder of the words he just demanded. "What just happened?" she whispered.

A soft chuckle escaped him, but he simply adjusted his grip, bouncing her higher so he could look her in the face. "I think we sort of just had our first fight."

"You're a shitty fighter," she said. "And I totally won."

"Not much of a victory considering I'm a shitty fighter and all," he teased back. He took a deep breath as he rested their foreheads together. "You scared me. I thought you had asked Alan for a way out."

She wiggled until he let her go. "I kind of did, to be honest, but for good reasons."

They settled on the rocks at the edge of the clearing, fingers still tangled, knees bumping.

Zach caught her chin in his fingers, gazing into her eyes. "First things first. I love you."

Oh my God. She swallowed hard. "Me too."

She caught the briefest flash of his grin before he leaned in and kissed her, putting action to the words that only he had actually said—*good fumble, Blushing.*

When they separated, she fixed her mistake. "I've been in love with you for a while, but it sank in clearly yesterday."

He brushed his thumb over her bottom lip. "So why did you get in touch with Alan?"

"Why did you get in touch with Finn? Because you needed to tell him the truth. Because you wanted him to make decisions based on the truth. That's what you just said, right?"

Zach nodded.

"Me too. I want to be with you, and I'm so glad you want to be with me. But, Zach, you *didn't* have a choice. I know you say you did, but you didn't. I called Alan to see if he could help me find a way to set you free to do what would make *you* happy."

It had been one of the most awkward conversations of her life, but staring into Zach's love-filled expression, it had been worth every embarrassing moment.

Zach's grin got wider. "So, let me get this straight. You phoned Alan and told him that you love me."

No use in feeling embarrassed about it now. "Pretty much."

He leaned in. "Good for you."

She supposed. She glanced over her shoulder to where the papers were now ocean litter. "We're not married anymore."

The sweet sound of his laughter rumbled around her. "We could do something about that. And I mean something that doesn't require tequila or BRIDE and GROOM T-shirts."

Her heart rate kicked up again. "Do you want to get married for real?"

The smile she received flashed sunlight bright. "I do. Thank you for asking. I am so going to gloat to everyone that *you* proposed to *me.*"

"Did I just—?" Oh my God, she had. Julia slapped a hand over her mouth for a second before grabbing hold of his shoulders and going in for a hug. "Okay, fine. We're going to get married for real."

But first she was going to savour the sensation. The complete rightness of being in his arms. Of being held tight and knowing that this was exactly where he wanted to be.

Knowing that they belonged with each other not because of some accident or twist of fate. Not because of liquor and circumstance.

Because of choice.

Speaking of which. Julia pushed back. "What do you think about a fall wedding?"

He lost some of his smile. "Um, really? I was kind of thinking beach wedding, this afternoon."

She shook her head. "We did the fast and *oops* type of wedding once. Maybe it would be good to take our time this go-round. Have our friends and family involved. Besides, that will give us something to look forward to."

"Then we can make it the fall. We need a memorable day— since there's not much about the first time we actually remember," he teased. His expression brightened. "But I do have one thing to make right now unforgettable."

He reached into his pocket and to her utter surprise, pulled out a shining blue ring that made her heart sing with happiness.

"It's gorgeous."

"Which means it's perfect for you." He slipped onto her finger.

She kissed him again, mostly because she could. Falling into his love and his caresses and caring.

A small cough sounded beside them, and they broke apart to discover Rita standing a few inches away. "Excuse me, Uncle Zachary. Grandpa wants to know if you're okay. I told him I thought you were because you were kissing Julia, and you shouldn't kiss somebody if you're not feeling well."

She turned her gaze on Julia and added very earnestly, "Germs."

"Very true," Julia whispered back. "Kissing is a dangerous business."

Rita shrugged then glanced back at her uncle. "If everything's okay, can you come back to the house? Everybody's waiting for your birthday breakfast, and Mom says I can't have whipped cream until you're there."

Zach tangled his fingers around Julia's. Both of them stood as he nodded seriously to his niece. "I'm very sorry we held up breakfast and the whipped cream. Everything is wonderful, so we'd better go get my birthday party started."

Only two steps down the path, Julia spotted the rest of the family. Their heads poked out of windows and around corners, a sea of worried expressions as they waited for their return.

Rita danced on ahead, leaving them a little privacy. Julia tugged on Zach's fingers. "Does your whole family know? About the divorce?"

"Just my dad, unless he told everybody."

Up ahead of them, Zachary Senior had taken a very visible position. He'd climbed on top of the fence and stood like a sentinel. But he had his finger pressed over his lips and offered them a wink.

"I think we're safe for now," Julia informed Zach. "Let's deal with your birthday first. We can let everybody know the rest of the plans in a couple days."

"Good idea."

A table full of people who loved him had gathered to sing "Happy Birthday." There were plates stacked high with pancakes and more than one bowlful of whipped cream and peaches waiting.

This time the bag full of names was left on the counter. Zach remained on his feet as the birthday song concluded.

"Since it's my birthday, it's my turn to share." He glanced down the table, making eye contact with each person there. "This year, I am thankful as always for my family. For how much each one of you means to me and how much you challenge me to be a better brother, son, uncle, and friend."

His gaze twisted to spotlight Julia. He caught her fingers and pulled her to her feet. "I am happy this year to be able to add another title to that list. We won't worry about the specific name, but it comes down to this—I am happy to be Julia's."

His sisters were *awwwing*. Petra wiped her eyes.

Not good. Julia felt her own eyes fill with moisture as Zach lifted her hands and kissed her knuckles. "I hope to spend the next fifty years learning what that means and how to do it better."

Family at the table or not, there was no way to resist. Julia leaned in and kissed him.

Hers. Because he made her happy.

EPILOGUE

Red Boot ranch, September 5th

Z ach took the stairs two at a time, glancing left and right to make sure no one spotted him. Everything went well until he hit the second-floor landing and came face-to-face with Karen.

He jerked to a stop. "Oh, hey."

Karen raised a brow. "Hey."

They stared at each other for a moment. Zach rocked on his toes. "Great day, right? Weather is totally cooperating."

"*Zach.*" She put so much disappointment into her tone. "Are you trying to pretend you're here to talk about the weather? Or are you going to admit you're trying to sneak in to chat with Julia when you know that's against the rules?"

"Fuck the rules," Zach murmured before offering a huge grin. "Come on. You just snickered. You don't care if I bend the rules just a teeny, tiny bit."

"No, I don't mind at all," Karen agreed. Then she leaned forward and lowered her voice. "But if you think I am going against your mother and sisters on this one? Hell no. I might've grown up with Lisa and Tamara tormenting me, but those hellions you're related to scare the bejesus out of me."

Figures. He was on his own for this one. Zach pressed a hand on Karen's shoulder and squeezed. "I give up. I'll wait to see Julia until later."

He turned and walked slowly down the stairs as if defeated, the heat of Karen's gaze boring between his shoulder blades.

Okay, he hadn't really given up. He took the first corner and rushed back out onto the porch, examining the back of the house.

Waiting nine months to get married had been weird at first, but as time passed, the delay had grown to be kind of special. His family had gotten into it, Julia's as well, and now that the day had finally arrived, it promised to truly be the celebration they'd hoped for.

Except, dammit, he wanted to see her *now* before meeting her at the altar to say *I do*. Only his sisters had decided tormenting him one more time was vital. Julia had vanished from their cabin early that morning. That was nearly five hours ago, and he was tired of waiting.

He examined the roofline of Finn and Karen's house more closely than he had over the past year.

"Don't you have somewhere you need to be?" Finn laid a hand on his shoulder. He leaned in and peered up at the house as well. "Or were you thinking about cleaning my eaves troughs?"

"Trying to figure out the easiest way to break into the second bedroom," Zach confessed. "I want to see Julia."

A snort escaped his best friend. "You just can't leave it alone, can you?"

"All the girls are set on us not spotting each other until the big moment. A true friend would help me find a way."

"A true friend would make sure you didn't break your neck before you officially get hitched." Only Finn lifted a finger and pointed. "Maintenance hatch to the attic. Access code is 3542. If you follow the ridgeline past the chimney, there's a ceiling hatch from the attic into the hall bathroom."

Zach grabbed him by the hand and pumped hard. "You're the best. I won't be long," he promised, already heading for the side of the house where the massive maple tree would give him a climbing base to get to the roof.

"If you're not in the guest house in thirty minutes, Josiah and I are coming to get you," Finn warned.

Thirty minutes should be more than enough time. Zach scrambled up the tree and onto the roof, sliding into the dusty attic space with zero hesitation.

Dusty, hot, and dark enough that he fished out his phone and turned on the flashlight. That let him pace the narrow wooden slats covering the length of the roof to where, as promised, the hatch to the second-floor ceiling waited.

He paused and listened. Feminine voices and laughter carried up to his ears, but they were far enough away he figured he was safe.

Zach was just about to lift the hatch when his phone vibrated in his fingers. Julia was calling him.

He sat back and answered. "Hey, love. What's up?"

"Why are you whispering?" she asked.

"I'm afraid somebody will take my phone away because I'm not allowed to talk to you until the wedding, or some such superstitious nonsense."

She snickered. "You need to get your phone checked. There's some sort of weird echo going on. And I'm sorry about the *no seeing each other* business. That's all Petra's fault, by the way. Your little sister is a bossy fart."

"This we knew. Have she and Lisa decided to take over the world yet?"

"Never mind that. Where are you?"

He glanced around at the darkness. "A little out of reach at the moment."

"I need to know," she insisted. "Or I will in about ten minutes. Keep your phone on."

And then she hung up.

Well. That was weird. Zach pushed away the questions he had and focused on the task at hand. He listened again then carefully lifted the board out of the way, revealing the bathroom at the end of the second-floor hall.

A moment later he had manoeuvred his way to the ground and closed the attic access.

He cracked open the bathroom door the slightest bit, peeking into the hallway.

Motion zipped back and forth between bedroom two and three at the top of the stairs, his mom and Karen traipsing back and forth with armfuls of flowers.

The room he wanted was situated three paces to the left...

He waited until the hall was clear then made his move. Rapidly darting to door number one, he slipped inside and turned—

The room was empty. Julia's wedding dress lay on the bed, all shiny white with tons of buttons. He'd seen a picture of it earlier and was already dreaming about undoing said buttons later that evening.

Which reminded him of the picture she'd given him last New Year's Eve. The one from her boudoir shoot—although the only similarity was she'd been wearing a nearly see-through white tank top...

Bad memory to think about if he didn't want to get all heated up with no time to do anything about it.

There were flowers, and a veil, and her shoes, but definitely no Julia.

He pulled out his phone, dialing her up and hoping his whisper wouldn't be overheard. "Where are you?"

This time she laughed. "I was looking for this sexy guy I met in Vegas, hoping I could get him to show me a good time. Only he seems to have vanished."

What the hell?

Before he could demand an answer to what was going on, Josiah's deep rumble took over Julia's phone. "I'd suggest you get down to the cottage ASAP. Take the direct route, though. Finn and the other guys can only distract the ladies for so long."

He hung up.

Zach shook his head. Sneaking out to give Julia a final *I love you* message had become far more complicated than expected.

A cheer went up from outside, and he glanced out the window to discover Cody had brought up a horse-drawn carriage. All the ladies had rushed out and were doing something with flowers—

He moved. Peeking into the hallway once before sprinting for freedom. Down the hall, leaping stairs. Dashing through the kitchen and out the sliding doors so he could race to the cottage next door.

He didn't stop until he was in the living room, where a pair of arms wrapped around him, Julia's laughter filling the space.

He caught her by the waist and lifted her, squeezing tight as her eyes sparkled at him. "You sneaky woman. What are you doing out of lockdown?"

"Look, baby. I'm not the one acting like a stealth agent. I sashayed down the stairs like a lady. When no one was looking," she admitted.

They grinned at each other, and then her hands were cupping his face. Sweet emotion was written all over her. The sweetest of emotions—because what they felt for each other had grown stronger over the past months.

"I wanted to see you one more time before we got married," Julia said. "I wanted to tell you how amazing you are. How good you've been to me, and how every single day, I'm so grateful you agreed to be my pretend boyfriend."

Laughter swelled inside him, but Zach had to share his own truth. He gave her a quick kiss, though, because he couldn't resist. He damn near spoke against her lips because he almost couldn't pull away. "I'm so glad you chose me. No matter what, I'm going to make sure you know how much we belong together. How much you mean to me. Even if you are kind of sex-crazed."

A sharp snort escaped her, and she covered her mouth with her fingers before grinning hard. "Your fault."

"I couldn't be prouder," he admitted before softening his voice. "But it's never just sex. Not with you. It's love."

She licked her lips, and he went in for a serious kiss. A wholehearted promise of what would come later. Not just that day, but next week, next month.

Next year, until the end of eternity.

Somebody coughed. Finn. "Time to get ready. I'm afraid your mom's waiting outside," he warned with a sheepish grin.

Julia stepped back, giving Zach's fingers a final squeeze. "It's okay. I'll sweet-talk her into not scolding you until after the honeymoon."

"Just don't let her start giving you advice of what to do while on our honeymoon," Zach warned as the door closed behind her.

He turned back to face his friends as Josiah walked into the room to join them.

"Are you ready for this?" Josiah asked.

Ready for Julia to become his officially, albeit for the

second time? This time he was going to remember every moment of it. "I can't wait."

∿

WHAT A DIFFERENCE. By now they'd watched the video of their Vegas wedding enough times that contrasting that event with what waited before her was natural. Part of the entertainment tonight would be showing that video to all their friends and family who had gathered.

That had been wild and impulsive. A mistake that turned out to be everything she'd ever wanted. Today was planned and solid. Yet equally sweet and infinitely more memorable because of the people joining them.

Julia rested her arms on the railing of the deck, stealing peeks toward where the chairs and wedding bower waited. "Soon?"

"Don't worry. Zach is not running away. Josiah has firm orders to keep his feet nailed to the front of the stage until it's official." A noticeably pregnant Lisa slipped beside her, curling an arm around Julia's waist. "A couple more cars showed up, so we figured we'd let everyone find seats before starting the processional music."

There was already a big crowd. Not only everyone she and Zach worked with at the Red Boot ranch, which started official operations in the spring, but all the people Julia had worked with at the fire hall the previous year.

Add in all the family members, between the Colemans and the Sorensons—Julia had never expected to have this many people in her life who all wanted to celebrate with her.

Karen appeared on her other side, adjusting the short veil attached to the tiara resting in Julia's hair. "You look happy," she said.

Julia straightened, twisting until she could see her sisters at the same time, Tamara as well, coming up the stairs to join them. "I have something to tell you."

The three of them tucked in close. Mirror images of each other and yet so unique. Karen had softened over the past year, and Julia was sure it was because Finn had been her constant champion. Karen had learned to take what she needed to be happy, and Julia had learned a lot from watching her older sister deal with past hurts.

Tamara's sturdy love had been offered and accepted in so many ways over the past months. Julia had spent tons of time with the Stone family, discovering they had their own strengths and weaknesses, but at the root of it, rejoicing that they were always there for each other.

And Lisa? Lisa had become the best friend Julia hadn't known she needed. Although her sister's mischief was a trifle more curtailed these days. Even now Lisa adjusted her stance, hand falling to the round swell of her seven-months pregnant belly.

Suddenly Julia wondered: what would her sisters see while looking back at her? Hopefully a woman who was learning the ultimate truth. Acceptance started within. Joy spread outward, and love expanded like multiplication tables gone wild.

Julia had spent nine months accepting the truth that Zach loved her unconditionally. That no matter what they needed to learn, they could do it together.

That family was a miracle.

She held her hands forward, her fingers instantly caught by her sisters. "People say being in the right place at the right time is all about luck. And I suppose one thing did lead to another, in a way. But walking into Silver Stone the day that Tyler was born was more than luck. It was breath into lungs and blood into veins. That was the day *I* was born into this family, as well, and I can never explain to you how sweet that is."

Dammit. She should've done this yesterday, because her eyes were getting wet.

"You don't need to explain," Tamara said softly.

Karen and Lisa nodded in agreement. "Nope. We pretty much know what you're talking about." Karen squeezed her fingers.

Lisa's hand was back on her belly, where even now another new life had begun. "We can never replace the years we missed, but we're going to enjoy every single day going forward."

Another truth. Julia took a deep breath. "Thank you for being my big sisters. I love you."

Arms surrounded her, squeezing her tight. Holding still in that sisterly bond formed not just by blood but by choice. They hadn't needed to welcome her in, but they had, and their decision had changed her world.

The music picked up in the background, and suddenly Petra was there. "Okay, darlin'. It's time to get my brother his just rewards."

Another favourite person in her world. Julia stepped back and accepted the tissue her almost sister-in-law offered. "You realize I'm going to find somebody from the ranch for you to fall in love with," she warned. "You need to move closer to Heart Falls."

"Ohhh, now there's a good idea." Lisa stepped away from Tamara. "Hey. No hitting the pregnant lady."

"No matchmaking," Tamara scolded.

"One wedding at a time," Karen said as she winked at Julia. "At least this year."

Her sisters led her down the stairs to the sturdy boardwalk path. Red Boot ranch now had a dedicated area to host weddings, and while this wasn't the first to be held there, it was the first for their family.

Julia glanced down the long row past all of the waiting guests. Past her future mother- and father-in-law, who were equal parts wonderful and embarrassingly terrible, just as Zach had warned. Past all of Zach's sisters, brothers-in-law, nieces, and nephews.

Past where Tamara slipped ahead to rejoin Caleb and the rest of the Stone family who had come to be a part of the celebration.

Julia's gaze stuttered to a stop, her feet as well, as she spotted the Elvis impersonator at the edge of one row. He lifted a hand and dipped his chin, and she outright giggled.

Her gaze snapped forward to where Zach stood at the front waiting for her with Finn at his side, Josiah as well.

Zach grinned. He knew why she was laughing.

"You got this?" Karen made a few final adjustments to Julia's dress.

"I do. I really do," Julia said firmly, focusing back on her sisters. She squeezed Lisa's and Karen's fingers one last time.

As her sisters started slowly down the aisle, Julia turned to where George Coleman stood waiting.

Another adjustment over the past months. She and her father were learning what kind of relationship they wanted. She didn't need someone to protect her, and she didn't need someone who treated her like a little girl. None of the Whiskeyteers did.

It hadn't always been easy, but between her and her sisters insisting he listen as well as speak, George Coleman had begun to change. His growth had been encouraged and influenced by Finn, Josiah, and Zach as well.

But what that meant here and now was that when her father held out his arm, she willingly slipped her fingers around his elbow. Joy was truly present in being able to have her father as a part of this day.

Tamara's daughter Emma and Zach's niece Rita walked ahead of them, tossing leaves instead of flowers. It was pretty and perfect. There was more than a bit of laughter when little Beau shook the pillow he was holding, the one with two rings tied to its surface, complaining loudly when he couldn't figure out how to make them fall.

It was family—oh, so much family.

But when they reached the front, it was all Zach. Everyone else could have vanished as far as she knew. Julia stared into his blue eyes and saw nothing but love.

They must've had the wedding ceremony, but it passed in a blink. Thank goodness somebody was recording it, because she would have really hated having her only memories be the ones from the Mile-High Chapel video.

They stood side by side on the deck post-wedding, Zach's fingers tangled around hers, firm and sure. He dipped his head and brushed his cheek against hers, murmuring in her ear, "I love you."

The instant shiver felt wonderful. She turned, linking her fingers behind his neck. "I love you too." She glanced out at the crowd preparing for them to open gifts. "I don't see Tony. I thought he was going to be here."

"He sent his regrets." Zach lifted her fingers and kissed them. "When I talked to him yesterday, he said his kids are down with the flu. He offered his congratulations and reminded me we have an appointment in two weeks."

"Okay." She curled against his side a little tighter. Therapy continued, with Zach joining her every other time. The fact that he'd begun meeting one-on-one with Tony every now and then had just been one more confirmation that Zach truly was perfect for her.

Pamela Sorenson clapped her hands and gestured people forward. "Bride and groom, come sit in your seats of honour."

It felt a little strange to spend time on presents, but considering the number of people who had travelled a fair distance to be there, at the last minute they'd decided to accept gifts while everyone was still around.

A lot of the presents were pictures, which thrilled Julia. Images from Zach's years growing up. Ones of her sisters during their Whiskey Creek days. A beautifully framed image of her mother that made Julia smile.

Pamela and Zachary presented her with a soft cotton sack.

Julia blinked for a moment before reaching in and pulling out two smooth stones etched with ZACH and JULIA. "Our own blessings bag. Thank you."

"That's the starter set," Pamela teased. "When you start having kids, we'll add their names. Now, since conception and pregnancy—"

"And we have the extended version for you, as well." Zachary Senior interrupted his wife, with a wink for his son and another much larger sack in his hand. "My etching tool got quite a workout. You know how many people are in our family now?"

A quick glance around the room said so, so many.

Not having wrapping paper on the gifts made everything go quicker as friends and family continued to come forward with small tokens. Hanna offered Julia a hug as Brad shook Zach's hand, then they passed over a ceramic cookie jar. Brad's big arm cradled his and Hanna's three-month-old baby boy easily.

As they neared the end, Petra came forward, arms loaded with three fancy metallic tins. "That's a bit overboard, isn't it?" Zach teased his sister.

"Not from me, bro. I found them over by the music station.

There are no names." She popped them all on the table in front of Julia. "Maybe someone had to leave early?"

Julia picked one up, examining it carefully. A pretty rural scene in pastoral colours graced the side. "Maybe."

Zach picked up another, and something rattled. "Cookies? I like cookies." He popped off the lid and peeked inside. An instant later he slammed the lid shut, grinning up at the crowd. "No cookies. We'll just put these aside. Thank you, whoever the gift is from."

Julia couldn't resist. She lifted the lid on her container to discover it was full of brightly-coloured condoms. Amusement filtered upward like bubbles in her belly. She leaned toward Zach. "Your mother?"

For a moment he paused.

Laughter swelled suddenly. Zach pointed across the lawn to where Lisa, Tamara, and Karen were hanging on each other and laughing themselves silly.

One, two, *three* tins...

Oh, dear. "Um, yeah. I'm not sure what's up, but there's probably a good explanation." Julia winked at Zach. "We're well stocked, that's for sure."

He grinned.

"That's it," Petra announced. "Time for the dance."

"Wait, one last present," Julia said, reaching under the table and pulling out one more picture frame. "For you."

She offered it to Zach facedown.

He took it with a grin, flipped it over and burst out laughing.

She'd framed a how-to image for "How to Replace a Roll of Toilet Paper." It included the clear instructions for the roll to go under, not over, because "the more economical usage of tissue is encouraged."

Zach placed the frame on the table then pulled her to

vertical, guiding her to the middle of the dance floor. "You win. After a year of battling it out, TP style, I admit defeat. Henceforth, all our rolls shall be loaded your way."

Julia wrapped her arms around him as the first strains of music rose on the air. Elvis strummed his guitar and sang softly, as if just for them.

"Love Me Tender?" Julia sang in Zach's ear.

Her husband, her heart, swirled them in a circle as he hummed along to the music. They fit, and after a year together, it wasn't random chance or even solid determination making this thing between them work.

They'd chosen each other, and that's why they would never let go.

"Love you true." Zach nuzzled his lips along her neck for a brief moment, shivers of delight filling her as he sang along, for her ears only. "And I always will."

～

New York Times Bestselling Author Vivian Arend invites you to Heart Falls. These contemporary ranchers live in a tiny town in central Alberta, tucked into the rolling foothills. Enjoy the ride as they each find their happily-ever-afters.

～

The Stones of Heart Falls
A Rancher's Heart
A Rancher's Song
A Rancher's Bride
A Rancher's Love
A Rancher's Vow

Holidays in Heart Falls
A Firefighter's Christmas Gift
A Soldier's Christmas Wish
A Hero's Christmas Hope
A Cowboy's Christmas List
A Rancher's Christmas Kiss

The Colemans of Heart Falls
The Cowgirl's Forever Love
The Cowgirl's Secret Love
The Cowgirl's Chosen Love

Heart Falls Vignette Collection
Three Weddings And A Baby

～

ABOUT THE AUTHOR

With over 2.5 million books sold, Vivian Arend is a *New York Times* and *USA Today* bestselling author of over 60 contemporary and paranormal romance books, including the Six Pack Ranch and Granite Lake Wolves.

Her books are all standalone reads with no cliffhangers. They're humorous yet emotional, with sexy-times and happily-ever-afters. Vivian pretty much thinks she's got the best job in the world, and she's looking forward to giving readers more HEAs. She lives in B.C. Canada with her husband of many years and a fluffy attack Shih-tzu named Luna who ignores everyone except when treats are deployed.

www.vivianarend.com

9 781999 495763